"Adam Palmer has a way with humor. *Mooch* is a witty and engaging read that will resonate with lives on a much deeper level. Who knew a paradigm shift could make you laugh out loud?"

—MARK STEELE, author of
Flashbang: How I Got over Myself

"Funny, unexpected, and entertaining!"

—CRAIG GROSS, founder of XXXchurch.com;
author of *The Gutter*, *The Dirty Little Secret*, and *Starring Jesus*

"What I first thought was simply an excellent modern comedy soon evolved into a masterfully woven tale of loss, redemption, adventure, forgiveness, and God's true love. I recommend this book to anyone who's been tempted to crash a ritzy party just for the prime rib (and be honest—that's pretty much all of us)."

—MARK G. KEEFER, MPSE, sound designer;
three-time-Emmy-award winner

Mooch
Adam Palmer

TH1NK
P.O. Box 35001
Colorado Springs, Colorado 80935

ISBN 1-60006-047-1

Cover design by Charles Brock, www.thedesignworksgroup.com
Cover illustration by Charles Brock
Creative Team: Nicci Hubert, Jeff Gerke, Erika Hueneke, Kathy Mosier, Arvid Wallen, Laura Spray

Some of the anecdotal illustrations in this book are true to life and are included with the permission of the persons involved. All other illustrations are composites of real situations, and any resemblance to people living or dead is coincidental.

Palmer, Adam, 1975-
  Mooch / Adam Palmer.
    p. cm.
  ISBN 1-60006-047-1
  1. Swindlers and swindling--Fiction. 2. Rich people--Death--Fiction.
3. Burial--Fiction. 4. Life change events--Fiction. 5. Christian
women--Fiction. I. Title.
  PS3616.A3388M66 2006
  813'.6--dc22
                              2006016770

Printed in the United States of America

1 2 3 4 5 6 7 8 9 10 / 10 09 08 07 06

For Michelle
I chose you. Thank you for continuing to choose me.

Acknowledgments

I HAVE A confession to make up front: This book started as a lark. Seriously. I wasn't trying to break into the publishing world or anything like that; I just wanted to see if I could write a novel in thirty days, following the format provided by the organizers of National Novel Writing Month.

I don't say this as a roundabout way of telling you how awesome I am, because I'm certainly not awesome. What I'm telling you, dear reader, is that I just did this to do it, and I was fortunate enough to have many people help me get from "manuscript vomited up in thirty days" to "bound volume in your hands."

So, for starters, thanks to Kevin D. Hendricks, who wrote his novel first and convinced me that it could be done.

Thanks to Nicci Hubert at NavPress/TH1NK for reading the early drafts of *Mooch* and finding something there to champion. Thanks also to Terry Behimer, Dan Rich, and the rest of the gang for taking a chance on me.

Enormous thanks to Jeff Gerke, my tireless editor, for helping me put muscle on the bones of this story. Your contributions were much appreciated, bro.

Enormous thanks also to the other Jeff, Jeff Dunn, who single-handedly put me in a higher tax bracket by providing so much stuff to work on and for introducing me to the folks at NavPress in the first place. Got anything else we can coauthor?

I would be remiss if I didn't mention the other folks who agreed to go on the thirty-day novel voyage with me, even though some of you didn't make it to the end: Michael Porter, Andrea

Jobe, Paul Zardus, Sean Lorenz, and Daniel MacIntosh. Special thanks go to Michael, who wrote his novel using voice-recognition software: You're an inspiration, and I'm so glad you're finally dancing with your Father God.

Thanks to everyone who read the initial draft and offered critical feedback, specifically Paul and Sean.

Thanks to the staff and clientele of the many coffee shops where subsequent drafts were fueled and written, specifically Aaron, Audrey, and Jamie at Shades of Brown. Dear reader, if ever you're in Tulsa and you want a fantastic cappuccino, visit this shop.

Also of note, the fantastic staff (notably Josh, Joe, Chad, Debbie, Shalon, Mary, Anna, and Vince) at Panera Bread, 41st: Thanks for the free wi-fi and the occasional free beverage.

Thanks to Mark Steele and Margaret Feinberg for being excellent writers in their own right and for helping me "get my name out there," as they say in the biz. You guys are an encouragement.

I must also offer thanks to a few writers I don't know personally: C. S. Lewis (of course), whose books made me want to be a writer to begin with; Elmore Leonard for teaching me a thing or two about dialogue; Michael Chabon for creating and sustaining such great characters; David Sedaris for being so gifted—when I met you in Tulsa, I forgot to tell you how much I enjoy your writing; Susanna Clarke for knocking it out of the park with her first published at bat; Tobias Fünke for being awesome; and Andrew Niccol for writing two movies that I always find inspiring—*Gattaca* and *The Truman Show*.

Thanks also to *Seinfeld* reruns for the nightly inspiration as I hunkered down to log my 1,800 words for the day.

To my extended family: Thank you for believing in me and supporting me. To my father, Jack: Thank you for being such a godly example and for instilling in me a love for the written word. You are missed. To my mother, Carole: Thank you for teaching me to read at an early age and for all those Saturday trips to the library that fed my tender imagination.

To my children, Emma, Noah, Dorothy, and Sterling: I love you guys more than I'll ever be able to show you. To my foster daughter, Marley: I'm so proud of you. I know you're going to do great things.

And lastly, to my wife, Michelle. Thanks for being my ultimate inspiration. Thanks for reading each day's work and giving me the hope in the dark days that this novel could actually turn out pretty good. Thanks for loving me despite my flaws, and thanks for extending all the unearned grace in my direction. After Jesus, you're the best decision I ever made.

One

The Adventures of Sedgwick

SEDGWICK WAS NEW in sales at The Cruz Agency. Oh, it's a boring story, how he got hired. Nothing special. He just knew someone who knew someone. But he sure was glad to be at the company party at the Downtown Hilton. Hard to turn down a nice dinner at a fancy hotel, even if you're new.

No, he didn't know very many people yet.

Why yes, he would like to meet a few new coworkers, thanks for asking.

Oh, but he couldn't do that right now because he needs to use the restroom. But maybe tomorrow at the office?

That sounds great.

Sedgwick was always dodging potential introductions like that. He didn't want to meet anyone; he wanted to remain as anonymous as possible. Half the company didn't know the other half, and Sedgwick wanted everyone to think he belonged to the half they didn't know.

And if he didn't meet anyone in HR, that'd suit him just fine.
He was only in it for dinner.

In fact, Sedgwick didn't even work there.

§

Jake Abrams made it through high school with a decent
complexion — afternoons and weekends comprising face-fulls of
steam kept his forehead and cheeks fully moisturized. He turned
the girls' heads, mostly because they were envious of his smooth,
acne-free face. It didn't hurt that he happened to be not-so-bad-
looking, in a scruffy sort of way.

But that not-so-bad-looking face was rarely seen outside of
school. Jake was too busy working his part-time job in the banquet
kitchen of the Downtown Hilton. His grandmother was in charge
of the housekeeping crew, and she'd vouched for him with the
banquet chef. He started off doing salad prep, cutting vegetables
and hard-boiled eggs, but he got a sudden upgrade to event staff
the day management booked a dinner for two hundred employees
of the Immigration and Naturalization Service.

Immediate positions opened up throughout the kitchen staff.
Housekeeping, too.

Jake's boss wasn't pleased with management's decision.
"Abrams, I suddenly have a lot of holes to fill on the line. You up
for serving a dinner to the INS in a couple of weeks?"

"Uh, sure."

Jake spent the last half of his junior year and all of his senior
year working on the line, standing over steaming troughs of green
beans with almonds, garlic mashed potatoes, and, occasionally,
Swedish meatballs. He artfully spooned them onto fine hotel

china carried by tuxedoed and ball-gowned guests, listening to conversations about their high-powered worlds, sometimes being interrupted by requests for "more Chicken Oscar please" or "not so much with the lima beans." He gathered these dialogue snippets and filed them away, never to be used again. Well, not for another decade, anyway.

Working on the line, Jake had a front-row view of corporate behavior, and he liked it. He liked how the people looked and sounded important to each other. He liked becoming a tangential part of their world for the night, observing their behavior like a fly on the rice pilaf.

But he liked the free food most of all. There was always something left over at the end of the night, and though it was supposed to get thrown out, Jake just couldn't watch all that food go into the trash while his teenage metabolism was revving away. He pilfered the leftovers when his boss wasn't looking.

"Abrams!" his boss had said one time as Jake was reaching for his third plate of Bananas Foster. "That's supposed to go in the trash, not your mouth."

"But," Jake said through a mouthful of ice cream, bananas, cinnamon, and alcohol-free rum, "it's just gonna go to waste."

"I know. That's the policy."

Jake swallowed. "Well, that doesn't make sense."

"Sorry I didn't get your approval on the rules before I made them."

"It would've been nice."

His boss gave him the stink-cye. "I see another one of those plates in your hand, you're gone." The INS dinner was a distant memory by now, and Jake was taking up expensive, minimum-wage-guaranteed room on the line.

He lasted less than a week. His love of spiral sliced ham did him in.

S

Ten years later. Magic hour, when the sun goes down and day bleeds into night. A very nice blue pinstripe suit, size 40 long, made its way down 7th Street. They were borrowed duds, but Jake needed to look nice tonight. He wouldn't tell anyone where he got 'em.

Jake and his suit rounded the corner and made the turn onto Cheyenne. A few more steps brought him to the familiar doors of the fabulous Downtown Hilton. He flat-out sauntered through and, after consulting a sign at the entrance, headed left toward Ballroom A.

Jake halted at the doorway, pausing for a moment to take in the spectacle. Hundreds of people, all dressed to the hilt, milled around holding little melamine plates and/or glasses of wine they hoped, wrongly, wasn't from a box.

Amplified small talk took hold of Jake's ears as he entered the vast cavern trying to pass itself off as a classy ballroom. Sadly, it was a scene Jake knew all too well: not-plush carpet with a busy pattern to hide food stains, high ceilings made of honey-combed patterns of shiny metal to better reflect the dim lighting, and accordion-style partitions that allowed the hotel to change the room size as they saw fit. Jake saw that all the partitions had been moved aside, so the whole room was in use. Good for him, too: The bigger the room, the better chance he had of blending in.

He reverted to his high school ways, listening for a few phrases that might help him through the night, but most of the conversation was drowned out by the DJ in the back crossfading between the greatest hits of the seventies, eighties, and nineties (and today!). A makeshift faux-parquet dance floor had been laid down, but since it was currently unoccupied, Jake estimated the party had been in swing for maybe twenty minutes. Time to hit the buffet.

Score. He never knew what would be on the menu, but Jake's behind-the-scenes experience taught him he could always count on something chicken- or meatball-based. However, tonight was the mother lode, the crown jewel of these banquets: prime rib. Yes, it was mass-produced and dry, but it was still roasted cow, and for that he was grateful.

He started to grab a plate, then stopped himself when he saw that the silver serving trays stretching across the skirted tables were covered by their matching silver lids, canned heat burning underneath. Too early. They weren't serving yet—just getting the meat ready to slice. Better pass the time with a trip to the restroom.

On his way out, he accidentally made eye contact with a late-middle-aged man who looked very much like he belonged there. The man cocked his head, narrowed his eyes, and extended his hand.

"Who are you and why are you here?" he asked, unsmiling.

"I'm . . . Sedgwick," Jake said. "Just started in sales."

The man looked down at Jake. Sized him up. "When?"

"Yesterday."

The man frowned and grumbled. His grip tight on Jake's hand. His other hand stroking his salt-and-pepper beard.

Jake evenly returned the man's stare.

"Awfully lucky of you to get hired right before the party," the man said.

Jake smiled. "I know! Hopefully I'm this lucky with my sales efforts, huh?"

Jake felt the man's eyes memorizing his face.

"See you around the office, Sedgwick." He let go, but not without giving Jake's hand a too-tight squeeze.

"Looking forward to it."

Jake booked for the doors and headed into the men's room across the hall, shaken by the confrontation. For a moment, he kicked around the idea of leaving, but the lure of free prime rib quickly convinced him to stay. He'd just have to avoid Mean Mr. McSurly for the rest of the night.

Jake had always hated this bathroom. It was much too small for a hotel this size. Seriously, Downtown Hilton, what were you thinking with just three urinals and two stalls? Nevertheless, it was the only one around, so he chose the first stall, walked in, closed the door, and sat down to pass a little time. He reached into the breast pocket of his jacket and found the pocket word search book he'd brought with him, then produced a pen from another pocket and got to work.

Jake half-focused his attention on a puzzle with the theme of "Things You Put Syrup On" (pancakes, hotcakes, griddle-cakes . . . he began to wish they were serving breakfast). He kept going back to that encounter with The Surliest Man Alive and felt lucky to be in one piece.

Though he hadn't worked at the hotel in a decade, Jake still visited often as a ballroom-crasher. In his lust for free stuff, he put his past observations to work for him, glad-handing party-goers and steering clear of managerial types. He'd learned to spot those almost immediately. He cursed himself for making eye contact with someone who obviously could call him on his ruse. No more mistakes tonight.

His thoughts were interrupted by a pair of yapping yuppie salesmen coming in to use the facilities, oblivious to the standard social customs of public restrooms. They breezed in, already mid-conversation, and continued to chat through their entire bodily-waste-ridding process.

Unfortunately for Jake, one of them needed the stall next to him. The man at least had the decency to close the door after himself, but he kept talking, literally placing Jake in the middle of their conversation.

"So, Loppy Boy is really coming close to ending the Penske deal," he said. "Could be good for us to leverage future strategies."

Jake surmised that the other man was sired by a camel, judging by the amount of time he'd spent at the urinal. "So when's he going to engage the project?"

"Pending a closing, the Penske deal will be engaged by the beginning of next week."

"What's he doing to envision the team?"

Jake already had his mental tape recorder rolling, though he knew he might stumble over some of these corporate buzzwords. It seemed like the fashionable terminology changed every thirty seconds.

"He's crafting a list of action items. Bullet points and headlines to give them some ammo in their whiteboard sessions."

"And who's pulling the trigger on those?"

"Paulson."

"Man. You gotta love Loppy Boy for setting up Paulson like that."

"Yeah, it's vintage Loppy Boy."

Urinal Man had already finished up and was washing his hands at this point. Stall Man eked out a few remains while smacking roughly five hundred feet of toilet paper off the roll. Flush. Zip. The jangle of a belt buckle. Door creak. Step, step, step, step, step-step.

"So, you see Louisa yet?"

From the steps and the timbre of the voice, Jake could tell that Stall Man was checking himself out in the mirror. Probably adjusting his hair, giving it that perfect hoping-to-hook-up-at-the-company-shindig look.

"Oh, yeah. Unspeakably hot."

"Relentlessly hot."

"Her hotness knows no bounds."

Stall Man sniffled. "Yeah, well, hands off. She's mine."

"Ha. She doesn't work here, Tom. You can't stake out a claim like usual."

"You kidding me? I'm a friend of the family, bro. That's all the claim I need."

Their voices faded out as they exited the room. Jake rewound his mental tape recorder and ticked off the highlights. Loppy Boy. Penske. Paulson. Louisa. Tom. Friend of the family.

Wait. Did that guy . . . ? He didn't. Jake realized that no water had run after Urinal Man had washed up. Stall Man, a.k.a. Tom, hadn't washed his hands. Ew. At least Jake had gotten a glimpse of the shoes so he had an idea whose handshake to avoid and who not to stand next to in the buffet line.

In Which Sedgwick (Sort of) Meets a Girl and Something Else Important Happens

THE PRIME RIB had been decent, but the asparagus was wilted and the mashed potatoes powdery. Jake was waiting around for some dessert and getting tired of the relentless keyboard pop booming from the speakers. He'd been able to blend in fairly well, following his usual MO: Sit at a table where everyone knew each other. They all talked to each other and seldom made any effort to include the outsider into their insider world.

Should the occasion present itself, Jake had a standard line for the question, "What do you do for (insert company name here)?" He was Sedgwick, and he'd just gotten hired in the sales department. Sometimes he'd be in the customer service department, depending on the company. In any given corporation, sales and customer service have a high turnover ratio, so it was entirely plausible that this strange man nobody had ever seen around the office was really just a new hire lucky enough to make the party.

Jake had another close call during dinner, right after he'd finished an overly dressed and iceberg-lettuce-filled salad. The sales department manager visited his table. Jake had just loaded up a plate from the buffet and was about to tackle it when Jerald, a resident of Jake's table and a not-so-helpful member of accounting, pointed him out to the manager and said something about Sedgwick the New Sales Guy.

The manager eyed Jake warily. "I didn't hear anything about a new salesman. Who hired you?"

"Oh, Paulson brought me on for the . . . Penske deal. Part of his, uh, team envisioning tactics."

The manager nodded. "Well, you have to envision the team. Paulson's a good man. He knows that."

A trace of a smile cracked Jake's lips.

"So," the manager continued, "what's your specialty, Sedgwick? What aspect of the team envisioning will you facilitate?"

No more smile.

"I . . . specialize in, um, a host of capacities," Jake said.

"Such as?"

"Well, specifically speaking, I guess you could say I'm a synergistic coordinator. Specializing in individual team member engagement and initial . . . iz . . . ation." Jake swallowed after the last bit, unsure if it was really a word. "Even eagles need a push, you know."

Now it was the manager's turn to smile. "Looking forward to seeing you around the office then, Sedgwick."

Crisis averted, Jake dove into his meal and ate it in peace.

And now he awaited dessert, almost assuredly something of the cheesecake variety. It was just a matter of time to see what fruit-related topping had been drizzled over it. There was always the off-chance that it was the dreaded "turtle" cheesecake, layered with its phony caramel and unidentifiable nuts, but after that prime rib, Jake felt sure he was due for some raspberry swirl.

He never got it.

He saw her instead.

The femme fatale across the room. The love of a lifetime. The take-one-look-and-you-have-no-idea-what-you're-doing-because-your-palms-are-sweaty-and-your-heart-is-pounding-and-all-you-can-do-is-stare type of woman.

Her.

Jake had never been much of a ladies' man. Too much work. And besides, he liked to jokingly say, he could never love anyone more than he loved himself. Consequently, he'd spent most of his adult life as a loner. In high school, he had plenty of friends who were girls, but never a girlfriend. Every girl he was ever interested in would giggle if he brought up the prospect of a date; he'd taken a friend to prom, and she'd paid her own way.

As an adult, Jake had had a few casual relationships, but nothing to melt anyone's butter over. He was worse than Jerry Seinfeld in the way he could root out even the tiniest flaws in women, so he never paid them much attention. He'd even gotten slapped once on a date, and all he'd done was mention how he'd borrowed the scarf from a snowman one day. He was cold, and the snowman wasn't using it—and that merited a slap? Nah, forget women.

But this woman . . . well, he couldn't put his finger on it. He knew in an instant this was the Louisa whom Urinal Man had labeled as "unspeakably hot." He also knew in an instant that Urinal Man had been understating the point.

Dark brown hair that matched eyes in a different shade of dark brown. Full lips. A hint of color to the skin. A killer black dress that effortlessly hit all the right notes without being brash. An intangible sass that created an almost tangible aura around her. She had something different about her, to be sure, something . . . how to describe it? Spicy, perhaps? Jake had never been smitten before, but he found himself now in a deep vat of smit. He knew that he must — *must* — meet this woman.

Ah, but what about his story? He couldn't very well meet her as Sedgwick the New Sales Guy — that guy was only around for dinner tonight. Besides, he knew nothing about her.

He looked at Jerald and pointed at Louisa. "Who's she?"

Jerald smiled. "Oh, that's Louisa Cruz. Boss man's daughter." He took a sideways glance at his wife, then lowered his voice. "She's quite a number, huh?" Jerald's wife heard him anyway and smacked him on the elbow. "What? I'm just trying to help young Sedgwick here get acquainted.

"Anyway, Sedgwick, Louisa is the last of Mr. Cruz's children and the only one he gets along with. He's a real SOB, hard to work for, and even harder to know. His sons wrote him off a long time ago, and so did she, but for some reason, she's been back in the picture lately."

"What's she doing at the party? Does she work here?" Jake asked, hoping the answer was "no."

"No." *Yes!* "She's just here for her dad. She always comes to the annual meeting to drum up funds for her NPO."

This was perfect. Now he could be anybody: a guest, or some female employee's brother. Someone's date, maybe? Mmmmm, maybe not. Perhaps with the catering company, or the hotel? Maybe he's *staying* at the hotel and happened to wander in not knowing it's a private party? He'd settle on something before he got there, but he knew he'd better start walking if anything was to come of this evening.

"Thanks for the info, Jerald." Jake got up to approach Louisa. She was talking to some clod (but honestly, any non-Jake guy she talked to would be a clod), and though she laughed and lilted and listened, Jake positively knew that she was just really, really talented at faking interest in total losers.

He picked his way through the crowd, trying to figure out his story while simultaneously loathing The Clod. How dare he try to chat up this wonderful woman when Jake was obviously exactly the man she was looking for? An undercover police officer, that's who Jake would be, and he would arrest this bumbling poser for Unprovoked Harassment of a Beautiful Woman.

Then he noticed the shoes.

And he stopped dead.

The Clod had Tom's shoes. Jake recognized them immediately — the pretentious, outdated tassel and butterscotch-colored leather was a dead giveaway. But worse than owning Tom's shoes, The Clod had Tom's filthy, unwashed hands. Hands that were now — gasp! — reaching for Louisa's to force some sort of awkward shake.

Alert! Alert! This had to be broken up immediately! Jake knew he was the man for the task; he'd practically been sent here for this reason, to rescue this damsel in distress, not just from this Clod, but from Clods everywhere. Some unknown power/deity/alien force had put him in this exact situation to keep Louisa's lovely, perfect hands from being stained by Tom's microbial fecal detritus.

A squall of feedback from the speakers pierced his eardrums

and forced his attention elsewhere. Realizing the music had stopped, he swiveled his head and saw a late-middle-aged man with a salt-and-pepper beard stepping up to a podium on a small portable stage, apparently getting ready to speak.

Mean Mr. McSurly.

Jake looked back toward Louisa, but saw only the swish of her dress as she moved away from Tom. Whew.

"Hello, everyone. Greetings, Cruz Agency employees, and welcome to the annual meeting."

Mr. McSurly was speaking now, and Jake gathered from the attention paid to him that he was Benjamin Cruz himself, the founder and namesake of the company and, according to Jerald, Louisa's father. Usually Jake tuned out the inevitable speaking portions of these events, mainly because, after satisfying his belly, he made for the door. Of course, usually he didn't wind up smitten with love at first sight, so he stayed, paying attention to see what he could learn. Mental tape recorder: on.

"I won't lie to you. It's been a rough year for The Cruz Agency. Business was down, and many of you performed very poorly in your positions. You should be thankful you're still employed. Nevertheless, we're still ending this quarter with net profitability, something we've done ever since I started this agency twenty-seven years ago."

Most of the crowd cheered, but, looking around, Jake could tell most of the applause was obligatory and half-hearted.

"I know I'm hard on you," Mr. McSurly-Cruz continued, "but most of you deserve it. Heck, if it wasn't for my daughter, we'd be having this thing at Denny's, and I'd make you all go Dutch."

A few people laughed. Mr. McSurly-Cruz didn't.

"But, we're still profitable, and I guess that means that the few of you who did a good job barely outweighed all the rest. So, congratulations. We're still around."

The crowd collectively held its breath.

"That's the part where you clap."

Obediently, the crowd responded.

"And now, if I may get personal," he said. "Louisa, come up here."

Louisa, onstage and slightly behind him, dutifully obeyed, flashing a wide smile in doing so. The smile caught Jake off guard, increasing his resolve to possess her.

"My daughter, Louisa, everyone." Everyone clapped again, for real, and Jake scoured the room with insane jealousy.

Louisa made the "Oh, stop!" motion to no one in particular. Her father motioned her toward the microphone, and the crowd cheered even more loudly. Appreciative bunch. Louisa gingerly approached the podium and waited for the noise to die down.

"Um, thank you." Her golden, honey-tinged voice seemed to find frequencies that resonated deep within Jake. "I don't really know what to say. I know Papa isn't the easiest person to get along with." At this, the crowd laughed, genuinely. "But he's still my father. And I'm glad I've gotten to know him better these past few months. And I'm proud of him for building this business. And . . . I'll see if I can't get him to lighten up on you guys."

More cheering, more applause. Jake loved listening to Louisa talk, despite her overuse of the word "and." He chalked it up to nerves.

Louisa stepped away from the podium, arms stretched toward her father as if to give him a hug, while he took a step closer to her.

And then he stopped.

His eyes and mouth widened.

His arm reached toward his chest, but never got there.

His knees collapsed underneath his weight; his body drew to the floor like metal to a magnet.

The crowd gasped. Louisa screamed and started toward her father.

Jake just stood there, dumbfounded.

He took a few steps backward, eyes on Louisa as she bent down to cradle her dad. Oddly, he wanted to help her. To rush the stage and comfort her. To administer CPR. Whatever it took.

Instead, he slunk quietly out of Ballroom A, out of the Downtown Hilton, and onto Cheyenne.

♪

He meandered home, mulling over the evening's events in his mind. When he finally reached his apartment, he changed out of the borrowed suit and into a T-shirt/shorts sleeping combo and attempted sleep, but the night only dragged on. He tossed and turned, all the while thinking of ways to get Louisa for his own.

Whether it was through determination or exhaustion, he mercifully found sleep after a few hours.

A Momentary
Monetary Complication

JAKE POLISHED OFF a bowl of Lucky Charms while bringing his mind around to the concept of being awake. Clink went the carafe to the cup as Jake poured himself an unusual second cup of coffee after his sleep-deprived night.

What little sleep he'd gotten had done him well; he now realized Louisa was way out of his league, anyway, so she could be easily forgotten. Right? She was hotness personified, sure, but there were tons of fish like her — *better* than her — in the sea. Ones that maybe wouldn't be so wrapped up in money, with rich daddies subsidizing their party-all-the-time lifestyle.

Of course, that Jerald guy said she ran a nonprofit organization. Probably something to do with cleaning trees or something. Oh, well.

Jake looked at the clock on his oven and quickly realized if he didn't hustle, he'd never get to work on time. Might as well get back to real life. He snatched up the suit, now residing in a folded garment bag, and headed out the door.

When it came to transportation over short distances, Jake figured it didn't get much better than his motor scooter, especially since his was the grandmother of 'em all, a Vespa, painted an alarming shade of orange that approximated a traffic cone. This was "Princess Tangerine": 150 cubic centimeters of pure potent fun wrapped in an ultra-hip package that always got a wave or two from the ladies.

Jake inserted the key, taking care not to scratch the finish, and gave the speedometer a loving pat. He stowed his coffee mug in a cupholder he'd attached especially for mornings and hung the garment bag on a hook protruding from just underneath the speedometer. Jake gave the bike a kick-start, folded his legs into the cramped space between the garment bag and the scooter's front, and set off toward work on two tiny wheels.

It was only then that he noticed the gas gauge teetering dangerously toward "E," so he changed course and headed to the corner gas station, killed the scooter's engine, and threw down the kickstand with his foot.

Gassing up the eccentric, dated scooter was a masterful task in itself. As with most scooters of her kind, Princess Tangerine hid her fuel tank under lock and key, underneath her seat. Jake had long ago acquired the skills of a snake charmer in order to access the gas cap. He carefully inserted the engine key into the lock on the back of the seat, and, performing a few maneuvers that would rival any FBI lock picker, he coaxed the obstinate mechanism into turning loose. He raised the seat forward and, a few twists of the gas cap later, fed Princess Tangerine her maximum gallon-and-a-half limit.

Jake closed the lid, transforming it back into a seat, and went inside to pay. He handed the clerk a five-dollar bill. "Pump six."

As he waited for his change, his eye caught a stack of that morning's newspapers, which caused him to think two things at once. First, he remembered that he hadn't borrowed the paper from his neighbor across the hall, part of his usual morning routine. (He always left the sports section — that was all the guy ever read and they both knew it.) He must've really been out of it.

Second, he noticed the headline, informing him that Benjamin Cruz's life had ended last night.

§

The smell. Always the smell. Jake had gotten used to a lot of things in his ten post–high school years earning a living at White Hall Funeral Home, but he'd never gotten used to that unpleasant olfactory weave of old carpet, older particle board, and embalming fluid that always found its way into his nostrils. The crying relatives, the hushed tones, the pea-green plush carpeting: These once-novel things hardly showed up on his radar anymore. But the smell got him every time.

Once, as a protest, he'd come in with a big comical clothespin clipped over his nose. "Jake, what're you doing?" Del, his boss and owner of White Hall, had said. "That isn't professional. Cut it out."

"This smell's killing me, man," Jake had said.

"You'll get used to it."

"What about a surgical mask? It doesn't get any more professional than a surgeon."

Del gave him a cautionary look back then. He was still giving them now.

And now here Jake was, ten years into the job, walking through the door in the morning and being assaulted by that smell yet again. He wrinkled the right side of his nose, juggled the garment bag and his coffee, and offered a half-hearted wave in the direction of Chiffon, the receptionist.

"Morning, Jake!" she said. She gave the gum she was chewing an audible pop. "How's your day going so far?"

Jake approached her desk and prepared himself for the inevitable vapid conversation that he and Chiffon had every morning. "Good," he said. "You?"

Her eyes lit up. "Awesome! 'Cause my guidance counselor? met someone who knows a producer on *Hamster Cage*?" Chiffon had that way of speaking where her voice periodically trailed up for no reason, making everything sound like a question. "And so I might get an audition?" The phone began to ring. "Or at least get my audition tape seen? Anyway, I'll tell you all about it later!"

She let out a giddy squeal, took a moment to regain control of herself, and then picked up the phone with her tan, fingernail-polish-slathered hands. "White Hall Funeral Home. How may I direct your call?"

Jake offered another wave in her direction, thankful that the phone interrupted their usual banter. Through the first ten minutes of each day at White Hall, Jake had compiled the following information about Chiffon:

She was barely out of high school and had been stationed at White Hall through familial relations (her aunt on her mother's side had a friend who knew some relative of Del—it was complicated), but it was hardly a chosen career.

She was currently pursuing a dream she'd had for months: to be a reality TV show contestant. She'd taken her first paycheck to a pawn shop and purchased an old VHS video camera, and since then she'd also gotten a video-editing program that she used on her mom's computer, as well as gained an extensive knowledge of the workings of the U.S. Postal Service.

Chiffon spent all her free time submitting audition tapes to every reality show she could think of. These tapes were generally about ten minutes of babbling about how her fashion sense and knowledge of fad diet trends made her a compelling choice for (insert show name here).

She'd sent in tapes to all the standard shows, but she wanted it so badly that she'd even auditioned for some of the non-network shows. Like the one where you have to live solely on things you win in contests. Or the one where you have to convince your family you're dating a camel. Or the one where you live among cockfighters and have your fate determined by warring chickens. She'd auditioned for shows that made you lose weight, shows that made you gain height, and shows that tried to find the world's best gumchewer. She'd gotten two callbacks on that one, but in the end the producers decided to cast a zookeeper for diversity.

But all those auditions were just practice for the main event. Because Chiffon's super-secret dream that she always talked about was this: She really wanted to be on one of those shows where you sing for mildly famous judges in order to get a recording contract. Like so many girls her age, Chiffon wanted to be a pop star. Or rock. She'd even do hip-hop if the right deal came along. Of course, she'd have to learn how to rap, but that's a small detail when there's stardom on the line. Regardless, she had recording dreams, and she thought reality TV was the best way to achieve them.

Could she sing? Did it really matter? Chiffon knew enough about "the industry" to know that a good singing voice wasn't necessarily the most important thing. Looks—that's what really mattered, and looks she had in spades. Attitude? Of course she had attitude; those funky lime green shoes didn't put themselves on. Stage presence? Jake wasn't sure if she'd ever been on a stage before, but the looks and attitude would probably serve her well there, too.

No telling what tomorrow morning would bring in the ongoing saga of Chiffon Brown's Quest for Reality Fame. Until then, Jake would just keep filing the newest bits with the old ones until he could use this information to his advantage. He always found a way.

Jake kept walking back, back, back to his workstation. He was a jack-of-all-trades here at White Hall, doer of all jobs, master of none. If it needed to be done, Jake would do it. Sometimes he spent days sorting through paperwork; other times he filled a day with odd jobs, like that one time he had to reattach a handle that had fallen off a casket (before it needed to be used, fortunately).

The farther back he got, the stronger the smell. Man, he really hated that smell. Finally, he reached his workstation, which was basically a small desk shoved into the corner of a large multi-purpose room whose main features were a line of filing cabinets, a framed print of the God's-finger-touching-Adam's-finger part of the Sistine Chapel, and the perpetual glow of fluorescent light bulbs, which Jake not so affectionately referred to as "the light of a thousand suns." He set down his coffee on the desk and began to sift through the pile of papers that lay atop the disco-era relic.

"Cardigan visitation tomorrow at nine," he mumbled to himself. "Better drop this off."

He took the suit through the double doors in the back, through a hallway, and into the Prep Room, where Jeremy, a prototypical twentysomething slacker, was sifting through some papers and sipping on a chai tea purchased from the deli next door, pausing before each sip to move his stringy, dirty blond hair away from his mouth. Jeremy took no notice of Jake's arrival, but absentmindedly pulled down his too-short, too-tight thrift store T-shirt. He scratched his lower leg through the camouflage pants that hung loosely about him. Jeremy's main diet of cigarettes and organic wheatgrass shots gave him little body fat to support clothing.

A simple stainless steel casket on a rolling cart inhabited the far corner of the room.

"Whaddaya think, Jeremy?" Jake held aloft the suit, which he'd withdrawn from the garment bag on the walk back. "It's for Mr. Cardigan."

Jeremy finally recognized Jake's presence. He worked to focus his eyes on the suit. "It's nice."

"Not bad, huh?"

Jeremy eyed the suit more closely, then glanced at the casket. "Those blue pinstripes are no good with his eye color. They totally clash. That the only suit the family has for him?"

"Yep. They dropped it off yesterday."

"Why am I only getting it today, then? The visitation's tomorrow."

Jake shrugged. "Sorry."

"Whatever."

"So," Jake said, "where you want it?"

Jeremy pointed to a nearby hook protruding from the wall. "Hook."

Jake complied as Jeremy took one of the papers from his hand

and walked to the casket.

"Seriously, dude," Jake said. "Did you just say that? About matching the eye color?"

Jeremy opened the lid of the casket and gestured inside. "Sorry, man, but Mr. Cardigan here is clearly an autumn, and that suit is made for a spring. It just doesn't work. It isn't his season."

"What season works best with those camo pants you're sporting?"

"Deer-hunting."

A big voice boomed from the door. "Jake! Where in tarnation have you been?! I've been looking all over for you."

Del had spoken.

♪

Jake took a seat in Del's tacky oak-paneled office and gave his boss a questioning look.

"What's, uh, goin' on, Del?"

"Sorry. I didn't mean to yell back there." Del sighed and leaned back in his chair, the buttons of his cotton/poly short-sleeve dress shirt straining to hold back his considerable paunch. He smoothed his bushy mustache—soon to be the only hair on his head—with his stumpy, thick fingers. "It's just that we have a bit of a situation here. You heard about Benjamin Cruz last night?"

Jake nodded. "Pretty crazy."

"Well, it's about to get crazier," Del said. "Ben and I went to business school together, and we both started our companies around the same time. Back then, we made kind of a deal that if our businesses were successful, we'd each frequent the other.

You know, he'd help me out and I'd help him out, and maybe we could help each other get started. This was when he was going to open a grocery store and I was going to get my own beer distributorship."

"Really?"

"Yeah," Del said. "Anyway, things changed, and we wound up doing what we do." He made a bewildered face. "Did, I mean. What I do and what he did."

"Got it."

"Well, you know we never had enough business around here to merit hiring a temp, and Ben . . ." Del took a deep breath. "I mean, we aren't really the type of company anyone ever *plans* on using."

"But Mr. Cruz intends to keep his promise?"

Del nodded slowly.

Jake leaned forward. "Del, how do you know he wants to follow through with this? It's not like he can tell you."

"I haven't been in business this long by being stupid, Jake," Del said. "It's in his will."

Jake felt like he was playing Scrabble and had no vowels. "Wait, they've already looked at his will? He just died last night, for crying out loud."

"Jake, the thing you have to understand about wealthy people like that," Del said, "is that financial affairs are one of the first things their people look at when they go. He probably had a team of lawyers who all had the thing memorized."

Jake nodded knowingly, as if he, too, had a team of lawyers memorizing personal information about him. There probably were, but it would be more credit card-related.

An uncomfortable pause followed as Del tapped his fingers on his heavy mustache, glazed eyes looking at nothing in particular.

Jake finally broke the silence. "Del, I don't see how this is a bad thing for you. It's high-profile business."

"Of course it is; that's why it's bad!" Del said, smacking his desk and causing Jake to jump in his chair involuntarily. Del clenched his teeth and drew a deep breath through them. "I've always been just fine being a small businessman. I like what we do, and I like our environment. I never wanted to own a big huge company or anything, and I never wanted this sort of publicity." He gestured out the door. "I don't have the facilities to deal with all this media attention."

"You don't have the personality, either." Actually, Jake didn't say that, but he thought it. What he really said was, "I'm sure we can figure something out, Del."

"I don't know, Jake. We just don't have the space. I mean, the viewings alone are going to be so crowded we won't be able to help any of our other customers." Del's eyes pleaded with Jake to agree with him. "Don't you worry about the other customers?"

"The other customers will be fine." Jake rose and patted Del's shoulder. "We'll take care of 'em. Don't worry about it."

Del breathed out so heavily and so lengthily that he emptied his lungs. After he'd drawn a deep breath back in, his eyes got nervous, like he was a submarine captain entering mine-filled waters. "There's more."

He shifted his eyes from side to side and leaned forward. Jake, more and more curious, took his seat again.

Del just stared, his eyes an impenetrable veil of secrecy.

Jake folded his arms.

Del licked his lips and started drumming his fingertips together. Finally, in a barely audible whisper, he said, "He's taking it with him."

"Taking what with him?" Jake's regular-volume voice sounded like a gunshot.

Del glared at Jake and kept his voice at a whisper. "He wants to be buried with his fortune," he said. "That's in the will, too."

"Yeah, so?"

"So, if that little news item gets out, this place is going to be crawling with a bunch of no-goodniks! Every thief, robber, and con artist in town is going to make a run for that money!"

Del's voice bordered on exasperation—his eyes wild with, was that fright? Jake thought he might start crying.

"I mean, I can't afford that kind of security, Jake. I can't go to bed thinking about how there's millions of dollars in my store and all that's keeping it there is a measly deadbolt and a sign that says Premises Monitored."

"Oh, come on, Del," Jake said. "Millions of dollars? That sounds like a bit much."

"Well, a few million at least! But the amount doesn't matter, anyway—people hear 'fortune buried,' and they'll go nuts."

Jake finally got it. Del was afraid of the big time. He'd taken a risk twenty-seven years ago when he started his business, and now that he was moderately successful, he was through with risks. Unfortunately, Benjamin Cruz was now thrusting this risk upon him from the grave, and Del was thrusting it right back.

Ordinarily, Jake would only worry about himself in this situation and decide not to really care about it. As long as he got his paycheck, he'd be cool. But as Jake thought about the drawbacks Del had mentioned, and they were indeed great, he saw a benefit to all this. An enormous, glorious, fabulous benefit.

The daughter, of course.

Jake could see it now: Louisa thanking him for honoring her

father's wishes; Louisa admiring how secure he'd kept the money; Louisa noticing what a good job Jake did taking care of the family, maybe crying her foxy little eyes out on his scruffy-but-lovable shoulder.

He took as tactful a tone as he could. "Del, don't screw this up." Um, maybe not the best start. Try again. "I mean, this is a great opportunity. The way I see it, we just have to keep this little tidbit about the will to ourselves, and we'll be fine."

Del frowned and scratched the back of his neck. "I don't know, Jake. It's too risky. I just know it'll get out."

"Who's going to tell anyone? You? 'Cause I'm not sayin' a word."

Wheels were turning in Del's mind. Rusty wheels, but wheels nonetheless. Jake leaned in to apply some mental WD-40.

"Don't worry about it, Del. I'll handle everything. I'll handle the family. I'll handle the arrangements. I'll handle the media. If anyone starts asking questions, I'll be the one to answer them." He leaned back in his chair with an air of victory. "I will be the face of White Hall Funeral Home."

"Well . . ." The wheels were turning faster and creaking less. "You do have a nice face."

"Are you kidding? It's the nicest face in town," Jake said without a hint of smugness. "And all those smaller customers you love so much are going to see me on TV and think, 'Well, that sure is a nice young man working down there. I'd love for him to take care of me when I die.' Mark my words, Del."

In Jake's imagination, he could see the wheels of Del's mind speeding up and slowing down.

"Del, come on. You made a promise to Ben."

Houston, we have achieved operational wheel velocity.

"All right, Jake," Del said. "But you do everything. I don't want to worry about another thing; I got plenty to worry about already."

"You won't have to lift a finger, Del. Honest."

"Okay."

For some reason, they shook hands. Ten years Jake had worked there, and the only other time he'd shaken Del's hand was about two seconds after he'd been hired.

Jake turned to leave. Then, playing it up Hollywood-style, he turned and innocently asked in a one-last-thing voice, "You have contact info for the family? Who should I talk to?"

"Oh, that'd be his daughter."

"Okay. What's her name?"

News from the Media
and News from the Lawyer

JAKE EXITED DEL'S office to a scene far different from the quiet, normal morning he'd been having. He wasn't sure, but there was a distinct possibility that every news station in town had suddenly discovered White Hall Funeral Home's existence and had sent a correspondent to White Hall's lobby to find out the details of Benjamin Cruz's funeral. Jake looked out the plate-glass front windows and saw minivans with logos from various stations lining the parking lot. A few of them even had antennae and satellite dishes craning up from their respective roofs.

Reporters and cameramen had crowded the not-spacious-but-not-tiny front area, adding a stifling heaviness to the already unpleasantly fragrant air. One lone, ambitious cameraman, cargo shorts stuffed with extra camera batteries and tapes, was grabbing random shots of the lobby, pointing his camera first at the faux-leather sofa, then at a display of "Good Business" citations that

31

hung in cheap frames on the cheap wall paneling, then at . . .

Oh, please no. Chiffon.

The crush of bodies had been so great that he hadn't seen her at first, but now he heard Chiffon's unmistakable, high-pitched voice making its way through the mass of humanity and clanging against Jake's ear with a thud.

"Oh, I've only worked here a few months? 'cause it's not, like, my *real* dream? which is to be on TV? Oh, are you pointing that camera at me?"

Jake's attention was torn from Chiffon when his shoulder was suddenly bumped forward by someone behind him. He turned around and saw Del, frozen in anxiety as he exited his office.

"Oh, dear," Del said.

Jake stepped into Del's line of sight. "Not to worry, Del," he said. "I'll take care of everything. You just hide out in your office until we're all done here."

"Good idea." Del retreated hastily into his office and shut the door like a master thief.

Jake turned his attention back to the mob scene in the lobby, just in time to hear Chiffon saying, "My guidance counselor? knows this guy?" He cleared his throat and raised his hand. "I'm assuming you all have questions regarding Benjamin Cruz's arrangements?"

He was unprepared for the sudden rush of newspeople, camera lenses, and shotgun microphones that all vied for his attention.

"What do you know at this time?" a chirpy and youthful female correspondent asked.

"Well, we know that Mr. Cruz passed away last night, and we're still coordinating the delivery of the body with the hospital."

"Anything beyond that? Schedule-wise?"

"Not at this time. We'll determine the funereal schedule of events as soon as we have a chance to meet with the family." Jake was proud of his use of the word "funereal."

Another correspondent piped up. "Mr. . . . what's your name?"

Jake smiled. "Jake Abrams."

"Sorry. Mr. Abrams, Benjamin Cruz was an affluent man with many resources. Can you tell me why he chose this funeral home?"

"Some years ago, Mr. Cruz made an agreement with Mr. Ciccolella, the owner of this funeral home, and his will stipulates that he intends to keep that agreement."

The correspondent looked around derisively. "But are you confident that your . . . establishment will be able to handle an event of this magnitude?"

Jake bristled, but kept it in check so the cameras wouldn't notice it. "Fully," he said through a smile he hoped didn't look as phony as it was.

"Excuse me?" a bright voice rang out from the sidelines of the impromptu press conference. Jake, the reporters, and a half-dozen TV cameras swiveled to see who was talking.

"What is it, Chiffon?" Jake asked.

"Um, I thought everyone would be interested in knowing? that the body has arrived?"

Jake turned back to the cameras and smiled broadly. "Great!"

S

That afternoon when the reporters had finally gone, Jake relaxed at his workstation, exhausted and ecstatic. He toyed with the idea of calling a press conference this evening as he was leaving. He'd need a reason for it, though. He wasn't sure what that could be, but he wanted to give the cameramen the opportunity to grab a shot of him and Princess Tangerine scooting into the sunset. That'd play really well on TV, a poignant metaphor for Benjamin Cruz's passing into the next world. Very artistic. Award-winning, even. If these news crews were worth their salt, they'd know what to do.

Jake had also spent considerable time that day keeping Chiffon at her desk instead of chatting up one of the many correspondents that flecked the halls of the funeral home. Every time he turned around, he saw her flirting with a reporter or offering a camera-wielding guest some coffee and then presenting it with a sing-songy "here you go" while popping up one foot behind her, like she was getting kissed for the first time in a movie from the forties. She'd even gone home during her lunch break and changed clothes. Obviously, she was not aware of who the star of the show was supposed to be.

"Chiffon," he'd said, "is that a different outfit than the one you were wearing this morning?"

"Yes. The other one had too many stripes? They look bad on camera?"

"Hmm."

Sadly, this was true. Jake recalled someone once saying that the whole world is a stage, words Chiffon was currently taking to heart. When White Hall was suddenly flooded with cameras and a built-in audience, Jake was also flooded with flourishes of Chiffon everywhere.

She left a stack of eight-by-ten glossy photos of herself next to the coffee machine.

She spent a half hour taping up her "Chiffon Brown, Actor/ Singer/Personality" business cards in various strategic locations around White Hall.

She fetched various things for various people, volunteering her services for anyone who might need them. Once, after visiting a news van to retrieve a fresh battery for a cameraman, she handed it to him, saying in a singsong way, "Here you go, here you are, a battery for you, from your car."

"Uh, thanks," the guy had said.

"I just wrote that!" she'd gushed.

Nevertheless, even with all of Chiffon's interruptions, Jake was still able to participate in plenty of glad-handing, smiling, and talking, all with the restrained sobriety his position required. He had been masterful, and now he was taking a rest, basking in the glow of his performance.

Of course, there was the matter of the money. At some point, Jake would have to come through on his promise to Del and actually start thinking about protecting Benjamin Cruz's money. But that could wait. Right now Jake was on top of the world, and he wanted to enjoy it.

A knock on the door disrupted his reverie. "Come in."

The door creaked open, and in came a very expensive suit wearing a smallish, mousy man. Speaking of Mr. Cruz's money. "Jake Abrams?" the man inquired.

"That's me."

"Hello, Mr. Abrams, my name is Edgar Kimbrough. I'm one of Mr. Cruz's attorneys overseeing his estate." He extended a hand, which Jake promptly took after realizing this was probably not a guy he should be a slouch toward.

"Nice to meet you."

"Same." Kimbrough withdrew his hand and pushed his wiry glasses farther up his nose. "Mr. Abrams, I have a very busy schedule, so let me just get right to it. Have you been apprised of the, how shall we say, 'situation' regarding Mr. Cruz's estate?"

Jake shrugged. "Yeah, pretty much, I guess." The lawyer's eyes were not confident. "I mean, Del mentioned something to me about Mr. Cruz wanting to be buried with his, uh, life's earnings."

Kimbrough grimaced. "Essentially that's the case. My client had no living relatives other than his children and was not especially prone toward social causes. Since familial relations were strained and benevolence was out of the question, he determined to see that, when he passed on, his monetary assets became as indisposed as he."

And Mr. McSurly had seemed so nice at the dinner. "Well, I guess if that's what he wanted."

"Indeed." Kimbrough squinted his eyes as if experiencing a massive headache, pausing momentarily to pinch the bridge of his nose with his thumb and forefinger. "Let's be brief, Mr. Abrams. As the executor of this will, I intend to carry it out to the letter. Therefore, Mr. Cruz's liquefiable assets will be converted to high-dollar treasury bonds that will be sealed in the casket with Mr. Cruz the evening before his funeral. For obvious reasons, the body will not be viewed during the memorial. At the cemetery, there will be a standard graveside service, then he will be interred immediately. I'll make the appropriate arrangements with the cemetery staff to ensure this occurs. Are we clear, Mr. Abrams?"

Jake took a moment to recover from the verbal barrage before he finally came out with, "Uh, sure."

"I'm glad we understand each other," Kimbrough said, completely devoid of gladness. "I'm sure you're wondering what role you will play in these arrangements, so let me answer that question for you."

"Actually, I—" Jake stopped himself. "You know what? Go ahead."

"You will be coordinating with me on security issues," Kimbrough said. "From the moment that money enters the casket, I will post a round-the-clock watch over Mr. Cruz's remains to ensure that they stay undisturbed. I trust you have already determined to have security of your own?"

The last time Jake was caught off guard was when he laid eyes on Louisa Cruz less than twenty-four hours ago. This time he was caught off guard, but in a completely different way. His idea of security was just not telling anyone about Mr. Cruz's odd arrangement. "Of course."

"Good. I'll be in touch, then, Mr. Abrams."

"Okay," Jake said. "See you later."

"Good day, then." Kimbrough turned and walked out, all business.

Jake sank back down into his chair, slowly realizing how much work this was going to entail. He was a decent enough worker, always got his job done and everything. But Kimbrough's assertion of "round-the-clock" security was just too much for Jake to handle on his own.

He wasn't thrilled with the idea of enlisting any of the other employees to stay overnight, but he also wasn't too thrilled with the idea of hanging out at White Hall with some security guy all night long. Plus he already had a full schedule for the week: two company dinners at the Downtown Hilton, an insurance adjustors' conference at the Radisson, and he'd heard rumors of an eighteenth birthday on the top floor of the Petroleum Club.

Depending on when the funeral was scheduled, he could be missing out on some good eating.

But who to get? Del was out — too high-strung and emotional about it. Besides, Jake had already told him it was all under control. Chiffon? No, he'd hate to do that to the poor security guy. She'd just go on and on about her career aspirations. That left Jeremy as his only other option. Jake wasn't too comfortable with the idea of a slacker like Jeremy being the second line of defense of Benjamin Cruz's considerable wealth, but he was even less comfortable with the idea of that person being himself.

Jeremy it was. Jake took a deep breath and picked up the phone.

Five

A Man from the Past

LOUISA STARED AT her plate as she pushed around a few spoonfuls of rice and beans in a futile effort to make it look like she'd eaten at least part of her lunch.

Her brother Ramon, on the other hand, was sitting across from her, eating voraciously and expressing his sorrow in a different way. "Serves him right for never eating here."

"Ramon."

"Louisa, I'm not blind." Ramon gestured with his fork in no particular direction. "I know my place isn't the nicest around, just a hole in the wall, but it's mine."

"Well, you just slopped some of *your* beans onto *your* floor." Louisa pointed past the simple metal table to the black-and-white tile.

Ramon stooped down to wipe up the mess. "And I clean it up with *my* napkin." The job finished, he threw the napkin down on the table. "Not like Papa would ever know. He should be proud of his son. I open my own business, just like him."

"I'm sure he was, Ramon," Louisa said, putting down her fork. "I bet it was just hard for him to, you know, come in here and act like everything was okay."

"He don't get hard arteries eating my food," Ramon said. "He get it from that chef of his. He use too much butter, always too much butter. Taste terrible."

"Ramon!"

Ramon checked himself. "Sorry, Louisa. You know how I feel about the *comida*."

Louisa nodded. "Well, it is very good," she said, smiling wryly. "Why else do you think I'm in here so much?"

She understated the point. Her brother was a fireball in the kitchen, and he had developed his own personal twist on the wide range of food items that society at large labeled "Tex-Mex." Louisa liked her brother, but she really liked his cooking, which gave her a good reason to visit his restaurant every now and then. She could catch up with him, and he always served her up a plate of something special.

Today was different, though. Last night had been one nightmare atop another. The heart attack. The ambulance ride. The hospital. The waiting room. The official word. The crying. The heartache.

And she'd done it all alone. Her father was purposely difficult and guarded himself carefully from emotion, a tactic which had successfully driven away Louisa's mother; God only knew where. Her brothers still lived in town, but they stopped speaking to him ages ago. Stopped caring. Louisa herself had been on the outside of Benjamin Cruz's world until just recently. He had no relatives here in the States; he'd never brought them over. So in the end, it was just her at the hospital. Her and a very few Cruz Agency employees, loyal to the bitter end.

"You like the food?"

Louisa snapped out of her thoughts to see Ramon looking expectantly at her. She glanced down at her plate and noticed that while she was contemplating her life's upheaval, she'd managed to get down most of the rice and beans.

Ramon smiled at her. "You want some more? I'll get you some more." Ramon took her plate, and Louisa let him. Resisting seconds was just something you didn't do with Ramon.

"*Esta muy rica*, Ramon," she said, though she hadn't tasted a thing.

"*Gracias, mija*," Ramon replied as he wandered back into the kitchen. "I made it just for you. Very *especial*."

Ramon had hired a local Mexican artist to paint the restaurant an unhealthy color that looked either orange or pink or both, depending on the light. Right now it was midday, so the natural light of the sun tipped the color meter to orange. Interspersed throughout were cartoonish renderings of cacti, sombreros, classical guitars, and, along the main wall, the crown jewel of artistry: a completely disproportionate mariachi band. Their noses were too big for their heads, their heads too big for their bodies, their instruments too small and slightly rounded. Their knees showed no bend and their feet no depth. It was hokey and amateurish and beautiful.

Louisa also got a kick out of the Mexican flag painted on the window. The Cruz family wasn't Mexican; they were from Costa Rica. She'd asked Ramon about it once, and he'd brushed it off, saying, "It's for the *gringos*. Make it more *auténtico*." Ramon knew his target audience, and he knew that most white Americans thought all Hispanics were Mexicans. Why tip them off and possibly send them elsewhere? He'd just play the game.

Ramon returned with Louisa's plate, this time with its rice-and-beans capacity filled. He set it down in front of her, and she gave him a look.

"What am I supposed to do with all this? I barely ate the first plate."

Ramon shook his head. "It's good for you. Look at you; you're too skinny. Eat."

A bell jingled as the restaurant's door swung open. Ramon turned his head to greet the customer and stiffened slightly. "Santi?"

Louisa whipped her head around and saw that, yes, the tall man at the door, wearing the handsome black suit, was indeed her other brother.

Santiago was the middle child, younger than Ramon and older than Louisa. Neither of them had seen him in at least two years, since he fell in with some unsavory companions who always seemed to be on the wrong side of the law. There'd been a big sibling-sized argument about Santiago's choice of business associates, and he'd disappeared since then.

Santiago strode up to them. "*Hola*, Louisa. *Hola*, Ramon. *Puedo comer?*"

Ramon's eyes narrowed for a moment, then relaxed as he shrugged his shoulders. "*Sí, sí.*" He shuffled off to the kitchen to get a plate for his brother.

Santiago flopped down at Louisa's table as if his appearance was a daily occurrence. "So, sis, what's happening?"

"Why are you here, Santi?"

Sanitago chuckled. "Nice to see you, too."

She hoped the look she gave him could lower the room temperature several degrees.

He continued, undaunted. "I don't know. Pay my respects or something."

"Mm-hmm," Louisa said. "Or something."

"Easy, sister."

Ramon ambled back into the dining room holding a rice-and-beans-packed plate for Santiago. He set it down in front of his brother, then sat himself down at the table. "Here you go."

Santiago clapped Ramon on the back. "Looks good, brother." He unwrapped a packet of silverware and dove in.

Ramon managed a smile at his long-lost relative. "Glad to see you like it."

Louisa leaned toward Santiago. "So, Santi, what is it? Ramon and I would like to know why you're here."

Santiago paused a moment to finish chewing his food. After a swallow and a wipe of the mouth with his napkin, he muttered, "Can't a man want to patch things up with his family?"

Ramon placed his hand over Santiago's. "Of course."

"Of course," Louisa said, "if he really wanted to. So why the sudden change of heart, Santi?"

"Okay, I'm an honest man," Santiago said. "I'll level with you."

"Honest? Hardly."

"So much ill will." Santiago shook his head. "And speaking of wills . . . what do you know about Papa's?"

Louisa let out a disgusted chuckle. "Of course. It's always about money with you, isn't it?"

"No. I'm sad about Papa's death, just like you," Santiago said, "but I'm also a practical man—a businessman. In need of funds."

"Let me write you a check."

"More funds than that, *mija.*"

Louisa's chair shuddered backward as she stood up. "I wish I could help you, Santi, but I don't know anything yet. You're just going to have to wait for your withdrawal."

She turned to Ramon. "Thanks for lunch."

Ramon nodded. "*De nada.*"

And without another word, Louisa left. A few hard clacks of her heels on the floor and a violent jingle of the door bell were all she left behind.

Six

Negotiations and
More of the Same News

"DUDE, I DON'T know, man," Jeremy said.

Jake covered the phone receiver so Jeremy wouldn't hear his exasperated sigh. "Come on, man," he said. "Help me out."

"I don't want to hang with some security dude all night, though, man. I got a life, you know."

"What are you going to do with this life you supposedly have, Jeremy?"

The pause that followed spoke volumes. For a moment, Jake had wondered whether the phone line had gone dead.

"All right, I'll do it for a hundred bucks."

"*What?*"

"You gotta make it worth my while, man."

"Hold on." Jake hung up the phone and took the short walk to the Prep Room. "Worth your while?"

Startled, Jeremy turned around in his chair to face Jake, the phone still against his ear. "Yeah, man. I can't be doing this for free."

"Jeremy, first of all, put the phone down." Jeremy complied. "Second, a hundred bucks is a bit steep. How about fifty?"

"Seventy-five."

"Sixty."

"Seventy-five."

"Come on, man."

"Seventy-five, dude." Jeremy folded his arms. "That's my ceiling."

"Don't you mean, like, your floor?"

Jeremy's eyes went blank as he pondered his word usage.

"You know what?" Jake said. "How about sixty, and I let you use Princess Tangerine on your next date?"

Jeremy smiled toothily and rose from his chair to give Jake a high-five. "Now that's what I'm talking about, dude! It's on!"

Jake returned the grin. "Great." As far as he knew, Jeremy hadn't been on a date in a long, long time.

S

Jake had a mental to-do list regarding the Benjamin Cruz funeral, and he had just crossed off task number one: "Sucker Jeremy Into Overnighter." So now to the second item: calling the next of kin, a.k.a. Her Royal Hotness Louisa Cruz. He flipped through some paperwork from the hospital and, after a bit of searching, discovered Louisa's cell phone number. He started to dial it, then stopped himself.

First contact.

What to do here? First contact was difficult as it was, under ordinary dating-type circumstances. But here Jake was, approaching it as some sort of regular work task, not considering the merits of what he was about to do. For starters, this was no ordinary woman. This was Louisa Freaking *Cruz*. And he had not obtained her phone number by dropping some cheesy line at a singles' function, but by taking it from hospital paperwork about the woman in question's recently deceased father. And Jake wasn't just some schlub, either—he worked at the funeral home and was in charge of her father's remains and funereal arrangements—he gave himself a few more points for his second use of his favorite highbrow adjective. The complete lack of ordinariness of this situation began to hit home with Jake, and he started to do the unthinkable. He started to lose his nerve.

He vacillated for a good three or four minutes, sitting in his chair, looking at the number. Over and over in his head he thought the conversation through, trying to imagine how it might go, what he might say, how she might react. Finally he decided he'd better just get on with it and be as professional as possible. He didn't have to sell her on himself over the phone, anyway. He was much better in person. Probably should have her come in to White Hall to, um, discuss her father's funeral. Yeah, that would be it.

Several beeps later, he was listening to Louisa Cruz's cell phone as it rang.

S

Ugh, not again. Louisa couldn't take any more calls. She was tired of well-wishers from The Agency trying to console her. She knew they meant well, but she was avoiding all human contact right now. She didn't recognize the number, anyway, so she switched her cell phone's ringer to silent mode and let the call go to voice mail.

She set the phone down on her desk and leaned back in her chair as if surveying her tiny office. She welcomed the break from the sudden work that accompanied her father's passing and that now fell on her shoulders to do. As if she didn't have enough going on her life. Though it didn't pay very well, Maria House took up a lot of her time.

She'd always been a dreamer, ever since she was a little girl. Her father's business was already very successful by the time she came along, so she never knew what poverty felt like. But for some strange reason, she felt a connection to the impoverished. She didn't know why, but she'd always had a humanitarian streak running through her.

She'd been spunky as a kid, and one day she got a sense of mission in Sunday school, when the teacher told her a story about Jesus, and how Jesus had told the rich man to sell all his things so he could go to heaven.

She wanted to go to heaven, so she decided to have a yard sale.

The next Saturday morning, while her brothers were watching cartoons and her parents were sleeping in, little eight-year-old Louisa Cruz dragged a few dolls, some shoes she didn't like, a smudged plastic rocking horse, and a quilt out to the front yard for a little sale.

Hoping for some variety, she also rummaged through the garage, found a few items, and took those to the front yard as well. Business was booming until Papa and Mama woke up.

"*Mija!* What are you doing?" Papa had said.

"I'm going to heaven," Louisa had replied simply.

Papa surveyed the damage and soon discovered that he'd be replacing the lawnmower, the weed eater, and half his toolbox. He failed to see the bargain of trading those in for a free pass to heaven.

Things were so much simpler then. That was right before business at The Agency had gone through the roof, and to Papa's head. They moved to a larger house, one surrounded by gates and fences to keep out the riffraff. They kept out the regular kids, too. There were no neighbors, no one to play with. Louisa was stuck with a private tutor and too much free time; she quickly learned how to be lonely.

But not for long. In her teenage years, Louisa put her new driver's license to good use and began to explore the city, seeing what it had to offer. She was a young woman, driving her new car downtown, hoping to find a friend. Surprisingly, this did not end poorly.

§

Louisa was still getting used to her new wheels, and she kept getting distracted by looking at her driver's license, which she'd propped up on the dashboard as a makeshift altar. She decided to stop at a little eatery, having grown mentally exhausted from the combination of her not-yet-developed driving skills, the unfamiliar vehicle, her goofy-looking grin staring at her, and the decidedly non-suburban pace of downtown traffic.

She'd chosen the eatery because there were three empty parking spaces in a row, right in front, so no parallel parking. Great. In a matter of moments, she was inside, seating herself at the counter and striking up a conversation with the halter-top-and-miniskirt-wearing woman next to her.

"What're you having there?" Louisa said.

"Oh, just a cup of coffee," the woman replied. "Just trying to stay warm."

Louisa nonchalantly regarded the middle-aged woman's choice of outfit. "I think some different clothes might help," she said kindly. "Maybe a coat?"

The woman laughed hoarsely, her voice shredded from years of acting as a conduit for cigarette smoke. "Oh, honey. Can't be done."

Louisa looked at her with puzzled eyes.

The woman must've sensed Louisa's bewilderment, and elaborated. "I won't make any money wearin' a coat."

The proverbial light bulb — this one about a thousand watts strong — turned on inside Louisa's head. "Oh," she said. "I . . . see."

The woman either sighed or blew on her coffee. "I'm sure you do."

The two sat there in silence, the woman sipping her beverage and Louisa fiddling with, but not really eating, her pie.

"So," Louisa said, "what's that like? You know, working the street?"

The woman half-laughed. "You're a curious one." She looked around suspiciously. "Why, you interested?"

Louisa did a poor job hiding her shock. "Oh, my! No. No." She immediately regretted it. "I mean, not that you . . ."

The woman nodded. "I know exactly what you mean."

"No, really. I — I'm sorry. You just caught me by surprise." And that was the moment when her life changed. She couldn't explain it, but for some reason, she suddenly felt emboldened to just lay it all out there. "I've never met anyone like you before; I was raised . . . in a different part of town, where people hide their mistakes and flaws, hide their hurts. I've never been exposed to anything outside my sterile world; I've never been taught what to say to someone—a human being, a living, breathing *person*—like you."

The woman's eyes had filled with tears. "Bless you, child."

Louisa leaned in to her, purposely invading the woman's space. "What's it like, ma'am?"

The woman absentmindedly traced circles around the rim of her coffee cup with her pinky finger, the nail cracked and swathed in tomato-red nail polish. "It's a job."

"There are plenty of other jobs."

"It's the only one I can get." Her chin was trembling.

"Why?" Louisa asked.

"'Cause I . . ." the woman's croaky voice trailed off, coming back only when she'd composed herself. "There's this stuff I need. And he gives it to me."

"What's your name, ma'am?" Louisa said, reaching out her hand to touch the woman on the arm.

The woman was full-on crying now, and she said through a sniffle, "Helen."

"I'm Louisa, Helen, and I have a question for you." Louisa gently reached out to take Helen's shoulders, squaring them up so the two women were face-to-face. "Will you come live with me?"

Now it was Helen's turn to be shocked. "What?"

"I can help you, Helen," Louisa said, her eyes locked on Helen's like a cat's on the neighbor's dog. "If you truly want to be helped, I can help you. My father owns an employment agency;

we can get you job training, new clothes, rehab, whatever. We have plenty of room in our house, so you can stay with us until you can afford to be on your own. You can start over. But only if you *really* want it."

§

Back in her office, Louisa chuckled at her teenage self, full of naïve bravado that had served her well.

Helen had been a good start, though, and because she'd stuck with the program, she was a good influence on the girls who came through the doors of Maria House. Hard to imagine.

Louisa was just about to not answer another call when there was a knock on her office door. "Come in," she said.

To the uninitiated eye, the man who walked into Louisa's office could be mistaken for a well-dressed badger. Instead, he was a lawyer.

"Edgar."

"Hello, Louisa," Kimbrough said as he sidled into her cramped workspace. "I love what you've done with the place."

Louisa sighed. "What do you want?"

"I've just come to deliver some news regarding your father's estate. I trust you'll be interested in hearing it?"

"Sure, Edgar," Louisa said. "I haven't even buried my father yet; I'd love to spend this time of mourning discussing how I can lust after his money more efficiently."

The Badger just stood there, blinking. He pursed his lips, as if waiting on her.

"Sit down," she said.

A smug smile turned up Kimbrough's lips. "I know you've

been spending a lot of time with your father these last three months, correct?"

"Yes."

"But before that you had a, shall we say, strained relationship?"

"It wasn't the best."

Kimbrough nodded. He thought for a moment, then continued. "Your brothers . . . would you consider their relationship with your father to be strained as well?"

Louisa rolled her eyes and leaned farther back in her chair. "Get to the point, please."

"I'm trying to determine why your father decided to leave all of you out of his will."

Oddly, Louisa first thought of Santiago and how mad he would be. The satisfaction from this thought helped cover her shock. Unfortunately, her body did not get the same satisfaction, as it was tumbling backward and banging its head against the bookcase behind its owner's desk.

Louisa sprang to her feet. Good thing, too, because Kimbrough remained motionless.

"I'm okay. Really. Just fine." She reached back and massaged her neck. "Just a little, you know, head wound. Nothing to worry about."

"Louisa, I really don't want to compound your pain, emotional and physical," Kimbrough said with all the feeling of a vacuum cleaner, "but there's more."

"Great," Louisa said in a voice that meant the opposite. "Are you trying to get me to throw myself out the window? 'Cause I'll have to have one put in first."

Kimbrough just looked at her, and Louisa began to wonder

if his computer-powered robotic brain had suddenly experienced the blue screen of death. She shrugged. "Go ahead, Edgar."

"In addition to cutting you out, your father's will also stipulates that his fortune is to remain with him."

Louisa cocked her head quizzically to the side. "I don't get it."

"He's taking it with him, Louisa."

"He wants to be buried with his fortune?"

Kimbrough nodded.

Louisa started to speak, then stopped to think, then started again. "I'm not sure I understand."

The lawyer shrugged and removed his glasses. "He came into my office several years ago and approached me about this. Said that he didn't want his wealth to be used on anything but him." Kimbrough breathed on his glasses, wiped them on his shirtsleeve, and replaced them. "Personally, I don't understand it, either, but it's my job to carry out my clients' wishes, not to be their collective conscience."

Louisa stared at him, her brain growing as numb as her head.

"I can see you don't really know what to do with this information," Kimbrough continued, "so let me be of assistance. You are to do nothing. This was your father's wish."

Louisa remained silent. Her head throbbed.

"Good day, Louisa." He turned around and was gone as quickly as he came.

The alarm on her cell phone buzzed. She had a message.

Seven

The Internal
Hooking-Up Coach

"UM, HELLO. THIS message is for . . . Louisa Cruz? Hi, this is Jake, uh, Jake Abrams, from, um, White Hall Funeral Home, and I was just calling to set up an appointment for us to talk about the arrangements that we need to discuss and make regarding your father's proceedings. Could you please do your best to call me back as quickly as possible so that we can begin these discussions and arrangements? Thank you."

And thus the message had been left. Jake was glad his legs weren't double-jointed, or he would've been very sore from kicking himself. All the worse: Louisa's voice mail didn't allow for re-recording, which Jake had counted on when he heard how lame he was sounding. Why hadn't he prepared something and then called back? Why did he attempt an extemporaneous message? Why?

He was powerless now. The message was sitting there, just waiting to be retrieved. He had no other choice but to be fatalistic.

She would probably listen to it and think he was just some prud-ish, seriously uncool guy a-workin' down at the funeral home. Oh, well. So be it. It was time for lunch anyway.

Jake had brought in some leftover pizza. Two nights ago he'd gone out to eat with his aunt and uncle—their treat—and on the way out he'd noticed the people at the table next to them had accidentally left the restaurant without taking their boxed-up leftovers. But now, standing in the official White Hall break room heating up the pizza in the official White Hall toaster oven, the realization struck him: *He had no soda.*

Now Jake was a pretty mellow guy, but there were certain things he couldn't abide, and one of those things was eating pizza with no soda. Preferably Coke, though Pepsi would do if push came to shove. He scoured the office minifridge in the hopes of finding something, but Jeremy was a green-tea drinker during the day (he'd been known to have a carbonated beverage or two in the evenings when he was feeling crazy), and Chiffon only drank diet. Del had long ago gotten used to Jake's bumming ways; he kept a private stash under lock and key.

Rebuffed, Jake went to his workstation and found a half-full Styrofoam cup from a few days ago that looked relatively dent- and scratch-free. He quickly emptied and rinsed it in the bathroom sink, then took a walk to the deli two doors down from White Hall.

The lunchtime crowd filled the deli to capacity, so Jake was able to make his way undetected from the door to the self-serve soda machine in the far corner. He filled his cup with ice and Coke, then turned to walk away.

He stopped suddenly, sloshing a small wave of his refreshing carbonated beverage onto his index finger.

Louisa? Is that you?

He was transfixed by a pile of brown waterfalls cleverly disguised as bountiful hair viewed from the back. The hair was right. The build was right. Good shoulders—not too bony or pointy, not too rounded or shapeless. She wasn't entirely facing away from him; maybe a third of her face was visible. He studied the outline of her cheek, the way her chin sloped, the semicircular beginnings of an engagingly large brown eye.

He stood there studying her, willing her to look his way so he could verify this woman's identity as the true Louisa Cruz. Time froze as he stood there.

And then she turned.

Not Louisa.

Not even close, really. How had he even for a second thought that was her? He shook his head imperceptibly and began to walk out, stopping for a moment to replace the lid on his cup and to lick the soda off his finger.

Wait! In line! There! That must be her, right? Jake didn't really see Louisa as a pantsuit kind of a girl, but there she was in line, wearing a pantsu—oh, not her. Again.

What was happening to him? Why did he keep thinking he saw Louisa? Had she returned his call yet?

The last question drove him out of the deli as quickly as he could walk without arousing suspicion. He ran/walked back to White Hall and promptly checked his voice mail. Nothing.

And his pizza had burned, too.

S

Jake's phone didn't ring until 3:23, long after he'd begun digesting his lunch of charred pizza toppings and a package of powdered donuts he'd shaken out of the office vending machine. He lunged at the phone with a vengeance the second he heard the digital ringtone, rapping his knuckles against the keypad as he picked up the receiver. "Ow! Hello?"

Instead of Louisa's smooth voice, he heard a chirp he couldn't immediately place. "Mr. Abrams? Everything okay?"

"Yeah, I'm fine," Jake said. "Just, uh, listening to some James Brown."

"This is Cindy Pennington, Channel 9 News. Wondered if you had time for a few questions?"

"Oh. Absolutely."

"Great."

Jake heard some papers shuffling in the background and remembered this reporter. She'd asked the first question this morning; he wondered why she would be calling him now.

"Have you had a chance to meet with the family yet?"

"No, ma'am. I've placed a call, but have not yet connected. As soon as we iron out the details, however, we'll let you know what those are."

"Excellent." He heard another paper shuffle. "And which members of the family will you be meeting with?"

"I'm sorry?"

"Mr. Abrams, it's well-known that Mr. Cruz did not have strong familial relations with his wife or children," Pennington said, devoid of emotion. "I'm just curious who you would be meeting with. If anyone."

"Well, if the family wants you to have that information, they'll be glad to supply it to you. I'm not at liberty to divulge it."

"Mr. Abrams," Pennington said, "surely you understand that our audience demands these sorts of details. Mr. Cruz was a wealthy, well-known man and one of the city's largest employers. People want to know."

"Well, people won't hear it from me."

"I'm sympathetic to the family's situation, Mr. Abrams, but I also have a job to do."

"So do I, Ms. Pennington." Jake wished he was in a movie so he could just hang up for effect. Fortunately, he was bailed out when the second line on his phone began to ring. "Excuse me, I have another call."

"I understand. Get back to work. I'll be in touch, Mr. Abrams."

Jake clicked over to the other line, peeved. "Jake Abrams!" It came out like a bark.

"Yes, Mr. Abrams, this is Louisa Cruz, returning your call?"

"Oh!" No! "Yes. How are you, Ms. Cruz?"

"I'm . . . all right. Considering."

"Of course, of course," Jake said. Man, she had a wonderfully great voice. He'd heard hints of its greatness at the party, and then again on her outgoing voice mail message, but actually having a conversation with that voice, having a part in the words it uttered . . . oh, yeah—the conversation. "You sound like a tough young woman."

It was at this point in the conversation that Jake became noticeably aware of a persona within him, a voice that guided him on the ways he should relate to women. Jake had long ago dubbed this persona his Internal Hooking-Up Coach, his IHUC, and, at times, it could be brutally honest with him. This was such a time.

"A tough young woman?" it mocked. "*A tough young woman?*"

That was all the IHUC needed to say. Anything more would have had less impact (and impeded the actual conversation Jake was having with the "tough young woman" in question).

"I get by," Louisa said after a moment. "You know how it is."

Smooth. Smooth. Just be smooth. Think industrial-strength blender. "Definitely. I do know. How it is. And how it can be." The IHUC abandoned the blender metaphor and went straight to something Jake could understand: Mayday! Mayday! Pull up before it's too late! "Anyway, Ms. Cruz, I—I hate to do this to you so soon, but we have a few things we need to discuss regarding your father's arrangements, and, um, forms to fill out and whatnot, and so, well, we need you to come by here for about a half hour to take care of this stuff." There, that wasn't so bad, except for the unwelcome *whatnot*.

"Oh, um . . . well, how soon do you—"

"Whenever is most—"

"—need me to—"

"—convenient for you to—"

"—come in?"

"—come in."

Fortunately, Jake heard Louisa chuckle as they stepped over each others' words, so he gave a laugh, too.

"I can come by today," she said. "Would that be helpful?"

"Absolutely, Ms. Cruz," Jake said. "Whenever you want."

"Okay. I'm in my office right now, but I should be done around five. Is that okay?"

The time Jake would normally be going home for the day. The IHUC made the decision easily. "That'd be great. I'll see you then."

"All right."

Jake was roughly one million miles in the sky when he hung up the phone, sailing once more on the S.S. Smit.

He got nothing done for the next hour and a half as he awaited Louisa's arrival. He wanted immediately to go to the lobby to look for her the moment she got there, but he stifled the urge and instead spent the time looking over the same sheet of paper roughly 570 times as his mind raced with random thoughts about her.

Finally, the magic time arrived when the intercom on his phone beeped and Chiffon's voice announced, "Jake? There's a Ms. Cruz here to see you?"

Jake's throat went dry. "Be . . . I'll be right there."

So that's where the moisture in Jake's mouth had gone: to the palms of his hands. What in the world? He was unaccustomed to feeling so fluttery, especially since he'd never had a face-to-face conversation with the woman who was driving the flutteriness in him. So, completely unprepared, he stepped out of his door and into the hallway, getting ready to introduce himself to the most beautiful woman in his world. Just before he reached the lobby, he remembered to smooth his palms against the legs of his pants.

And then there she was.

He approached her, extending his hand along the way. "Louisa Cruz?" Stupid. Guys are never supposed to offer their hands first, forcing the woman into a shake. Wait for her to offer her hand. Jake's IHUC let him know he'd botched the Initial Physical Contact.

"Yes." She extended her hand to meet his, gripping it not too firmly, not too softly. Just right, like Baby Bear. "Mr. Abrams?"

"That's me." Was that too cavalier? After all, she's here to talk about her dead father. Must be more sober — serious — if she's going to buy the act. "Um, if you please, follow me and we'll get started."

"Absolutely." Yes, that voice was absolutely gorgeous, absolutely perfect, absolutely right here in the room with him. Excellent.

Jake led Louisa into a conference room of sorts, known as the Interview Room, a simple area with a big table and a few chairs around it and Van Gogh and Monet prints on opposing walls. Del didn't like to welcome people into his oft-messy office, so he'd established this room as a way to sit down with clients without exposing them to the clutter of his world. Jake used it now because the tiny desk at his workstation, with its pitiful office chair and equally pitiful four-legged stool, were certainly nothing that would impress someone of Louisa's stature.

He gestured to a chair. "Have a seat?"

"Yes, thank you." Louisa placed the small handbag she was carrying on the table. "How have you been today?"

"Um, not bad. You?" Stupidstupidstupidstupidstupidstupid. The IHUC was repeatedly smacking an internal palm against its internal forehead. With that line, Jake had officially joined the ranks of the Clods, proud member since about ten seconds ago.

"I'm doing all right, all things considered," Louisa responded with a slight smile.

That was a smile, right? The IHUC let up on the palm-smacking. Perhaps Jake needn't sign his Clod Membership Card just yet.

"Okay, then. Let's get started." The conference table had a drawer on one side, which Jake now opened. Inside was a stack of forms and a rubber-banded batch of pens; he took out one of each.

"Let's start with the basics. What was your father's full name?"

"Benjamin Martin Cruz."

And so began the first conversation of what Jake hoped would be many. He finally settled down and got comfortable with Louisa, asking her all sorts of questions that pertained to his form. Louisa patiently answered them all in her smooth, sweet voice.

"Okay, now we need to talk about headstones," Jake said. "There are many varieties of stone to choose from: granite, marble, stuff like that."

"I think granite's good," Louisa said. "It's hard, right?"

"One of the hardest. Are you worried about durability?"

"No," she said, "I just want it to be consistent with his character."

Jake chuckled. "He was a tough guy, huh?"

Louisa nodded, smiling slightly.

"Yeah," Jake said, "I think that sounds like a good choice, then. We do have a special option for pushovers and softies, but it's just a big pile of sand."

She laughed. A legitimate, heartfelt cackle.

At Jake.

The IHUC was up in arms. No need to make that wisecrack! It was completely inappropriate, not to mention offensive. And she was laughing only because she was a nice person who felt sorry and embarrassed at his rudeness.

Jake didn't quite believe the IHUC.

Because, oh, that laugh. Jake had heard the word "lilting" to describe a laugh before, but he'd never really comprehended the meaning until now. Louisa had what could only be described as a lilting laugh, almost a physical presence that could carry Jake aloft as he floated on it. He wished he could think of another funny thing to say, but his brain locked up and he decided not to risk making a wisecrack without the aid of his higher reasoning.

The closer Jake got to the bottom of his form, the more he drew out the questions, elaborating and lengthening and all-around stretching them out. He didn't want this moment to end. Ever. The bottom of the form loomed like an executioner drawing ever closer. Finally, as it had to, the end came.

"Well, I think that just about does it," he said. "Thank you for your time. I know this was probably very hard for you."

Louisa shook her head. "It was easier than I thought it would be. You helped a lot."

The IHUC blushed. Jake just smiled in an aw-shucks sort of way. "Can I show you to the door?"

Louisa smiled. "Sure."

Jake smiled. "All right, then." He desperately wanted to ask her out, to capitalize on this magical moment, but the IHUC put the immediate kibosh on that notion. One hundred percent inappropriate. That would never do, no matter who she was or how many times she smiled or laughed. She would see right through him! How dare Jake even think such a thing?

They walked to the door in silence. When they reached it, they stopped and faced each other. Jake waited for Louisa to extend her hand, which she did. He shook it and said, "Ms. Cruz, thank you for coming on such short notice."

"Please, call me Louisa."

"Oh, okay. Great." Oh, come on, Jake! That's the best response you can come up with? And could you have said it in a dopier voice? Internally, Jake withered under the force of the IHUC's blows.

Another smile from Louisa. "Okay."

"Okay," he repeated, hoping she wouldn't realize he was still holding her hand.

"Say, Mr. Abrams. Jake," Louisa said as she let go. She let out a quick breath and slumped her shoulders. "This may seem forward, but would you like to get some dinner?"

Jake's eyebrows went skyward. "Dinner?"

The IHUC had no response.

Jake did. "Yeah. Sounds great."

She smiled. "Okay, great. Do you like Mexican?"

He'd never been a big fan. "Love it."

"Great. I know a really good place. Ramon's Mexican Kitchen. Do you know it?"

"Can't say I've ever been there."

"Well, you will soon. It's at the corner of Beacon and Oxford."

"Beacon and Oxford. Got it." Jake was doing well to contain the backflips his heart was doing.

"I'm going to run home and freshen up," she said. "Meet you there in, say, an hour?" She glanced at her watch. "And a half?"

"Sounds great."

"Great."

She gave a half wave and began to walk out the door. Then she turned around and called over her shoulder. "Oh, by the way. My brother owns the place, so it's my treat."

"Great." This was Jake's kind of woman.

"We both like to say 'great,' don't we?" Louisa said. "Looks like we have something in common."

And out she walked. Jake stood in the lobby and watched her make her way toward a black Volvo sedan.

S

The whole way back to her car Louisa fought the urge to turn around.

Something about this man piqued her interest. He'd seemed sweet in his voice mail message; that's why she'd called him back today. Talking on the phone with him, he sounded like a nice enough man, but when she got here and saw him in person . . . Well, she was impressed.

Scruffy, but still good-looking. And she could see a spark of mischief in his eyes, mischief he seemed to be repressing for her benefit. She liked his forwardness and instant comfort with her. She liked how he talked like a regular person, not a customer service rep.

And he made her laugh. She'd originally laughed at his first joke as a knee-jerk reaction, and though it seemed wrong at first, laughing in the midst of her sorrow, she'd become more comfortable with it the more deeply she examined her feelings. It was something she needed. And though Papa was gone . . . well, life still continued for Louisa. She ached for her father, but the laughter had given her a slight reprieve from that ache. She'd wanted to take Jake in her arms and thank him for that laugh. She'd used her eyes instead.

And then when he announced that the interview was over, she realized she was sad. As odd as it seemed, she'd enjoyed her time with him, reliving her father's mostly good memories. She was learning to treasure the last three months she'd had with him, and talking to Jake reminded her of those ninety-two days, to be exact.

Mischievous, funny, good-looking . . . It was a combination she needed right now.

She reached her car, unlocked it, climbed in, and shut the

door. Behind the safety of tinted windows, she looked to see Jake still watching her. Yes, this was going to be an interesting evening.

S

Yes, this was going to be an interesting evening. Jake saw Louisa turn her head, barely visible through the window tinting of her car. But he saw it. She'd actually asked him out, then turned and looked for him after she got in the car.

As he attempted to repress this strange puppy love-type feeling, he had a mental image of an enormous ocean seen from above. The waters were gentle, warm, placid, and sweet. There was a tiny speck on the surface, and as his mental camera zoomed in, it also changed directions to see the speck from the side. It was his ship, the fine sailing vessel he'd crafted from her laughter, her eyes, her smile. A magnificent creation it was, and he stood in the prow, one foot on the side and chest thrust outward as he smelled the smell of open water.

His mental camera panned along the side to see a figure being launched into the air. It was Jake's Internal Hooking-Up Coach being thrown overboard.

In Which a Lot of Stuff
Happens on the Way to Fajitas

JAKE'S IMAGINARY MOVIE was interrupted by Del's meaty voice. "That Ben's daughter?"

Jake raised his eyebrows and turned to face his boss. "Yeah."

"She seems nice."

"Yeah, from what I could tell."

"You get everything worked out for the funeral?"

"We got a start on it."

Del looked around, then leaned in. "Does she know?"

Jake looked around and leaned in, too. "Know what?"

Del lowered his eyes at him and whispered, "About the money."

Jake lowered his eyes and whispered, "What money?"

Del gave Jake the "come on" face.

"See," said Jake, "I'm so good at keeping secrets that I forgot what you were talking about. That's how much I'm *not* letting it out."

"She'll know eventually. And then she'll make trouble for sure."

"Her?" Jake said, incredulous. "No way."

"Never underestimate the power of money," Del said. He wagged a finger in Jake's face. "Don't let her bat her eyes at you and get you to let your guard down."

"It'd take a lot more than an eye-bat to do that, my friend." He thought of mentioning Del's ex-wife, but stopped himself. He knew Del was speaking from past hurts, and he also knew his boss had dropped a sizeable alimony check in the mail earlier in the week.

"So, how's the press?" Del asked.

"Just fine. A little inquisitive, but nothing I couldn't handle."

"Really?" Del said in an urgent whisper. "What were they asking? Did you tell them anything?"

"No, Del. Relax." Jake took a deep breath in the hopes that it would encourage Del to do the same. "Just some questions about Louisa. Stuff I didn't really think would help our situation."

"But you kept your mouth shut."

"Absolutely."

Del looked around again. "Okay," he said, sighing heavily.

"You all right?"

Del dismissed the question with a wave of his hand. "I'll be fine. Just glad when this is all over."

"Me, too," Jake said, not meaning it.

S

Jake scooted home in a bit of a daze. He couldn't believe that Louisa Cruz had actually asked him out. It was like she was practically begging him to hook up with her. He was so out of it from licking his dating chops that he missed a gear on the final turn toward his building and popped an accidental wheelie that almost gave him an early appetizer of pavement and pebbles. Fortunately, the act of his front wheel going in the air snapped him back to reality, and he pulled the clutch lever in time to disengage the gears and bring the roaring beast back on all twos. Now his heart had two reasons to be racing.

As was his custom, he parked his scooter on the sidewalk right by his front door, then darted up the stairs to his second floor bachelor pad. He was mentally flipping through his wardrobe catalog, trying to remember what was clean, what needed to be washed, and what was dirty but still useable. After all, wearing a pair of jeans once didn't necessarily make them dirty, just broken in. Shirts, the same. Socks . . . that was stretching it, but Jake could go two days on a pair of socks. Underwear was the only place he drew the line — those were one-day wear only.

Okay, sometimes he'd go two. But only during the winter, when he didn't sweat so much.

Once inside, he clicked on a hideous brown glass lamp that had once been his prized possession since he found it in a dumpster behind a thrift store. Jake was fond of accessorizing his cramped studio apartment with found objects, and each new find became his latest prized possession. Since the lamp, his prized possessions had become, in order: a giant candle in the shape of a gnome, a hand-drawn black-light poster of a unicorn riding a jet ski, a wok with no handle, and his newest — a three-foot-tall ceramic monkey with a sturdy, flat head. He used it as a pedestal to display the gnome candle.

He began sorting through the pile of clean/dirty clothes

that generally stayed somewhere around the corner of his bed, frequently mutating into different shapes, densities, circumferences, and heights. He'd done a wash less than a week ago, which meant most of his good stuff was still available. He pulled out a snazzy pair of jeans and a very wrinkled black dress shirt, sniffing them both to make sure they hadn't picked up the scent of slightly moldy oranges (one had fallen behind his refrigerator a couple of weeks ago—he'd rather put up with a hint of wayward citrus wafting through every cubic centimeter of his bachelor digs than move the refrigerator). Satisfied with their fragrance-free status, he grabbed a couple of empty hangers from the closet and headed to the bathroom.

Squeak, squeak, squeak. FFFT—shhhhhhhhhhhhhh. Now that the shower was running, Jake put the shirt and pants on their respective hangers, hung them on the towel rack, then jumped out of his current clothes and into the shower.

Jake loved the shower. Maybe more than most people. He mainly liked it because it allowed him time to himself, only to himself. Of course, he lived alone, but there was something about the close proximity of the pale green tile and the slightly mildewed green striped shower curtain that made him feel secure. Add the refreshing spray of scalding hot water, and the shower became a downright cozy place. He did some of his finest thinking there.

And this night, just before his first official date with Louisa Cruz, the potential lust of his lifetime, he had a thought that took him so by surprise and occupied his brain so completely that he depleted the hot water tank. He'd been aware enough of the temperature to keep turning down the cold faucet, but when the water ran lukewarm and the cold faucet would turn no farther, Jake decided to put his thought on ice. And after all the steam had worked its way through it, his shirt was now immaculately smooth.

S

Jake spent the rest of the hour pondering. He pondered as he toweled off. He pondered as he dressed. He pondered as he put on deodorant. He pondered as he checked himself in the mirror, making sultry faces like an underwear model in an über-fashion magazine.

Fully ready, Jake bolted out the door, hopped on Princess Tangerine, and made haste toward the corner of Beacon and Oxford, whose names indicated they contained something far from a Mexican restaurant. Nevertheless, within ten minutes, Jake was standing in front of Ramon's Mexican Kitchen, looking around the parking lot for a black Volvo sedan.

He checked his watch. He was four minutes early. Should he go in? Should he wait outside? He didn't know what was the right thing to do — whether she would appreciate his being early or feel bad for her being late. He decided to wait outside, sitting on his scooter, still wearing all his riding paraphernalia. That way it at least looked like he'd just gotten there and hadn't had time to take off his helmet, goggles, and gloves. Yeah . . . she'd like that.

S

Louisa glanced at the dashboard clock. She was going to be late. An hour and a half just wasn't enough time to get home, check her e-mail, check her voice mail, find a cute but romantically nonspecific outfit, shower, dress, dry her hair, apply limited makeup, check her voice mail again in case the phone had rung while she was in the shower, check her e-mail again, find her keys, and be out the door. She had definitely done all that in record time, but she was still going to cut it close.

She hated the thought of Jake sitting in there waiting for her, but there was another thought she hated more, so much that she kept pushing it out of her brain every time it came up.

She wasn't sure this was such a good idea, meeting Jake at Ramon's restaurant. Especially with Santiago haunting the place earlier today—what if he was still there? And what about Ramon? What would he think of Louisa being out with some *gringo* the night after their Papa had passed away? Shouldn't she be doing something else right now, something more sober and full of mourning?

But for some reason this occasion seemed right to Louisa. She felt like Papa would approve somehow. Like, if he'd met Jake, he'd like him. Louisa felt sure that Papa would want her to be right here, right now, on her way to have dinner with this man. She'd considered the possibility that she was only telling herself that as a way of skirting the emotional pain of her father's death, but she didn't care. She was tired of being the strong one. She wanted just one evening to relax and let someone make her laugh. It didn't hurt that this particular someone was also easy on the eyes.

She had to do this, regardless of what her brothers thought. They were hardly family anyway. They barely had a relationship, and what they had was only what Louisa had fought for. She'd been unable to get in contact with Santiago since he went criminal, and while she visited Ramon's restaurant often, he never returned the favor with a visit to Maria House. Or even her own house.

It was understandable that Papa had decided to do what he

did with his money. His children didn't care for him, didn't care for each other. They were all so busy living their own lives they forgot to be a family. Deep down inside, though, there was a part of her that felt hurt. Had the last three months meant nothing to Papa?

Her cell phone rang, interrupting her deep meditations. She sighed and retrieved it from the passenger seat where she'd casually thrown it earlier in the day. She glanced at the number and saw that it was Thomas Chenoweth, one of the VPs at The Cruz Agency. Her thumb reached for the "answer" button.

Beep. "Hello?"

"Louisa? Tom Chenoweth."

"Yeah, hey. What's up?"

"Hey, I just got off the phone with Edgar Kimbrough. He wanted to talk about The Agency and what stipulations Ben had in his will about it."

"Yeah?"

"Yeah. So I'm on the phone with him and he tells me about the estate. You know, your dad taking it with him and all."

Louisa was silent for a moment, cursing him for unknowingly attempting to ruin her evening. Her broken voice eked out: "Yeah."

"Man, I'm sorry, Louisa."

"Thanks."

"I don't really know how to tell you this, but . . . . well, your dad didn't mean for that to happen."

The street, the other drivers, the car, the steering wheel faded away as Louisa's brain rushed to make sense of what Thomas Chenoweth had just said. "Wh-what?"

"The fortune going down with him, that was for real. But

that was his old will, and he'd told me just last month that he was going to change it. I only know because I'd kinda helped him the first time around when he drafted the original. So he told me he was going to have it changed to have his estate go to Maria House."

Louisa's car was on autopilot now.

"I guess he just didn't have the time to make the change," Chenoweth said. "Sucks."

Louisa then said the most mature thing she'd probably ever said in her life. "Well . . . I guess that's just the way it goes sometimes."

"Yeah, I guess so. Anyway, I talked to Kimbrough about it to see if there was something he could do, but he said it'd be wrong to alter the will, seeing as how Ben had done it right the first time. That one has to stand."

"That's . . . okay."

"I feel awful for you, Louisa. I mean, I know you could've done a lot with that money. I guess you and your old man really patched things up something good in the past few months, eh?"

Louisa wasn't really paying attention. "Sure, Tom. Sure. God'll work it out."

"Yeah, well, God doesn't have a legal degree," Chenoweth said. "Kimbrough does, and he says it's a no-go. Anyway, I just wanted to let you know that your dad really was thinking of you there toward the end. He wasn't a total tightwad."

"Well. Thanks."

"Say, Louisa, what are you doing? You want to grab a cup of coffee, maybe a cheeseburger, talk this over?"

Jake. Louisa's subconscious reminded her that she was in her car, driving to meet Jake at her brother's restaurant. The reality of her current situation hit her, and she realized she was already parked in the parking lot, engine running, talking on the phone.

"Oh, thanks, Tom. Actually, I have plans already."

"Oh. Oh, okay. All right." There was a pause. "Maybe some other time?"

"Sure."

"Good night, Louisa. Take care of yourself."

"Talk to you later."

Beep. Funny how a life can change so drastically in less than twenty-four hours.

The thought of canceling the evening's outing flickered through her mind, but was quickly whisked away when she saw Jake standing outside her window, motorcycle helmet under his arm, eyes squinting to peer through the tinted window at her. Right now she needed him more than she'd realized.

Conversation
(With a Side of Rice and Beans)

JAKE FIGURED LOUISA was on an important call, but he still felt dorky standing outside her door while holding his gear. He'd been waiting for only a few minutes. When he saw her car pull in, he'd gone through his act of taking off his stuff and paying no attention to her or her vehicle. He figured she'd have parked and been to the door by the time he leisurely removed his protective outerwear, but when it was all off and she was nowhere to be seen, he was forced to look around for her, a task made harder by the oncoming dusk and the faint aroma of grilled meat and dishwater emanating from the restaurant's back door.

He had an idea of where she'd parked, and he'd do anything to get away from the smell, so he looked in that direction and saw her car in a space. He heard the whir of the engine fan and realized the Volvo's immaculate engineering was still running. Maybe she was finishing out a favorite song on the radio; Jake had done that tons of times, back when he still had a car. He decided he looked more stupid standing next to his scooter than he did approaching the car, so he settled on the latter.

When he got there, she was on the phone. She didn't look too enthused. *Deflated* would be a good word. He didn't really know what to do, so he gently rapped on the window just as Louisa was hanging up.

"Sorry I'm late," Louisa said as she opened the door.

Jake brushed it off. "No big deal. Everything okay?"

Louisa gave an easy smile. "Oh, yeah! Just fine."

Jake wished he knew her well enough to know for sure whether she was fibbing. "Well then," he said, attempting to get past the awkward silence that had descended, "shall we?"

He offered her his arm, wedding usher-style, and she took it.

"Nice helmet," she said, pointing out its face shield.

"Thanks," Jake said. "Gotta keep this face pretty."

Louisa laughed. Jake began to think that it was addictive, that laugh. He'd just heard it a little over an hour ago, but he'd been craving it ever since. Hearing it again . . . well, he hoped he'd hear it a lot more tonight.

They walked into the restaurant and looked around. It didn't look very busy. Jake wondered if it ever got busy here. Other than a portly middle-aged couple just finishing a fajita platter and a trio of Mexican cowboys with three beer bottles lined up in front of each of them, they had the place to themselves. And what a place; the combination of the harsh fluorescent lighting and the freaky murals convinced Jake that he now knew what carnival fun houses looked like south of the border.

It smelled awesome, though. Better than the Downtown

Hilton, anyway. Especially without the dishwater smell to complicate the fine aroma.

A Hispanic man probably in his early thirties approached them. "*Hola, mija. Quien es esto?*" he said, gesturing them toward a nearby table.

"Hi, brother," Louisa said. "This is my friend, Jake. He works at the funeral home; he's taking care of Papa. I thought I'd better take him out to meet the family so he does a good job."

The man's eyes widened.

"Jake," Louisa said, "this is my brother, Ramon."

Ramon extended his hand. "Nice to meet you," he said in a voice that didn't match the words.

"Uh, same to you," Jake said. They were the first words he'd uttered to Louisa's brother, and they seemed like the wrong thing. Still, he shook Ramon's hand.

Ramon let go of Jake's hand, then took off toward the kitchen. He called over his shoulder, "I bring you chips and salsa."

Jake and Louisa sat down to await their Tex-Mex staple. Jake didn't know where to begin, conversationally, so he went the obvious route.

"I don't think Ramon much cares for me."

Louisa let out a chuckle. "He's trying to rattle you by talking in Spanish, but you don't need to worry about him. We aren't very close, anyway—I only come here because his food is so good." She gave him a wink, which he took to mean that she was kidding. Mostly.

"Well, I'm looking forward to trying it. What's good here?"

Louisa glanced at the menu with a devious look in her eyes. "It depends on what you're in the mood for. If you want something soupish, I'd suggest the *menudo*—so good. Or if you want something roasted meatish, try the *birria*. If you want something *picante*—spicy—you can't go wrong with the *mole poblano*. And if you're looking for something on the light side, try the *ceviche* salad."

Jake's eyes were crossing as he tried to find the different items while Louisa rattled them off. The menu was complicated and varied, with big, capital-letter descriptions under each item, making it an ocular obstacle course. Finally, he decided to fold his menu up and get the answers straight from the source. "What was all that you just named?"

Louisa laughed. "It's all nasty. *Menudo* is soup made from intestines, *mole poblano* is a pepper with a chocolate and chile sauce on it, *ceviche* is raw fish with lime juice, and *birria*—you know, actually, *birria* is pretty good."

Jake had felt his expression contorting into progressively more grotesque versions with each item she named, and now he was afraid to solve the mystery of *birria*. "Yeah, but . . . what is it?"

"Roasted goat."

Jake's very American palate retreated in fear. Outwardly, though, he was determined not to show signs of weakness. "Oh. Sounds, um, interesting."

Louisa laughed again. "Oh, don't worry, I'm not going to make you eat it."

Ramon approached with the chips and salsa and set them on the table. "*Que quieres comer, Louisa?*"

"Combo fajitas, Ramon. We'll share."

"*Bueno.*"

Louisa gave Jake a slight wink. "That suit you better?"

Jake breathed a sigh of relief. "Much."

"Oh, come on. Where's your sense of adventure?"

"For food? I sold it to McDonald's a long time ago."

More laughter. And more conversation. And more witty banter between the two of them. And more chips and salsa. And more conversation. And more laughter. And more, more, more.

♪

Jake leaned back in his chair and patted his full tummy. "Man, your brother knows how to cook a mean meal."

"No kidding," said Louisa. "He's a genius."

"So," Jake said, "I understand you run a nonprofit organization."

Louisa froze. "How'd you know that?"

Jake knew it because Jerald had mentioned it to him at The Cruz Agency company party. Something about how she started and ran her own NPO. This information might be contained in the very thick file on Benjamin Cruz that currently sat on Jake's desk, but he hadn't really read past the first page. "I read it in your dad's file," he said. "Just that you had something to do with a nonprofit organization."

She nodded. "Makes sense."

"What's that like?"

"Oh, it's a challenge," Louisa replied. "Every day, there's something new going on."

"I bet."

"Like, today, I couldn't get back with you earlier because I had to head out to the hospital."

"Everything all right?" Jake leaned in, squinting his eyes. "You look okay to me."

"Oh, yeah, everything's fine with me," Louisa said, reaching a hand across the table in reassurance, but leaving it short of making contact. "No, I had to go out there for one of the girls we're helping out." She withdrew her hand and reached into her pocket, producing one of those cloth-covered rubber band things that women use in their hair. Jake never knew the actual name of those things. Ponytail holder? That sounded about right. She pulled her bountiful hair behind her head in a ponytail.

"So, what do you do?"

Louisa leaned forward. "Jake, do you have any idea how many hurting people there are in the world? How many people are out there, in our own city, just cast aside by society because they don't fit in?" She was speaking more rapidly, tapping the table with a very tense finger. "How many women are forced into a lifestyle of addiction and emotional humiliation after being promised the moon? Do you?"

Yikes. Jake just stared.

"I try to help those women," Louisa said. "I try to help them right themselves, teach them a trade, get cleaned up. Heal them emotionally."

Jake lowered his voice. "You mean, like, uh, women of the night?"

"Prostitutes, Jake. You can say it out loud; people won't think less of you." Her arms were resting on the table now. "And you don't even have to make air quotes around the word." Which, of course, Jake had done when he said "women of the night."

"Sorry," Jake said. "Force of habit, I guess."

Louisa breathed out heavily and relaxed her body back into her chair. "Oh, I'm sorry," she said. "I'm a little passionate about it."

"I noticed," Jake said. "Continue."

"Okay. Let's see . . ." Louisa said, rapidly drumming her

fingers on the table. "Oh, yeah. Hospital." She took a bite of chip and continued. "Well, like I said, we help women get off the street, if they want to. On a few occasions they want to get off the street because they've gotten pregnant. If that happens, we can help them with a place to live, a labor coach, parenting classes if they want to keep the baby, or we can help them find an adoptive family if they want to go that route.

"So, we had this girl who was in that situation, and we hooked her up with these adoptive parents who were going to, you know, raise the child. Now, the only concern on their part was that the man who was going to be the grandfather is an extraordinary racist. He's all for them adopting, but he wants to make sure it's a white baby. Now, this girl is white, and she said she figured the father was white, so everything should be good, right?"

"Right," Jake said. "Except it wasn't."

"Oh, heavens no," Louisa said, shaking her head and chuckling. "Anyway, the girl goes into labor today, and I rush out to the hospital to greet the baby—they're so sweet when they're new—and to help out wherever I need to. Well, I got there just as the baby was being delivered, and I'm telling you that kid came out, and I about lost it. Because he was about as black as you could imagine."

"Oh, man."

"Yeah."

"What'd the mom and dad do?"

"The adoptive parents? Oh, they didn't care. They just snuggled him up, and thanked her for being so brave, and took to him right away—since he's totally cute and they're great anyway, so of *course* they did—but the grandfather didn't even know yet. He was in the hallway."

"So what did you do? Was he pretty scary?"

"He was a pretty big guy, yeah. But I just went out in the hallway and said a little prayer that God would point me in the right direction, and then I went up to him and said, 'Mike, you know what? Your grandbaby's just been born, and I think maybe the birth mother didn't quite know who the father was, because he is biracial.' I could tell he was about to get angry, so I didn't even give him a chance to talk. I just kept going. 'You know what that means, though? That just means that God's going to heal you from being a racist today. Isn't that wonderful?'"

"No," Jake said, eyes and mouth wide open. God? Heal? Uh-oh.

Louisa nodded. "Oh, yeah. And I said it really cheerfully, like he'd just won the lottery or a free car or something."

"Did he go ballistic on you?"

"Not at all. He just stood there for a second, thinking—"

"Is that what he looked like?" Jake asked, because Louisa was scrunching up her face like she was the one doing the thinking.

"Yeah, probably," she said.

"You do a good impression. It really adds to the story."

"Thanks."

Jake nodded demurely. "Sorry to interrupt."

"No problem," Louisa said. "So he just stood there thinking; then he turned away from me, walked into the room, and asked to see his grandson."

"Wow."

"He was holding him in a rocking chair when I left."

Jake shook his head incredulously. "That is an intense story, man."

"Pretty cool, huh?"

"Definitely."

"It's just amazing to me," Louis said, "how people can totally change, just like that, when faced with the proper circumstances. It's such a mystery."

"Maybe that's why you got into this whole, you know, field of work," Jake said. "You like mystery stories, so it just makes sense that you're working with these people and seeing the human mystery up close."

"Oh, yeah," she said, looking him dead in the eyes, "I love a good mystery."

Jake returned the look, matching her intensity. "Me, too."

Time stopped.

Jake turned the moment over in his mind, trying to decide his next move. His mouth made it for him. Maybe the silence got to him; maybe in the back of his mind it'd been gnawing away at him. He didn't know why, exactly, but he said it. "That's a heck of a thing your father did to you." And immediately he regretted it.

Louisa's face registered her shock. "Yeah."

Rushing in to repair the damage, Jake said, "Sorry. I mean, I just—I think that—well . . . I don't know how he couldn't give you anything."

Louisa's shoulders slumped as a sigh escaped from deep within her lungs. "Actually, he did. Just not in real life, not in legal terms."

She told him what had happened with the two wills.

"I see," Jake said. Then he checked her reaction. He was afraid his "I see" was delivered in a way that might've tipped his hand, that might've said there was a lot more behind it, a whole film festival's worth of behind-the-scenes footage currently being screened inside his brain.

And he almost held the premiere right then and there. He

immediately went back to that thought he hadn't been able to get out of his head at home. He'd moved it to one of his farthest back burners (the Thought Stove in Jake's mind had several burners—and no timer), but it had been forcing its way to the forefront of his mind all evening long. Should he mention it? Was it too soon?

The last thing Jake wanted to do at the moment was anger Louisa. He was too busy enjoying her lovely face and perfect nose and full-moon-sized eyes. It was too much of an ego-booster, being with her; he didn't want to ruin it—and his evening—by forcing anything.

"Well, I'm sorry to have brought the whole thing up," he said. "I don't know what I was thinking."

Louisa shook her head, "No, it's okay. Don't worry about it."

Jake awkwardly picked up a chip remnant from the table and munched on it while counting how many empty bottles the Mexican cowboys had left. They were alone now, and night had settled in completely, making the restaurant's already bright lights even brighter by contrast. He swallowed and returned his attention to Louisa. "Hey, thanks for dinner," he said. "It was great."

Louisa nodded, a slight smile gracing her lips. "Oh, you're welcome. I had fun."

"Me, too," Jake said. *Until I totally screwed it up with my big fat mouth.*

"Well . . ." they both said.

Jake suddenly panicked. What was the etiquette here? A handshake? A kiss? A polite curtsy? Had this been a date? A business dinner? Though he'd been mostly at ease through the meal, she was still a client and he was still a businessman, two people who would have to see each other in nonrelationship situations over the next few days. What should he do next?

As they stood up to leave, Louisa answered his question by leaning across the table and giving him a peck on the cheek. "Thank you, Jake. I needed this today."

That'll do.

"Maybe we can do this again sometime," Jake said. "I don't have any relatives in the foodservice industry, but I'm sure I can scrounge up enough cash to treat."

"I'd like that."

Okay. That was definitely a plan. Jake resisted the urge to grab a large stone, a hammer, and a chisel so they could set a definite date and time right then and there. Instead, he just walked her out the door and to her car.

"See you," he said as she climbed in the driver's seat.

"Bye," she replied, offering it with a slight wave and lips upturned at the edges.

The door closed, the engine started, and the car pulled away.

♂

Take it.

That's all Jake's thought had been. Just two little words that had popped into his mind earlier in the evening, two words that kept bouncing around in there no matter how hard he commanded them to rest.

Take it. Take. It. There was nothing remarkable about either of those words. One of them was a useful, even flexible, verb; the other an extremely common pronoun. He'd heard them in his head many times before—when faced with a magazine he really liked at the doctor's office or a tray full of ketchup packets when he knew his refrigerator was condiment-free. There was nothing special about the two words "take" and "it" combined into one imperative command.

Nothing special, except for what the "it" stood for. The fortune of Benjamin Cruz rattled through Jake's brain like the chains of a haunted mansion's ghost. He scooted home thinking of that fortune. He walked upstairs to his apartment thinking of that fortune. He pulled on some jammies thinking of that fortune. He lay down in bed thinking of that fortune. Mmmm . . . fortune.

The first time the thought had hit him, his head had begun to wander into fantasyland, thinking what life could be like as an ultra-wealthy stud. And in his mind's eye, it looked pretty dang good. Yes, legally the money was supposed to go down into the ground with Benjamin Cruz. But Benjamin Cruz had changed his mind. Louisa knew it. Jake now knew it. Even that guy at her father's company knew it. So Edgar Kimbrough, attorney-at-law, was determined to stick to the rules. So what? Let him. Jake couldn't abide the thought of all that money lying in the ground going to waste.

What would happen if he took it? Who would it hurt? No one. Who would know? No one. This sort of thing was a no-brainer for Jake when it came to sodas and extra buffet servings and waiting room publications. If it didn't hurt anyone (well, to the point where they'd know it, anyway), Jake would do it. Sure he was selfish, but he knew about other people on the planet, even if he didn't care too much for them.

He couldn't stand the thought of Louisa's inheritance just sitting in a box like so much buried treasure. Some mutated form of chivalry was rising up in him, and he was ready to slay dragons and unhorse filthy knights to restore order to the universe and give Louisa what was rightfully hers. For an even split of the profits, of course.

He'd known Louisa Cruz for only half a day, but he also knew at this point that if he mentioned it to her, she'd immediately frown upon the idea. It'd probably upset her and ruin his chances of ever hooking up with her.

Which led to the dreaded question: What if she wanted a serious relationship? He liked his life the way it was; he wasn't sure he wanted some woman barging in and mucking things up.

But if he played his cards right, if he could pull this off, he could get the money and the girl. Two birds, one stone.

The Hatchings of a Plan

THOSE BAGS WOULD be tough to conceal. And the redness. And the overall droop around the edges, caused by lack of sleep. Louisa stared at her own eyes in the bathroom mirror, barely awake from a restless night of tossing, turning, and crying.

Her buoyant time with Jake had done her good, she knew, but when she had gotten home last night, the sorrow and pain had come flooding back to her, compounded by the knowledge of what might have been. Not the inheritance. She'd rather have her father.

Louisa pondered her reflection, examining her face more closely than any human being really should. She noticed the imperfections, the way her nose tilted slightly to the right, the way her eyes were just the tiniest bit off-center, the hatchlings of crow's-feet beginning to form at the edges of her eyes. She felt very . . . mortal.

It was a ritual she did every three months or so, something to reacquaint herself with her actual face, the one nobody saw because they weren't allowed to study it so deeply. She was curious about what changes she was undergoing as she aged, and she kept a mental catalog of every new wrinkle, every fine blemish that wasn't there last time. She wasn't obsessive about it, merely a fact-gatherer on an exploratory mission.

She knew she was still young, but she could already see differences between her face and the faces of those who came to Maria House. The teenagers (usually) still had hints of baby fat in their cheeks, smooth and apple-like. Their eyes glowed with the naïveté of youth, despite the very grown-up actions that had brought them to her. They had no trace of crow's-feet, but those eyes always—every time—showed the fear that gripped them. The older women showed signs of soul abuse, their faces an extreme palette of being overpainted and overworked night after night. They came to Maria House so Louisa Cruz could ease that fear and give them a hand. And they were the only family she'd had since she started Maria House.

She also studied the mirror to find the similarities between her and those girls, some common ground she could use in her mission to help them and the little ones they sometimes carried. It was a comparison study, usually. But today, it was less a study and more an avenue for introspection.

As Louisa stared into her eyes, she reflected on the turns her life had taken the past two days. If she'd had to put one word to it, it would've been "overwhelmed," and though she was used to having all the answers for the girls at Maria House, she now understood a little bit better the fear of the unknown they faced.

A knock at the door forced her away from the mirror. She threw on her robe and shimmied from the bathroom to the door, pausing to stuff her feet into some old slippers. "Just a minute!"

She opened the door and found herself face-to-face with Santiago. He'd ditched the suit and gone for a stereotypical look, including a crisp, pale blue *guayabera* shirt, khaki slacks, and dark, designer sunglasses. He even had his hair slicked back. He reeked of Corona and Old Spice.

"Hello, Santi. What are you doing here?"

Santiago smiled, tilted his head to one side, and said, "Hello, too. I was just wondering what you'd found out about the will."

"Santiago, we've been over this."

"Come on. I figured you'd found out *something* by now."

Louisa leaned against the door frame. "You can't fool Little Sister. Don't act like you haven't already heard."

"Heard what?"

"About Papa's money."

Santiago removed his sunglasses and looked directly at Louisa. "What about it?"

"That he wants to be buried with it," Louisa said, exasperated.

"What?"

"Yep. Sorry. Thanks for stopping by. Come back in another couple of years." She began to close the door, but Santiago blocked the motion with his arm.

"Louisa, listen—"

"No. I don't want to listen. I don't know what you're up to, but Papa had a way he wanted things done, and we have to respect that way whether you like it or not."

"Papa did not respect me, so I see no need to respect him now. Respect must be given to be gotten, and since I can no longer get it from Papa, I do not need to give it."

Louisa narrowed her eyes. There were so many things she wanted to say that she could think of none. Instead, after a slight pause, she said, "Okay, Santi. If you want to hire a lawyer and contest the will, you're more than welcome."

"You know I'm not exactly the courtroom type."

"Then what do you want?"

"Aren't you going to ask me in?"

Louisa snorted. "What. Do. You. *Want?*"

"You know the man in charge of Papa's body."

"Yes."

"I need to speak to him."

"No."

Santiago adopted a patronizing smile. "Louisa, I would give you your rightful share."

"No."

"Don't tell me you haven't already thought about it, Louisa," Santiago said. "This money, it should go to us."

"Oh, yeah? Well, what about Pati, then?"

Santiago wagged a finger in her face. "Mother remarried and you know it. She has no legal claim here. Just us."

"I thought you didn't care about legality."

Santiago hesitated. Louisa began to wonder if she'd left the toaster oven on when she'd heated up her toaster pastries (strawberry, unfrosted) earlier.

Finally, Santiago spoke. "Okay, *mija*. If that's the way you want to be, that's the way you want to be. We'll respect Papa's wishes."

"Thank you."

He nodded. "*Adios*, little sister."

"*Adios*, Santi."

Louisa closed the door as Santiago turned and walked away. She didn't believe him for a minute.

§

The phone at Jake's workstation greeted him that morning with a blinking red light, saying, in its polite, nondescript way, that he had a new voice mail message. He didn't see it until after he'd made a pot of coffee (there'd been a sample of a new Costa Rican blend in his neighbor's newspaper this morning — Jake took it as a sign) and had stared at his computer for a few minutes doing Internet searches on last wills and testaments.

When he retrieved the message, he was delightfully surprised to hear Louisa's voice talking to him, asking him to please call back soon. The sweetly robotic female voice that controlled his voice mail gave him some options, and he chose to press two to save the message, just in case he wanted to hear Louisa's voice again later. He dialed her number and had to wait through three rings before Louisa answered.

"Hello?" she said shortly.

"Louisa? Hey, it's me. Jake."

"Oh, hi," she said, not so shortly this time.

"Hi. I just got your message. What's up?"

"Well," she said, trailing off at the end and waiting for a minute, like she was psyching herself up to rip off a Band-Aid, "I just needed to talk to you about something. Relating to my father."

This had something to do with last night, didn't it? "Okay, have at it."

"Last night when I told you about my father's true wishes for

97

the money, what were you thinking?"

Yikes! "I was thinking," Jake said, trying to think up a decent lie about what he was thinking, "about how I'd feel if my dad did that to me."

"And?"

"And what?"

"And how would you feel?"

He sighed. "Hard to say; it's such an odd situation, you know?"

"Yeah."

"Of course you know."

There was an awkward silence while Jake's ears strained to hear the faint music of Louisa's breath. He let the silence continue for a few seconds, then, "Why do you ask?"

"My brother came to visit me this morning."

"From the restaurant?"

"No, not Ramon. My other brother, Santiago."

Jake wasn't sure, but he thought he could sense her eyes rolling when she said *other brother.* "Oh," he said, "dropping by to check up on you?"

Louisa let out a soft snort, and Jake discovered that even supposedly unladylike sounds from Louisa were angelic. "No, not quite."

"What then?"

"Jake, he wants the money. And he specifically mentioned you."

Ahhh. This was starting to make sense. Louisa was worried that Santiago would somehow contact Jake and misrepresent her. "Don't worry, Louisa. I'm sure I can handle him."

"No, Jake, you don't understand." Her voice had taken on a pleading edge. "Santiago has not been known to keep the best company. And he's as bullheaded as my father was. He'll do everything he can to get it."

"So he'll get the best lawyer he can find; no big deal."

"Jake. I'm afraid he'll do something drastic. He's that way."

She was worried for him. How sweet. "It's cool, Louisa. I can talk him dow—"

"Jake," she said, the franticness of her voice stopping him midsentence, "he is a criminal and a thug, and he will resort to violence if he has to."

Whatever. People always talked big; hardly anyone ever backed it up. "Is he really a break-your-kneecaps type of guy?"

"Yes," Louisa immediately replied. "That's why he separated from the family in the first place. Papa found out he was dealing and told him to stop. But Santi enjoyed the money and power too much."

"And now he wants more?"

"Yes."

"For his big narcotics empire?"

"Something like that."

"Then let's take it." Jake didn't know exactly what he was thinking, or if he was thinking at all, but the time for thinking was over, and, with Santiago providing the perfect excuse, the time for action had arrived. She'd given him the open door, and now he was going to walk through it.

"*What?*"

Jake wished he wasn't talking on the phone so he could see Louisa's face. There were so many different ways to interpret *What?* and most of them relied heavily on facial expressions.

"Let's put it in safe hands. Keep it off the street."

"Jake, that's unconscionable!" Louisa said. "Besides, what

about the will?"

"Yeah, it says it has to go down with him, but there's nothing there that says it has to *stay* in the ground."

A different, non-phone-speaker voice entered Jake's ears. "Jake, what in tarnation are you talking about?"

Jake whirled to see Del standing two feet away.

"What's that?" Jake said.

"What?" Louisa said.

"Hold on one second," Jake said to Louisa. He put the phone on his shoulder and fully addressed Del. "What'd you say?"

"What on earth are you talking about?" Del said. "Are you taking drugs, young man?"

"Um, no."

"I heard you, Jake. Don't try to deny it." Del gave a fatherly shake of his head. "I heard you talking about drugs. Keeping 'em off the street. Who're you talking to? Is that your pusher?"

Jake suppressed a chuckle. "No, Del. No, I don't have a pusher."

"Well, I need some answers."

Jake reluctantly put the phone back to his ear. "I need to . . . handle something right now. Can I call you back in a few?"

"I'm coming over," Louisa said, "so we can talk."

Jake hung up without saying anything more.

"Come on, Jake," Del insisted. "I'm waiting."

Jake looked around mysteriously, fingering the phone cord as his mind raced. "Can you keep a secret, Del?"

Del's face became wary. "Yes."

"I was just talking with a media associate of mine, someone deep in the organization."

"The organization?"

"Mm-hmm. Very deep."

"How deep?"

"Deeper than deep. So deep we can't really talk about what we mean when we talk on the phone."

"What you mean?"

"Exactly."

Del looked perplexed, which was pretty much what Jake was going for. "So you have to talk in code or something?"

"Del," Jake continued, "I can't really go into it, but let's just say that I'm still in the middle of handling things."

"What things?"

"You know—" Jake arched an eyebrow—"*things*."

"Things that need to be handled?"

"Now you're getting it."

"By people deep in the organization?"

"Bingo."

"They can't talk to you about what they actually want to talk about?"

"Right on." Jake patted Del's shoulder. "You'd make a great spy, Del. You *get* it, you know?"

"Just keep 'em away from me, Jake. And watch yourself with these contacts of yours. You never know who you can trust. There are people out there that'd just as soon break your kneecaps."

"Hey, you don't have to tell me twice."

❦

Louisa leaned back in her office chair, taking care not to go too far. She couldn't believe what Jake had just suggested. Of all the nerve!

Still, he'd seemed pretty certain about the wording of the will. She'd probably need to get a copy, read through it, see what it really said. Where could she get it? Tom or Edgar might have a copy.

She looked around the sardine can that passed itself off as her office and began to think about how much that money could benefit Maria House. They could get decent offices, where she wouldn't be bothered by the sound of the phone ringing and all the general reception area chatter that inevitably filtered in. She wouldn't have to remind women to be quiet when they got emotional in her office.

And then there were all the unknown people that would benefit if Jake and Louisa kept the money out of Santiago's hands.

And her father really had wanted it to go to her anyway.

She'd call Tom. No, Edgar. He'd definitely have a copy.

Louisa reached for the top drawer of her desk to retrieve her address book. She seemed to recall having Edgar's card in there. In her earnestness, she tugged outward and upward at the same time, wrenching free the already loose drawer handle and causing her hand to fly backward and bang into the bookcase behind her desk.

This had the unfortunate consequence of knocking loose a support from the secondhand bookcase, causing the top shelf to collapse, spilling three different translations of the Bible, three books on overcoming pharmacological addictions, a collection of Dorothy Sayers short stories, four books on politics and pop culture, several back issues of *Vibe*, and a small jar containing miniature bars of dark chocolate at Louisa's feet.

Well, she *could* use a new office.

Ramon could get some of the inheritance, too. His restaurant would be so much better with a little cash flow. He could afford to advertise, spruce up the place, hire a waitress. They could both use the money, and Papa had really wanted it to go to her, probably because he knew she would share it with Ramon and not with Santiago.

That big bookshelf spill was probably a sign from God, showing her how much she needed the money.

A quiet inner voice told her not to go through with what Jake was suggesting. After much trying, she succeeded in not paying attention to it.

∫

"Jake, can you shoot me, please? Just for, like, five minutes?" Chiffon stood in the doorway of Jake's not-office, holding out her video camera to Jake with one hand and applying lipstick with the other.

Jake glanced at his watch. He'd gotten off the phone with Louisa two hours ago; she should be here by now. "I'm kind of busy, Chiffon."

"Come on, Jake. Jeremy won't do it 'cause he doesn't believe in TV? And Del isn't here?"

"Jeremy doesn't believe in TV? Like, that it doesn't exist?"

"Stop kidding around and shoot me, okay?"

"Fine." Jake reluctantly grabbed the camera from her hand. "Here, why don't you stand in front of the God and Adam picture there? It adds class."

"Ooh! Good idea?" Chiffon said, hastening to the desired spot.

Jake slipped the camera over his palm, aimed, and pressed the record button. "You're on."

Chiffon put on an ultra-chipper smile and gave the camera a big wave. "Hello, producers of *Hamster Cage*! My name is Chiffon Brown, and I'm like, totally good for your show, because, um, I like running on a treadmill? and that's kinda like running in one of those big wheels?" She looked down at the floor and wrinkled her nose and eyebrows as if in deep thought. After a few very long seconds, she looked back up at the camera. "Oh! I like taking the subway? which is totally like those plastic tubes that hamsters get in? and, I drink out of this sport bottle all the time?" She held up a quart-sized plastic water bottle. "Oh—and my last name is Brown, and hamsters are brown? so, like, I'm halfway there! Anyway, I would be really, really, really good, and . . . great . . . on *Hamster Cage*? Bye!"

Jake clicked the camera off. He blinked his eyes rapidly to lose the tiny image of Chiffon that was burned onto his right retina after staring into the viewfinder for so long. Looking over, he noticed that Louisa had entered during the taping. He gave her the "hang on one second" hand gesture as he handed the camera back to Chiffon.

"How'd I do?" She was bubbling over with excitement.

"Great, Chiffon. If anyone should live in a big hamster cage for a month, it's you."

"*Hopefully* a month? I don't want to get voted out."

"Of course not."

"Thanks, Jake." She turned to leave when she saw Louisa. "Oh, hi, Ms. Cruz! What are you doing here?"

Louisa had taken a seat on a nearby stool, watching as Chiffon wrapped up her audition. "Oh, I just stopped by to talk to Jake about a few things regarding my father's burial."

Chiffon immediately went into Empathy Mode. "Aw, poor

thing? I'm so sorry you have to do that."

Louisa smiled as her eyes moistened. "I am, too."

They stared at each other for a few seconds, sharing a girl moment.

"I hope you get to live like a hamster, Chiffon."

Chiffon switched back into Reality Show Hopeful Mode. "Thank you! You are so sweet? See ya." She veritably skipped off to the reception desk.

"Does Chiffon really like hamsters?"

Jake chuckled. "Chiffon really likes the thought of being famous. Doesn't matter how, so long as she eventually gets around to her singing career."

"I see. She any good?"

"You know, I've never heard her. She's auditioned for a couple of singing-type talent shows, though. One of them even called her back for a second look."

"Well, that's something. I like to see girls like her at least attempting to do something with their lives."

"Oh, definitely," Jake said. He looked conspiratorially at the doorway, making sure Chiffon was completely gone. "So, you said you wanted to talk?" he said in hushed tones.

"Yeah, sorry I took so long." Louisa reached into her purse and produced a photocopied document. "I stopped by my father's house to check out his copy of the will. I looked it over and you're right, there isn't any mention that the money must remain buried with him."

So much for "unconscionable." That was the word she'd used, right, about this whole idea? It's amazing how many "unconscionable" things became *un*-unconscionable in the warm light of money. "So, are you actually on board here?"

"Maybe." Louisa didn't look up at him, instead pointing to a portion she'd marked in pink highlighter. "There's a lot of legal jargon there, but basically it just says that the contents of Papa's bank accounts and his investments were to be transferred into treasury bonds, placed in his coffin, and buried with him. His personal property is to be turned over to The Cruz Agency to do with as they please."

"Wow."

"Yeah, Tom'll be happy about that one."

"Who's that?"

"One of the higher-ups at The Agency."

Jake nodded his head, vaguely aware of the surfer-dude posture he took on. "Right on. So I guess we just have to dig it back up once it's been buried, and we're free and clear."

"If we were going to take it, yes."

Jake didn't like that "if" there. Although, now that he was actually discussing it with Louisa, it didn't seem as cool or risky as he'd originally thought. It didn't even seem wrong; it seemed silly. It felt like something kids would think up as a way of playing treasure hunter, looking for a shoebox full of snack cakes they'd placed in a shallow hole only a few hours earlier.

Except this treasure was quite real and would be quite large. And have fewer calories per serving.

"Jake, I haven't decided," Louisa began, but halted before explaining further.

Jake reached out his leg and propped his right foot on one of the stool's rungs. "Yeah?"

"Should we do this?"

"I don't see any reason not to," Jake said, leaning back in his chair and crossing his left foot over his right, "as long as we can respect your father's past and present wishes *and* keep the money away from Santiago."

"I don't know. . . ."

Jake looked at her, unsure of where to steer the conversation. He wanted to get the money, if only because he'd set his mind on it, and also because it was an affront to his freeloading lifestyle to let it sit there and rot. He removed his feet from Louisa's stool and leaned forward to look directly in her eyes.

"Look, Louisa, the funeral isn't for three more days," he said. "Maybe you should take the rest of the day to think it over. I'll let you have the final say on whether we do it or not."

Louisa nodded quietly. "Thanks."

Jake let out a slow breath. She was the best-looking sucker he'd ever seen.

A Complex Dish
of Sugar and Sand Crab

LOUISA WAS CURRENTLY relying heavily on Volvo's sterling reputation for sturdiness. As she drove back to her office, her mind was elsewhere, upping her chances for a fender bender and proof of her car's toughness.

Louisa's mind was at a Ping-Pong match of its own devising, where it was attempting to determine the appropriate course of action regarding Jake's idea. Back and forth, back and forth, the topic bounced around from pro to con and back again. Louisa made a mental note to take a couple of aspirin when she got to her office; she was getting a headache.

A few minutes later, Louisa was walking through the doors of Maria House, expectantly heading to her office to find that aspirin. Instead, she found a young girl sitting on the couch in the foyer. Helen was apparently at lunch, and this girl had made herself at home, reading a magazine with her feet up on the coffee table.

"Can I help you?" Louisa said. This sight was nothing new at Maria House; hundreds of women came through here each year, and many of them tried very hard to act like they didn't care they were there, that they were indifferent to their situation. They were, of course, fooling no one.

"I need to talk to Louisa Cruz." The girl smacked some gum in her recently de-braced mouth.

"That's me." Louisa began sizing up the girl immediately. The black and pink striped halter top did little to hide her doughy midsection, which Louisa's visitor had tried, ineffectively, to tuck into her ultra-tight white capri pants, the ends of which met the tops of some very worn, white, high-heeled boots. Her broad, bare shoulders had hints of body glitter, as did her hair, which was plastered to the sides of her head, finishing in a bunched-up ponytail protruding upward and falling slightly to the side. Louisa made her assessment in a flash before continuing. "Let's go into my office."

The girl lazily dragged her compact frame from the couch and followed Louisa into the tiny room. Louisa took a seat at her desk, and the girl clumsily spilled herself into the chair opposite.

"What can I do for you?" Louisa said.

"I might need a little advice," the girl said with an accent that was half-street, half-Southern belle.

Louisa chuckled internally at the girl's use of the word "might." Every woman who came through those doors needed advice; there was no "might" about it.

"Well, if you've never been here before, you'll need to set up an appointment to talk to Carolyn," Louisa said. Carolyn was a Maria House volunteer who often did the precounseling for the girls before sending them on to Louisa.

"No, I don't wanna talk to anyone but you." The girl's shifty eyes darted back and forth across the office. She stirred uncomfortably in her chair.

Louisa blinked. "What's going on, sweetheart? What's your name?"

"Sugar."

Louisa's heart sank. She was hoping to connect with the real girl, not the phony woman she pretended to be on the street at night.

"Sugar. Okay. How old are you? Seventeen? Eighteen?"

"Eighteen."

Lie. This girl wasn't a day over fifteen, and Louisa knew it. She could tell by the shakiness in her voice; Sugar hadn't been on the street long enough to develop that much confidence in her story, or maybe she wasn't used to telling it during the day.

"Eighteen-year-old Sugar," Louisa said, to reassure the girl that she believed her story. In these interviews, Louisa also usually attempted a girl-to-girl connection by complimenting some part of their wardrobe. "I like your boots."

The girl smiled wide. "Thanks, I got 'em on sale. They were only seventy-five dollars." A little small talk always helped girls like Sugar forget their other life, the one where they were slowly killing themselves—the part that mattered, anyway—for a little money that they never got to keep. Although this girl didn't seem like so many of the women who got involved walking the street to support a drug habit. She was too new; too clean.

"Wow, that's a good deal."

"Yeah, I was pretty excited."

They both nodded for a moment.

"So why are you here, Sugar? Why do you need to talk to me?"

The girl's smile vanished as a hint of fear showed through her exterior confidence. She shifted nervously again. "I got a problem," she whispered.

"Go on."

Sugar hesitated. "Maybe I should just leave," she said, starting to stand up.

"You been working the street?" Louisa said quickly.

The girl nodded and sat back down.

"You want out?" Louisa asked. "Is that why you're here?"

The girl barely shrugged her shoulders. "I guess I do, maybe, but that's not why I'm here."

Louisa feared what the girl was going to say next. She leaned forward. "Why are you here?"

"You help out pregnant girls, right?"

Louisa leaned back with sadness. She'd have been shocked, too, if this didn't happen so often. "Yeah, we can. We can get you off the street, find an adoptive family for your baby, or provide you with assistance if you want to keep it. . . ."

The girl got up again. "Keep it? Adoptive family? I just want the problem to go away. I don't—" She sat back down as her knees buckled and her eyes filled up with tears.

Louisa got up from her desk and kneeled beside the girl's chair. She put her arm around her and held her in a half embrace for a few moments.

"Sand Crab said I shouldn'ta come here," the girl said.

"Sand Crab? He the one who got you into the business?"

The girl nodded again.

Louisa was furious. She was always furious at the pimps for picking on underage girls like this one, girls who probably had difficult home lives and were just looking for a way out. The Sugars of society were always promised the world and always ended up with nothing but a drug habit and a shell of a soul. Louisa usually went after the pimps, if she heard their names enough. She knew almost every working pimp in the city, both by their street name and their real name.

"What's his real name, Sugar? Can you tell me that? That'll help me help you."

The girl wiped a tear from a heavily lined eye, mascara clumps coming off onto her long pink fingernails. Her voice trembled with emotion and the breathiness that comes from a heavy cry.

"His name is Santiago. Santiago Cruz."

In Which Wheels Get Put into a Very Halting Motion

"LET'S DO IT."

Jake almost dropped the phone. "Seriously, Louisa?"

"Yes."

"Are you sure?"

"Jake, stop asking. We *have* to get that money. We have to keep it out of Santiago's hands."

The determination in Louisa's voice was unmistakable. Jake hadn't expected the phone call so soon, but he had expected it. In his mind, there was no way around this caper—it had to be done. He wondered what Santiago had done to trigger Louisa's strong acceptance of the idea, but he didn't really feel like asking, afraid too much digging would make her change her mind.

"Well, okay," Jake said. "I'm down with that."

"Good," Louisa said, voice trembling. "What's next?"

"Not sure," Jake said. "I've just been sitting here getting a

preliminary plan together, so I guess I just keep working on that."
He twisted the phone cord through his fingers. "I'll just call you
when I have a few ideas, and then we can maybe go over them
together, figure out the best one?"

"Fine," Louisa said. "Sure. Yeah. That works."

"All right, then," Jake said, sensing the end of the conversation
and feeling an irrational panic that he wouldn't wind up getting
his fingers extracted from the phone cord. "I'll be in touch."

"Great. Talk to you later."

Must . . . get . . . fingers out. Can't . . . hang up. "Hey,
Louisa!"

"Yeah?"

"Um, well, I was thinking that, you know, well—" Stupid
fingers! Jake tried to keep the phone to his ear and mouth while
pulling it as far away from his hand as possible, but the cord only
stretched longer, refusing to release his fingers. "—do we have to
wait until the money's buried? Can't we just sneak it out earlier
and be done with it?"

Louisa sighed. "No, Jake. If we're going to do this, we have to
follow that will down to the last letter."

Success! Spreading his fingers wide, Jake finally managed to
extract them from the cord. "Oh, yeah. That's totally what I was
planning on. I just wanted to make sure with you."

"Mm-hmm," she said. "Anything else?"

"Nope," Jake said quickly. "I'll call you."

"Bye, Jake."

"See ya."

Jake became a model of productivity, working through lunch
and stopping only momentarily to snack on crackers and government peanut butter (one of his neighbors was into free stuff,

too: She bent the rules on her taxes so she could qualify for food assistance from the government, and she'd offered a little extra to Jake last month to keep him quiet). By midafternoon, he had the workings of a decent plan.

Benjamin Cruz was due to be interred at Brownstone Avenue Cemetery, one of the more popular lots in town for wealthy folks. Jake had handled many transactions there and was buddy-buddy with the main groundskeeper. He figured he should have no problem slipping him a few bucks and securing a small backhoe to make the dig go easier. He also decided they should do it at night. It was safer, and the fewer people who saw them, the better.

He really wished he could snatch the money before the actual burial. He supposed he admired Louisa's integrity and all, but right now it was really cramping his style.

A chirpy voice derailed his planning train. "Mr. Abrams?"

He looked up to see a young, smartly dressed woman who'd gone overboard with her makeup and her bottle of knockoff designer fragrance. "Can I help you?" he said, conveying as little interest in her as possible.

The woman approached him and extended her hand. "Cindy Pennington, Channel 9 News."

"Oh, yes, hello." Jake stood and shook her hand begrudgingly. "How'd you get in here?"

"The receptionist let me back."

He silently cursed Chiffon and her popularity-craving ways.

"I was wondering if you had time to answer a few questions?" Pennington said.

"Do you always say that?"

She smiled. "Probably."

Though he wanted to kick her out and get back to scheming,

Jake figured he'd better be nice. He didn't want some snoopy reporter messing up his carefully orchestrated plan. He then made fun of himself for using the phrase "snoopy reporter" in his own thoughts.

Instead of giving her the boot, he got up, snatched a chair from the corner of the room, and moved it closer to his own. He gestured toward it. "Have a seat?"

"Thank you."

"Can I get you anything? Coffee, water . . . ?"

"I'm fine."

"Good, 'cause we don't have any of that stuff anyway."

She offered him a courtesy chuckle. "Mr. Abrams, I was just curious to find out what you know about Mr. Cruz's will."

Way to dispense with the pleasantries, lady. "Only what I've been told. Certain burial procedures he desired."

"And what would those be?"

Jake put on his best patronizing face. "I wish I could tell you, but I'm afraid those details are confidential. You'd need to speak with Mr. Cruz's attorneys."

She bristled. "I've spoken with them already."

"Yeah, I can't elaborate on anything they said. They'd be the ones to go to." He waited for her to ask about something else, hoping this one question wasn't the entire reason for her visit.

"Rumor has it Mr. Cruz is seeking to be buried with his estate," she said.

"Is that so?" he said without flinching. "First I've heard of it."

"I'm sure it is."

"I don't know where you're hearing your rumors, but it sounds like someone's pulling your leg, Ms. Pennington, to see their hoax on the news. Although I wish it were true; it'd make a great story for you."

"Well, these things happen. Just thought I'd follow it up."

Jake's phone beeped and Chiffon's voice came charging through the intercom. "Jake? Someone's here with a delivery for you?"

"Okay, thanks," he said.

"You have work to do, Mr. Abrams," Pennington said. "I'll excuse myself and let you get back to it."

"I'll walk you out."

Jake's mind was racing. How much did this reporter know, or *think* she knew? Mentally occupied, he made his way to the front desk and saw a slack-jawed man in a shirt with the words "Cedar Valley Casketry" embroidered in cursive script on the left chest. It took Jake a second to read it, though, since it was distorted by the round shape of a can of snuff being carried in the front pocket.

Like any business, White Hall Funeral Home tried to keep a moderate inventory of their main product, which in this case happened to be caskets. But Del had once had a falling-out with the primary manager of Cedar Valley, so he hadn't used them since. Jake wondered why they were here now.

"Can I help you?"

"You the one in charge of the Benjamin Cruz funeral?"

Cindy Pennington, halfway out the door, halted immediately.

"Yeah. Jake Abrams."

The man shook Jake's extended hand.

"Pleased to meetcha. I got his casket in the truck."

Jake furrowed his brow. "I thought we already had his."

"Prob'ly not, sir. He had this one made special, just for him."

A little alarm bell went off in Jake's head. He turned and saw that Pennington had stealthily made her way back to the pair of men and was not-so-casually eavesdropping.

"Man, these rich guys, I tell you," Jake said to the delivery man, glancing at Pennington out of the corner of his eye. "Never want anything the same as us commoners." He lowered his voice slightly. "I need to check some paperwork to find out more about this special casket of yours."

Jake hurried back to his workstation and retrieved Benjamin Cruz's file from under a can of soda he'd bought with change pilfered from various coin returns in the area. He sifted through the contents (of the file, not of the soda) on his way back up front.

He'd been so preoccupied with Louisa and his plan over the past two days he hadn't bothered to really read the file—to do his job, essentially. And it was here that all his planning from earlier in the day began to unravel.

Benjamin Cruz had, in fact, ordered a special casket from Cedar Valley, and once Jake had looked over the paperwork, he could now see why.

It had a built-in safe.

Jake arrived back in the lobby and noticed the reporter chatting with the delivery man. He overheard the man say, "Oh, I dunno what's so special 'bout it. Alls I know is, it's s'posed to come here. I don't make 'em; I deliver 'em."

"Hey, man," Jake interrupted. "Sorry about that. Go ahead and deliver it to the back. Normal spot."

The man thrust a clipboard at him. "You'll hafta sign for it, friend."

"Sure thing." Jake picked up a pen from Chiffon's desk and signed the carbon copy document, giving Cindy Pennington a smiling look the whole time. "Benjamin Cruz's casket being delivered. Big news there."

He handed the clipboard back, and they both watched the deliveryman exit.

Pennington looked back at Jake. "I'll be in touch, Mr. Abrams."

"I can't wait!" He smiled until she got out the door, then hurried back to his workstation, picked up the phone, and dialed.

"Louisa? We have a problem."

δ

"It's hard to look at," Louisa said, staring at the casket in the Prep Room at White Hall. "Knowing my father's body will be there forever, starting in three days."

"I bet. That has to be quite a thought to carry around."

Louisa nodded.

"You were close?" Jake didn't want to get too personal right here, right now, but it felt like the right thing to say.

"Not for most of my life. He was a hard man to please, and an even harder man to know." A tear started to form in the corner of her eye. "But I did get closer to him just before he . . ." She looked like she was stumbling over the proper terminology to finish her sentence. Jake had heard them all: "passed away" or "went to heaven" or "left us" or any of those other euphemisms people use when they don't want the harsh-yet-best "died."

Jake placed a comforting hand on her shoulder. "It's okay." It was the only thing he knew to say. He'd been around the funeral business long enough to know that sometimes the best thing to do at this point was to conjure up a favorite memory and turn the emotions from sheer sadness to fond sadness. "What happened in those last three months with him? What changed between you two?"

"Not a whole lot, really. We both lived the same lives we'd been living, but we just started living them with each other more in the picture."

"Why's that?"

Louisa shyly looked down. "It sounds kind of silly. Like, so overdone, but it's true." She glanced back up at him.

His eyes met hers. "What?"

"We both, um, found Jesus, I guess."

Jesus? Okay, first she mentioned God, no big deal, but now Jesus? The religion stuff was starting to get a little uncomfortable.

"You found Jesus, huh?" he said. "I didn't know he was missing."

Louisa gave him a playful punch in the arm. A very hard playful punch, that maybe wasn't as playful as it looked. "Jake, I'm serious."

"Sorry." He wasn't sorry about half-insulting her religion. He was sorry he'd gotten hit for it. "Tell me about it."

"Oh, there's not a whole lot to tell," she said. "We were all raised Catholic, so I had, you know, foundational basics, I guess. I knew the whole story—dying on the cross, coming back to life, saving sins, all that."

"Sure."

"Well, sometimes I like to go to flea markets and things like that, looking for cheap antiques I can use to decorate my apartment. About four or five months ago I was looking around a flea market and saw a big, gaudy Bible. It reminded me of one we'd had when I was a little girl. It was an illustrated family Bible, and I used to love flipping through it to look at the pictures. Happier times. This Bible took me back to that part of my childhood, so I bought it and took it home.

"I don't know, I guess I was trying to recapture those moments, those simpler times when my brothers and I would play and my mom was still around and the whole family got along. I opened it up and started looking at the illustrations. But these were different than the ones our old Bible had. These seemed more . . . alive. I went from page to page to page, taking in the illustrations of all the stories I'd learned as a child. Adam and Eve. Noah's Ark. Abraham. Jacob. Joseph. Moses. David and Goliath. Jonah. And so on.

"And then I got to the pictures of Jesus, and, this is going to seem strange, but I just fell in love with His face. The way the artist illustrated Him, He was so beautiful and strong and peaceful and full of courage." She chuckled at herself. "Listen to me, I sound like a little girl with a crush on the latest singer or whatever. But I don't know, this was different from infatuation; it was more comforting, more real."

"Makes sense, I guess," Jake said.

"So I started reading the parts in that Bible about Jesus. And it was really the first time I'd ever read those parts, truly read them. And I loved them. I wanted more. I decided I wanted to learn more about Jesus, so I went to a church near my house that weekend."

Jake had been nodding the whole time, admiring her good looks, but tuning out what she was saying. He was glad for her, that she had a nice little Jesus crutch, whatever it took to make it through the day. But to Jake, while religion was fine, Louisa was finer. "So what about your dad? How'd that come about?"

"I took him the Bible to give him a happy memory of those older times. When he saw it, he started . . . not really crying. It was from further down than that. It was, like, actual weeping. He was so sad. I asked him what was wrong, and he said he wished for those old times to be back and exchanged for the times he had now. He was very regretful for the life he'd lived up until then, for the way he'd treated us kids and our mother. I don't want to make this too cheesy or anything, so I'll just say that I talked him into coming to church with me. I don't know how much you know about all the Christian terminology and stuff, and it sounds kind of silly if you don't know what it means, but we both invited Jesus into our lives, and we were close ever since."

"That's a great story, Louisa," Jake said. "Really."

"It was a great three months, while it lasted. I'm just happy to know that I'll see Papa again."

"Of course you will," Jake said, panicking internally. What had he gotten himself into here? Okay, the childhood Bible stories, those were fine, but all this "invited Jesus into our lives stuff" was so . . . Jake didn't know how to describe it. Louisa was a cool girl and all, but this kind of talk ran so cross-grained to Jake's psyche that he began to doubt what exactly he was doing with her.

He did know one thing, though: He was going to rob her dad, with her help. "So, what are we going to do about this safe?"

The casket was made of highly polished mahogany with gold accents on the outside and regal purple lining within, which hid the safe in question. Jake gave the satiny fabric a tug near the area where Benjamin Cruz's head would reside, and some elastic gave way to reveal a long, thin, flat metal box, securely fastened to the casket's interior. It had a large, dial-style combination lock in one corner, and the door was being held slightly open by a small plastic clip gripping the inside lip of the safe.

"I have no idea," Louisa said. "I could try finding out the combination at The Agency, but I doubt anyone there knows anything about this. Do you think the Cedar Valley people would know?"

Jake shook his head. "I asked them already. They said it came that way from a safe manufacturer. Your dad had contacted the manufacturer directly and given them a combination, along with orders that no one know the combination but him. So they put that clip on there and sent it along. Once the clip comes out and the door closes, no one's opening it back up without cutting into it."

"Well, maybe he told Tom."

"Wait a minute," Jake said abruptly. "Do we really want to go telling people about the safe in your dad's casket?"

"Tom already knows about the money going in there. I don't think it'd hurt to tell him about the safe. It might help us."

"Think you can find out without tipping him off?"

Louisa nodded. "Don't worry. It's worth a shot."

Jake relented. "Okay. Try it out, then."

Louisa retrieved her cell phone from her purse, found Tom's number in her contact list, and dialed. "Here, let me put it on speaker," she said, punching the appropriate button.

The sound of the ringing drove the phone's tiny speakers to distortion before Louisa adjusted the volume. She was still fiddling with it when a vaguely familiar voice crackled into the room.

"Louisa," the voice said, sounding pleased.

"Hey, Tom," Louisa said. "Caller ID?"

"Yep. What's up?"

"Well, I'm here at the funeral home checking on Papa's casket, and . . . well, it's kind of embarrassing."

"I won't think any less of you," he said.

"Well, did you know there's a safe inside there?"

There was a pause on the other end. "I had no idea. Inside the casket?"

"Yeah. I guess it's where the money's going to go."

"Oh, that makes sense. Keep away the riffraff."

"Probably. Anyway," Louisa sighed despairingly, "I kinda accidentally locked my car keys in it."

"What?"

"Well, I was looking at it up close, and I set my keys in there to see how big it was, and the door accidentally swung shut." Louisa was sounding progressively more agitated. "And now they're locked in there and I have to leave in a little bit so I don't know what I'm going to do without them because I need them and they also have my house key on there *and I just don't know what to do and IreallyhopeyoucanhelpmebecauseI'mstartingtofreakout!*"

She flashed a "how am I doing?" look at Jake, to which he gave an enthusiastic thumbs-up.

Tom, by comparison, was in crisis mode. "It's okay, Louisa. Calm down. Relax."

"Sorry. I'm just . . . freaking out here, and I thought you would know about this safe and maybe have the combination."

"I don't think I do. Let me check, though."

"Okay."

Jake gave her a double thumbs-up this time. He thought about segueing into some finger guns, but checked the impulse before his gesticulating got out of hand.

"Car keys," Jake whispered. "Nice."

Louisa smiled at her off-the-cuff subterfuge and leaned in close to Jake's ear. She smelled like spiced apples—in a good way. "That's what I get from hanging out with a devious guy like you," she whispered. "You're rubbing off on me."

For a moment, Jake's diaphragm forgot how to breathe. Maybe he would play this relationship game out for a little longer.

The moment was interrupted when Tom's voice taxed the volume capacity of the speaker phone again. "Hey, Louisa."

"Please tell me you have good news."

"Yep. I found it."

She breathed an overeager sigh of relief, "Oh, *thank* you."

"You're welcome."

"That was fast."

"I got lucky looking through some papers labeled 'emergency.'"

"I'll say," she said.

Tom read off the combination to her as she copied it down onto a scratch pad Jake had just handed her.

"Thanks again, Tom. I *really* appreciate it."

"No problem," he said. "I'll, uh, talk to you later?"

"You bet."

"Great."

She ended the call silently smiling, a mischievous glint in her eye. Jake was now sure she'd fully committed to their little caper.

Good thing, too.

It was about to get a lot harder.

The Conversation
Turns to Things Above

BEFORE THEY STARTED to work through the plan, Louisa had opted to go to the deli to get a bite for the two of them while Jake scoured the rest of her father's file.

That left Jake alone in the Interview Room — alone in the whole place, actually. It was getting late, and Jeremy, Chiffon, and Del had already gone home for the night. Jake heard the door open and automatically assumed Louisa had returned from her deli run sooner than he expected.

Instead, he was face-to-face with a well-dressed Hispanic man. Designer suit — three-piece, charcoal gray pinstripe, which seemed to be the current style of choice for men who liked to flaunt their wealth. Easily three-hundred-dollar dress shoes. Three hundred bucks for some shiny black leather and a couple of pieces of vulcanized rubber — the nerve. The sunglasses seemed a little desperate, and the guy clearly didn't need them to give off confidence. He already had that. In fact, the sunglasses made him seem less confident.

"You must be Santiago," Jake said. He'd been expecting a visit ever since Louisa had told him about Santiago's appearance at her house. He was surprised it'd taken this long.

The man smiled and spoke in a smoky voice. "Louisa told you about me."

Jake shrugged. "Natch."

"Then I won't have to be long."

Jake sat still, holding his own in the testosterone contest with Louisa's brother.

"You," Santiago said, slowly removing his sunglasses and using them to gesture in Jake's direction, "are in charge of Benjamin Cruz, correct?"

A nod.

"Which means you," Santiago continued, "are in charge of the money that will be placed with him when he's buried."

Another nod.

"I want that money."

And yet another nod.

"And you're going to help me get it."

This time, Jake raised his eyebrow. "Really?"

"Yes."

"Okay, let's say I actually do that. What do you have in mind?"

"It's easy. You just tell me where he's buried, and I'll do the rest."

"You aren't going to the funeral?"

"I'm not big on public appearances."

"With that suit, you should think about it," Jake said. "It's quite nice. You'd be the belle of the ball."

"You're funny," Santiago said without laughing. "Are you going to help me or not?"

"What's in it for me?"

Santiago smiled again. "That's what they always ask," he said. "Ten thousand."

"Fifteen."

"Done."

"Great."

Santiago gestured vaguely around the room as he put his sunglasses back on. "Nice office. Could use some renovations, though."

"Well, this isn't really my office," Jake said, "but thanks."

Santiago continued like he hadn't heard Jake. "Nicer than my sister's office, anyway."

"What are you doing here, Santiago?" Louisa was back, her grip tightening on a white paper sack containing dinner for her and Jake. Her jaw was set, eyes riveted on her brother. "Or should I call you Sand Crab instead?"

"Ah. I knew you'd find out about that sooner or later."

"Get out of here, Santiago," Louisa said, voice trembling with anger. "I'm giving you one chance to get out and never come back. Otherwise, I call the cops on you."

"I'm disappointed in you, *mija*," Santiago said. "We're family."

"That's why I'm giving you the one chance."

Santiago slowly rotated toward the door and began to walk toward it. He paused to cast a glance in Jake's direction. "I'll be in touch." Calmly, casually, he walked out the door, through the lobby, and out of White Hall Funeral Home. After a few seconds, Jake hurried behind him and locked the door.

"What was that about?" Louisa asked as Jake hustled back into the room.

"Oh, nothing much. I've just been contracted to steal your dad's fortune for your brother," Jake said. "Good thing he doesn't know I'm already planning on stealing it for his sister."

"Jake, this isn't funny."

Louisa set the bag of sandwiches down on the conference table, then began to root through it as she sat down herself. She located Jake's sandwich and handed it over to him so they could munch while they figured out their next move. "Here's your turkey and bacon."

"Thanks," Jake said. "What'd you get?"

"Roast beef."

"Really? You don't strike me as the type." Jake made this assessment based on her diminutive figure, cleverly concealed behind a simple jeans-and-hooded-sweatshirt motif that still made her look desirable.

Louisa began to unwrap her sandwich. "Oh, I thoroughly enjoy all cow-based meats."

"I'm an olive loaf guy, myself," Jake said with a wink. "But I can never find it anywhere."

"I think you probably need to look in more elementary schools."

They both took bites from their sandwiches and chewed in silence for a moment.

"I've always made a point," Jake said (after swallowing), "never to let an indirect threat spoil my appetite."

"Amen to that."

Jake absentmindedly resumed looking through Mr. Cruz's file while they ate. "So is your brother really a big shot out there on the street? Lord knows he acts like the movie version of it."

"So far as I know. He probably doesn't really need this money. I'm sure with him it's the principle of the whole thing. He can't stand being disowned."

"I'm sure it hurts."

"It does." Louisa had stopped chewing.

Jake looked directly into her eyes, only to see them dart away from the attention. "I'm sorry. For you."

"It's okay. Really."

They shared a sweet look that made the silence between them appropriate. Though Jake had only met her a couple of days ago, he'd begun to feel something a little stronger than his usual ego-driven attraction. She certainly had a beautiful face, which Jake was fond of noticing, but he was also beginning to notice something else. Something deeper.

She had a beautiful heart, too. If he wasn't careful, he'd go soft and start—horror of horrors—caring about her. Not to worry, though, because she immediately reminded him of their incompatibility.

"What do you think of God, Jake?"

Jake repressed a sarcastic eye roll. Here she was again, shoving the Almighty into a perfectly good conversation. Jake took a deep breath. How to play this? "Well, I guess this question was going to come along eventually, wasn't it?"

What did Jake think of God? If he was to answer honestly, he'd have to say that he didn't know. There were millions of other things to think about during the day, and God never really crept to the top of the list. Working at the funeral home had numbed him to all the soul searching that people usually did when faced with the death of a loved one. Reflecting on it now, he realized that the Guy Upstairs was a big mystery.

"I'm down with God, I guess," he said. "He's like the president or something. Kind of in charge, but I'm not going to run into him anytime soon. He's off in heaven or Washington or wherever, and I'm over here just minding my own."

He didn't know what Louisa would do with this assessment of the Almighty. The more he thought about his answer, the more Jake realized he'd never really pondered the deep spiritual things of life. He was usually too busy working some angle to score free stuff. But he'd given Louisa an honest answer, which ought to be good for something. Surely the Man Upstairs would appreciate that?

Louisa smiled. "That's a start, Jake."

Jake returned the smile, certain that his had nowhere near the luminosity or vibrancy of hers. He began to have difficulty squaring the incongruities in his head. How could someone as incredulously hot as Louisa Cruz tie herself down to the Jesus stuff?

"Good. Starts are good, right?"

"They're a start," she said.

They shared a chuckle as Jake glanced back down at the file. He did a double take as his eye caught a word.

He double-checked.

He triple-checked.

He blinked his eyes as his brain automatically went back to the drawing board. He began beating himself up for being so interested in recent events that he wasn't doing his job.

"Oh, no," he said.

"What is it?" Louisa rose from her chair and joined Jake, looking at the file over his shoulder.

He pointed to the word. Louisa's eyes followed the length of Jake's extended finger.

Mausoleum.

A Safe as Big as a House— and Marble, Too

FROM THE FILE, Jake learned that when Benjamin Cruz was alive, he had become fascinated with his own legacy, specifically with preserving it. He had never gotten into the whole cryogenic freezing thing, though he'd considered it. Instead, he'd drafted a will that included no one but himself. He'd special ordered a casket for himself. He'd been very much interested in himself, and he'd thought that everyone else should be interested in him, too, whether they wanted to be or not. So in addition to the will and the casket, he'd contacted Brownstone Avenue Cemetery about constructing a small mausoleum in his honor, purchased with company funds, using a purchase order detailing the necessity for "preservation of the company legacy."

Thinking it a potential jinx on his life, he'd never mentioned it to anyone, except to the owners of the cemetery and to Del, who had put it in his file without really thinking about it. And there Benjamin Cruz's secret had sat for the last two years, waiting for Jake Abrams to find it and discover that his entire plan had gone out the window.

"This sucks." Jake's normally positive outlook on life was temporarily on strike.

"I thought he was supposed to be buried."

"Being put in a mausoleum *is* being buried, technically. It just isn't in the ground."

Jake reached for the copy of the will Louisa had brought earlier and began to look it over. A few quick glances showed him that the word "buried" never appeared. The document used the more legalesque and highbrow word, "interred." They'd gotten it all wrong and had assumed something that wasn't true.

Jake reread the directions listed in the file. Mr. Cruz was to be laid to rest inside a mausoleum on cemetery property, which was then to be sealed up immediately. It was Benjamin Cruz's clever way of protecting his fortune from the literal gold diggers he knew would come looking for it. A nice, safe, secure mausoleum, where he could rest surrounded by a foot-thick wall of high-dollar stone and a four-inch-thick bronze door.

Jake let out an audible sigh. "We're going to need stronger shovels."

"What are we going to do?"

"I don't know yet. But this certainly puts a crimp on things, doesn't it?"

Louisa nodded. "I think that's an understated way of saying it, yeah."

"Well, look at the bright side, Louisa. There's no way your brother will get it now."

"Oh, he'll find a way," Louisa countered. "He'll bribe a guard, put pressure on someone from the cemetery. He'll blow the thing up if that's what it takes. He's very determined."

"A family trait, I've noticed."

They both leaned back in their chairs and assessed the situation. Jake was the first to speak.

"So you're saying you believe, no matter what, Santiago will make every attempt to get this money. Out of the safe that's in your father's casket that's sealed in this nearly impenetrable mausoleum located inside a well-guarded cemetery."

"Yes." At least she was to the point.

"So we have no choice, really."

"No."

"Hmmm . . ."

"You're already working something up?" Louisa said.

Jake rubbed his hands through his hair, then started gnawing on the tip of his forefinger. He repeated this pattern a few more times, hoping it would make an idea appear out of thin air.

Finally he sat up. "I need some inspiration."

§

Jake parked Princess Tangerine in the shrill glow emanating from what seemed like miles of neon tubing around Video Palace. Louisa needed sleep, so she'd gone home, giving Jake the opportunity to visit the video rental store, a traditional brick-and-mortar structure that stood alone in the parking lot of the Target down the street from Jake's apartment. The place was a multicolored assault on Jake's eyes, especially at night, when management spent an unhealthy amount of electricity powering the store's exterior lighting.

Nevertheless, their DVD selection was fairly good, and they always seemed to have several copies of the most recent releases. Back at White Hall, Jake had remembered an ad he saw in his neighbor's newspaper that promoted the movie *Potato Thief*, recently released on DVD and available to rent at any of three convenient Video Palace locations.

Jake had seen *Potato Thief* during its original theatrical run, manufacturing his own double feature after paying for, and watching, a matinee of *Destruction Force*, a passable action thriller in which many things got blown up real good. He hadn't been satisfied with *Destruction Force*, so after the show ended, he spotted a large, empty bag that had been used for popcorn, took it to the concession stand to get his free refill (it was theater policy; that's how they sold so many large popcorns), and then plunked himself down at a different screen to hopefully get his money's worth watching *Potato Thief*.

The reason Jake now hoped to catch *Potato Thief* on DVD was simple: It was a movie about a grand, well-planned theft. The gimmick was that all the criminals nicknamed their targets after vegetables, and themselves after garden pests. Hence the title of the movie.

Jake walked through the self-opening doors of Video Palace and into the harsh, garish store, filled with rows and rows of home videos and DVDs, walls adorned with posters of new releases that looked just like posters of old releases. He took a left and walked along the "new releases" section of the deserted store until he got to the area where *Potato Thief* should be.

He found a bunch of empty display boxes instead.

He went up to the counter, where a teenage boy in jeans, a white polo, and a Video Palace vest was studiously watching an in-store movie, playing on the ten or so TVs strategically located throughout Video Palace. Oddly enough, the movie was *Destruction Force*. The teenager greeted Jake with extreme apathy. "Yeah?" he said, without turning away from the rampant fireballs onscreen.

"Hey, man," Jake said. "I was wondering if you had any copies of *Potato Thief* available?"

The teenager looked blandly at Jake. "Did you see any out there?"

"No."

"Well, if they're not out there, we don't have 'em."

Jake pointed to a slot cut out of the countertop. "What about in the drop box? Anything in there?"

The teenager sighed heavily and meandered to the drop box. He slowly bent down, opened a door on his side of the counter, and looked in. "Nope."

"Can you check the drive-up drop box? The one outside?"

The teenage clerk closed the door and made his way back to Jake. "I checked it, like, an hour ago. I'm not due to check it again until close."

"Come on, man."

"Sorry." The teenager turned back to watch his movie.

Jake just shook his head and exited the store quickly. He climbed aboard Princess Tangerine and was about to start her up when he saw a car approach the exterior drop box, which was basically a mailbox with a bigger slot and no postage fees. It was set quite a ways away from the store, toward the perimeter of the parking lot.

Jake leapt off the scooter and ran toward the drop box. He wanted to see what the people in the car were returning, but he was too late. The car drove off before he got there, but the whole scenario gave him an idea. He planted himself next to the drop box and waited for the next car to arrive.

He only had to wait a couple of minutes before a Honda SUV pulled up. The driver, a man in his midthirties wearing a sweatshirt, gave Jake a quizzical look.

"How're you doing this evening?" Jake said. He didn't wait for a reply. "Listen, we're having some problems with the drop box tonight. It's . . . clogged. So, I can take your movie for you and run it in."

The man smiled. "Oh, okay." The man grabbed a DVD from the passenger seat and handed it to Jake. "Here you go."

"Thank you, sir. Enjoy your evening."

"You, too."

The man drove off, and Jake looked down at the movie he'd been given. *Destruction Force.*

"I suppose it was too much to hope for the first one out of the chute," Jake said.

Fifteen minutes and three cars later, Jake had received three more copies of *Destruction Force* and half a candy bar that one driver wasn't particularly fond of. He was about to give up his quest when a small Ford hatchback pulled up, driven by a tiny woman who could very well have been one hundred years old.

"Hi there, ma'am," Jake said. "We're having some trouble with the drop box here, so I can take your movies in for you."

The woman gave him a toothy grin. "Oh, this isn't my movie. This is my grandson's, but he rented it on my card, on account of he has a lot of late charges on his."

"Well, I will take especially good care of it then, ma'am."

The woman handed Jake her grandson's movie, which Jake

could already see was *Potato Thief.* "Thank you so much," she said. "You're very kind."

"You're welcome, ma'am," Jake said, smiling back. He waved as she drove off, waited for her to get out of sight, and then hopped on his scooter, taking a moment to stash the DVD in his glove compartment.

He looked at his watch. 9:15. If he hurried, he could get home, watch the movie, and have it back before midnight. He couldn't bear the thought of that sweet woman getting a late charge because of him.

♪

This was no good.

Potato Thief was nowhere near what Jake had remembered. He reclined on his couch, head propped up on a cushion, lights off for that perfect theater atmosphere. He was prepared to focus all his attention on what *Potato Thief* could teach him, but at the moment, all he was learning was that the filmmakers were lazy and gave their heroes a bunch of impossible gadgets to accomplish their break-in and subsequent theft.

And then his eyes locked on the television and not just because, like most bachelors, his TV screen took up a lot of room. The movie featured a handsome man and pretty woman, and through the course of the film, they'd flirted with each other, then fallen in love. Now, at the end, after they'd successfully lifted the potato diamond, the guy was—he was dumping her!

Jake sat up, eyes fixated on the screen. She wasn't taking it well, obviously, but they knew it was for the best. They were sitting on a bench in a crowded park. She asked for her share of the loot, and he handed her a compact briefcase. "It's all in there," he said. Then he walked away, disappearing into the crowd. The movie cut to her going home and opening the briefcase.

It was empty.

And then a shot of the guy, sitting on a tropical beach with a cigar in his mouth, laughing. The perfect crime. And that was how *Potato Thief* ended.

Maybe Jake had learned something from it after all.

∂

Louisa sat inside Ramon's at 7:30 the next morning, waiting for Jake's arrival. He'd promised to work out a plan the night before; then they were going to talk it over here this morning. Jake had originally suggested picking up some bagels and taking them to White Hall, but Louisa had insisted Jake try Ramon's *huevos con chorizo*, eggs with a special Mexican sausage.

"How's the funeral planning going?" Ramon was a busy bee as usual, nosing into everyone's business.

"Fine."

"Something wrong?"

Louisa stirred some sugar into her coffee as she tried to figure out the best tack to take. "Why'd you tell Santiago about Jake?"

Ramon looked bewildered. "He called me asking about you, so I mentioned that you came in the other night with the man from the funeral place. Why? Is that not okay?"

"No, it's fine, Ramon," Louisa assured him. "But Santi—he's going after the money, whether we like it or not."

"He needs to let Papa rest in peace."

"You're right. You want to talk him into it?"

"Oh, *mija*, we both know Santi, and we both know nothing's going to change his mind now."

"Tell me about it."

Ramon grunted an unintelligible response and shuffled off to the kitchen to start cooking up some breakfast for Louisa and her friend who hadn't shown up yet.

While waiting for her *huevos*, Louisa contemplated the ridiculousness of the situation. All this rigmarole could've been avoided if her Papa had just made the change to his will in the first place. Sometimes he could be like that, though. Well, *had* been like that.

Where was Jake? What was taking so long?

ᡐ

Ding! A small bell chimed as Jake ambled into Ramon's Mexican Kitchen twenty minutes after he was supposed to be there. He was wearing the same jeans he'd worn yesterday, but at least he'd gone to the trouble of putting on a clean T-shirt. He hoped he didn't look like he was clearly missing the sleep he'd foregone last night.

"*Hola*, Jake!"

Jake looked toward the kitchen area to see Ramon's head peeking around the door, his arm extended in the air in an exaggerated wave. Jake mustered all his remaining energy to offer an "*hola*" in return. He shuffled over to the table and sat down across from Louisa.

"You're late, mister," she said.

"Well, in some time zones, I'm early," Jake responded. He pointed toward the kitchen. "What's up with Ramon being all friendly?"

"He feels bad for mentioning you to Santiago."

"Oh." Jake thought a moment. "Hey, he should give me some free food or something. Breakfast is on him," he said, smiling.

"You're only saying that because it is."

"No, I'd much rather it be my clout that bought this meal, not your family ties."

"So be it."

Jake formed a support for his chin, placing his elbows on the table and making his hands into a big fist. "Think I can have a sip of your coffee until Ramon gets here and I can order my own?"

"This is yours. I figured you'd need one after last night's master planning strategy session."

"That's very thoughtful," Jake said, eager to start sipping and get on with the day. He held the cup to his lips, smelled the coffee, then tasted a bit. "Thank you."

"You're welcome." Louisa looked around at the empty restaurant, then took a peek into the kitchen area. Jake followed her look and saw Ramon with his back to them, frying something that smelled spicy. Jake was caught off guard when Louisa leaned in to him and said, "So what'd you come up with?"

§

The hot morning sun began wooing beads of sweat from Jake and Louisa the moment they arrived at Brownstone Avenue Cemetery. Jake was friends with the groundskeeper, and they now stood in his maintenance shop waiting for him to show up. Size-wise, Jake was jealous of the shop, since it was twice as big as his office. On the downside, though, was all the landscape equipment it housed, which gave off enough two-stroke engine oil fumes to make a person dizzy.

It was only a matter of minutes before he did show up. He—Bo was his name, a kind, forty-ish fella in a basic blue uniform, like a mechanic or air conditioner repairman would wear—strode into the shop with purposeful movements, his black work boots a temporary green from the wet blades of grass that covered them, his hand already out in greeting. "Hey, Jake!" he said, smiling a huge smile that brought out the dimples on his baby-face. "I hope you haven't been waiting long. I've been doing some trimming this morning. Didn't hear my walkie at first."

Jake shook his hand with enthusiasm. "No big deal, Bo. No big deal."

"So, what can I do ya for?"

Jake gestured toward Louisa. "This is Louisa Cruz. Benjamin Cruz's daughter?"

Bo smiled toothily and extended a hand toward her. "It's a pleasure, ma'am."

Louisa smiled and accepted his greeting. "Thank you."

"Louisa and I have been going over the arrangements for her father's service," Jake said, "and we were just wondering if we could take a look at his mausoleum. You know, get a full, uh . . ." Jake searched for the right words, ". . . sensory sweep, if you will. So we can have a head start on the graveside portion of the service."

"Oh, sure, sure," Bo said. "Yeah, why don't you hop on the cart and we'll drive out there?"

They obliged and soon they were on Bo's golf cart, tooling down one of the many cement paths that wound through the cemetery grounds. The cool wind generated from the cart's motion was a welcome relief from the sun. Jake noted the multitude of headstones, varying in shapes and sizes, placed in neat rows throughout the wide-open grassland. Oh, how much easier that would've been.

"We're almost there," Bo said over the rush of wind. "It's in a nice, secluded corner of the grounds up here. Didn't have room for it anywhere else."

They made a turn and drove on a path that ran parallel to the cemetery's high wrought-iron fence. "Thar she blows," Bo said, pointing to what looked like a gleaming white doghouse. As the cart drew closer, Jake realized that the structure was actually much larger than a doghouse. The distance had thrown off his perception. It was impressive, if on the smallish side, rising ten feet in the air and looking like it was just wide enough to hold a casket and some very thin pallbearers.

"Nice, ain't it?" Bo said. "I remember when they built that sucker. I'd come by every day to check out the construction. It's solid, that's for sure."

"How long ago was it built?" Louisa said from the back.

"Um, let's see," Bo said, stopping the cart just to the side of the mausoleum. "Must be going on two years now. Maybe three?"

The three of them got out of the cart and approached what would be Benjamin Cruz's final resting place. "Wanna take a walk around?" Bo said.

"Sure," Jake said, casting a wary eye at Louisa. She returned it with gusto.

"These walls look like solid marble," Bo said, walking along the wall toward the back of the structure. "But they're really solid concrete covered in marble. The concrete core's about eight inches thick, and then there's marble over that, inside and out."

"And how thick is the marble?" Louisa said.

"Um, each side was about two inches, I think."

"That had to cost a lot."

Bo chuckled. "You got that right, ma'am. 'Course, your father had the money, I guess." They continued walking. "So, anyway, that's the scoop all around the perimeter here. And then I got this nice shrubbery along the back." He pointed to a three-foot high hedge that ran along the back wall.

"Yeah," Jake said. "It's nice."

Louisa pointed upward. "What about the roof?"

"Oh, that's more concrete, topped with granite," Bo said as they rounded the corner. "I think it's marble on the inside, though."

"Must be pretty heavy," Jake said. "I can't imagine it'll blow over in a windstorm."

Bo chuckled. "No, Jake, I don't think that'll be a problem. Besides, the walls and foundation go three feet down into the ground. This thing ain't going nowhere."

They took the last corner and finally saw the face of the structure. Jake had been expecting something ornate, with loads of references to Benjamin Cruz everywhere, but it was astonishingly simple. More marble, with the single word "Cruz" engraved in foot-high letters above the door.

That door would be a problem, though. "Bronze?" Jake said.

"Yep," Bo said. "That's some fancy stuff, there. Again, it's reinforced stainless steel on the inside, then coated in bronze. The handle's solid bronze." He strode up to it and gave it a rap with his knuckles. They landed with a dull, heavy thud. "I remember when they brought this sucker onto the grounds. Darn near tore up my sod with that truck of theirs."

"Does it open?" Louisa asked. "Can we go in, check out the inside?"

"Yeah, it opens," Bo said, "but you can't go in right now. Locked."

Louisa nudged Jake's shoulder. "Why don't you give it a little kick, Jake? See if it'll open up?"

"Sorry, I didn't wear my superhero boots today."

"Hey, check this out," Bo said, motioning them over to a keypad, cleverly set into a small alcove in the stone a few feet away from the entrance. "This is pretty cool. Electronic combination lock. Rick, the guy who owns the place? He's the only one who knows the code." He gave Jake a hard slap on the back and gave a gasping belly laugh. "That'll keep the criminals out, huh?"

Jake felt sick. Louisa looked determined.

"Well, I better get back to it," Bo said, ambling toward his golf cart. "You want a lift back to the gates?"

Jake waved him off. "Nah, I want to check this out a little more closely. Get some ideas for the finer points of the proceedings. We'll just walk out."

"Suit yourself, Jake," Bo said. He nodded at Louisa. "Ma'am."

"Good-bye, Bo."

He put his golf cart in gear and drove off. Jake watched him go, then turned back toward the mausoleum and the electronic keypad. "This is going to be a tough nut to crack." He entered a few random numbers.

"What are you doing?" Louisa said.

"I want to see what happens. Listen for alarms and stuff."

They both stood silently, listening. Nothing. No alarms went off; no security personnel came storming down the path to see what was the matter.

But Jake and Louisa did see something.

Over there, on the other side of the fence.

There it was again. A camera flash.

Someone was taking pictures. Of them.

"No way." Jake began sprinting in the direction of the photographer. Too late. The unidentified man had already vacated the bushes he'd been crouching behind and was making haste toward a nearby late-model sedan. Jake really had no chance of catching him, but he gave a valiant effort anyway, almost to the point of scaling the wrought-iron fence that separated them. But by the time he'd gotten a foot on the bars, the photographer's car was accelerating away.

Louisa hurried up behind him as he collapsed against the fence. She looked him over. "Boy, you're breathing hard," she said. "You okay?"

Jake nodded, because he knew if he tried to speak he would probably throw up all over her shoes. This is what he got from never exercising.

"Lousy paparazzi," Louisa continued. "I guess it was only a matter of time before they showed up. I'm kind of surprised I hadn't seen any of them before now."

Jake nodded again.

"What with me being the bereaved daughter of a well-known man in the community."

Jake nodded yet again.

"You sure you're okay? You're still breathing really hard."

"Yeah." The last part sounded more like a big gasp than an actual word.

"Do you need to lie down?"

"No." Jake was panting really hard. "Just (pant, pant) need to (pant) catch my (pant, pant) breath."

"Okay."

They both stood listening to Jake catching his breath.

"You probably should exercise more, you know?" Louisa said. "This is a sign you're out of shape."

"I'm aware of my non-in-shape-itude, okay?" Jake said. "I think, considering the circumstances, that was a pretty decent, admirable sprint."

"Yeah, it wasn't bad."

Jake took one last deep breath and then started to mosey back to the mausoleum with Louisa. "I guess that guy gave us a heads-up on something," he said. "If we're going to do this, we need to be extra careful about it. We can't afford to let our whole plan go to ruin by getting seen in the paper."

"True."

"So from now on we take extra caution. We're always looking around us to make sure there are no cameras pointed anywhere near us. Agreed?"

"Agreed."

"Okay." Jake didn't want to show it, but he was nervous. Cindy Pennington already suspected too much, and he didn't want to give her anything further. Once more, he was being forced to alter his plan. "We should probably just head back to the funeral home. You seen enough here?"

"Yeah."

❦

They rode back to the funeral home in the whisper-quiet silence of Louisa's Volvo. Jake sat in the passenger seat, in his own world, making alterations to his scheme like a master tailor working on a pregnant bridesmaid's dress. Distracted by a glint of light in his periphery, he looked over to his left just in time to see a tear wind its way down Louisa's flawless right cheek. It lost its grip on her jaw and plunged downward, joining several dark spots on her blouse.

"Are you thinking about your dad?" he said.

Louisa nodded.

"I'm sorry. I wish I knew something to say that could help you cheer up."

She threw him a glance. He couldn't tell if it meant "Shut up" or "Thank you."

"I guess 'cheer up' isn't really the best thing to say, huh? Maybe I should just stick to 'I'm sorry.'"

She chuckled quietly. "Thanks."

"Don't mention it," Jake replied. "You know, I see a lot of grieving people where I work, and there never seems to be a right thing to say. I mean, I hear a lot of trite things from well-wishers."

He shifted around so he could face her, leaning his shoulder into the back of the seat. "You know, 'He's in a better place,' or 'God needed another rose for His garden.' Stuff like that. I mean, I guess it's true, depending on what you believe. But it just always strikes me as awfully . . . meaningless. Seems like they don't know what to say, either, so they just say a lot of random, feel-good stuff."

"My father *is* in a better place."

"I'm sure he is. And good for him," Jake said. "But you're still here, and you're still crying, and you're still dealing with this sudden disruption of your life. That's all I'm saying." He thought of *Potato Thief* for some reason. "That's why I'm just going to stick with 'I'm sorry' and leave it at that."

Louisa sighed wearily and looked at Jake with gratitude in her eyes. "Thank you, Jake."

"I really am sorry, you know," he said. "I'm not just saying that."

"I know." Louisa blinked back a new set of tears. "You're sweet for telling me."

"It's all osmotic sweetness I got from you. I gave you some of my craftiness; you're giving me some of your legitimate heart. It's a great deal for me, but you really need to call your sales rep and ask for a refund, 'cause you're getting ripped off."

Louisa laughed and filled the spacious interior with melody.

Jake smiled mischievously. "It's going to be all right, Louisa." He looked into her eyes with sincerity. "Trust me."

A deep sigh was the only response he got for awhile. Then: "What's next, Captain?"

"Well, we're going to have to spread the word a bit. Hope you don't mind, but I think we need to call in some outside help."

Reinforcements and More

"OKAY, GUYS, WE'RE having some complications with the Cruz funeral, and I need your help."

Jeremy and Chiffon sat at the large table in White Hall's Interview Room looking unenthused. Jake had broken into their lunch plans, and now they listened halfheartedly, Jeremy leaning back in his chair and banging his head against the plastic frame around "Starry, Starry Night." Louisa had gone back to Maria House to try to get some work done while Jake rounded up a full-fledged crew.

"What's going on, man?" Jeremy asked in a voice full of disinterest and mistrust.

"What's the deal?" Jake said. "I'm about to freak out here asking for your help, and you both look like you'd rather be bleaching your shoelaces."

Jeremy and Chiffon rolled their eyes at each other.

"Jake?" said Chiffon. "Like, usually the only time you talk to me? is, like, when you say you need help? Well, you still owe me like five bucks, which is no big deal usually, but I totally need gas and could really use it because we don't get paid for another couple days?"

"Oh, come on. I don't need to borrow anything this time."

"Good," Jeremy said, "because I'm strapped until payday, too."

"Don't even worry about it. I got your hookup."

Jake explained the situation, telling them about the will and the money (which Jeremy already knew) and the new will and Santiago. When he got into the bones of his plan and their involvement in it, they both nodded their heads and seemed eager to join in on the fun.

After finishing his explanation, Jake leaned back in his chair and folded his arms across his chest, satisfied at the way he'd laid it out. It was the first time he'd said it all out loud, and it sounded even better when he heard it with his actual ears instead of his inner ones.

Jeremy was the first to speak up. "Sounds good, man, but what's in it for us?"

"Ten grand. Each."

Jeremy did a double take, while Chiffon's gum nearly fell from her suddenly open jaw. "What?"

"We figured it was worth it to pay you guys a little bit. It's only fair; if you help out, you should get paid."

"I guess," Jeremy said, "but that's a lot."

Jake nodded. "And you'll earn every penny. So what do you say?"

"I'll do it?" Chiffon said, getting a little tongue-tied as she rushed the words out.

"I'm in," Jeremy agreed.

"Great."

"When do we start?"

"The funeral's in two days, so we start now. I need to take a look inside that mausoleum, so Jeremy, I'm going to need a ride out to the cemetery."

"Right on."

They stood up to leave. Jake turned to Chiffon. "Hey, can I borrow your video camera?"

♂

Jake and Jeremy stood in the badly wainscoted office of Brownstone Avenue Cemetery's owner. It was a spacious place, though the furniture was probably rented, and that uneven wainscoting had to go. It was really bugging Jake, though not as much as the buzzing of a halogen floor lamp in the corner, the room's only light source aside from one of those classic green desk lamps that feature so prominently in public libraries in movies. Jake was carrying a black leather satchel, the shoulder strap finding a way to dig into his flesh, despite his shirt's valiant effort to prevent it.

"Can I help you?" the owner said, rising from his desk. He was a paunchy man with a pencil-thin mustache and a suit that looked like it'd been purchased from a warehouse-style clothing store.

Jake shook his hand, adjusting his satchel as he did so. "I hope you can. My associate and I are here from White Hall Funeral Home, and we need to take a look inside a mausoleum on your grounds. We were told you could do that for us."

"Well, I'm not sure," said the man smugly. He sat back down and rested his hands on his desk. "Which structure did you have in mind?"

"The mausoleum for Benjamin Cruz," Jake said.

The owner sat up straight in his chair, then virtually leapt to his feet. "How can I assist you, then? Mr. Cruz was indeed a very good client of ours."

"Well, good," Jake said. "We're in charge of Mr. Cruz's interment, as far as everything goes on our end, and we'd like to see the inside of the mausoleum for preparatory purposes. Would you be so kind as to show us?"

"Absolutely," the owner said, almost before Jake was finished talking. "We very much want everything to go well on our end, too."

A few moments later, they found themselves back in front of the mausoleum, preparing to enter. It was at this point that Jake reached into the satchel, still slung around his shoulder.

"What's your name again, sir?" he said, though he wasn't sure he'd ever heard it.

"Rick," the owner replied.

"Rick, I was just going to clear this with you." Jake produced Chiffon's video camera, slipping his hand into the handle and removing the lens cap. "Some of my associates back at the funeral home also need to see the interior of the structure. Hope you don't mind if I tape our visit."

Rick seemed uneasy, shifting his eyes back and forth as he mulled the proposition. "Hmm . . . I suppose that'd be okay."

"Great." Jake put the eyepiece up to his eye and pushed the record button with his thumb. "Let's go."

They'd taken only a few steps toward the building when Rick turned to Jake. "Sorry, sir, but I have to unlock it. I can't let you see this part."

"What's that?" Jake said.

"I said you're going to have to turn around. I have to enter a combination here to get in, and Mr. Cruz was adamant that no one know it."

Jake waved a conciliatory hand. "I understand, Rick," he said. "We want to do our best to respect Mr. Cruz's wishes."

"Thanks."

"Sure thing." Jake and Jeremy turned around while Rick turned his attention to the keypad.

Jake heard Rick fidget a bit, then six light taps. The lock beeped softly. "Here we are."

"Is it safe?"

"Yep. You can turn around now."

"Great." They complied, and Jake noticed that the door was now open a fraction of an inch. Rick grasped the handle of the massive door and, with some effort, swung it open. Jake eyed it with esteem. It was an impressive enclosure.

They walked inside and examined the interior. Lots of smooth marble. Hardly any rough edges. It was a simple layout: essentially four walls surrounding a small platform that rose from the middle of the floor. Most mausoleums had space to accommodate several family members, but Benjamin Cruz had plainly built this to be all about him and him alone. His casket would rest on the platform, smack in the middle.

Jeremy clapped loudly, and the sound echoed for a brief moment before dying out.

"What was that for?" Jake said.

"Testing the acoustics," Jeremy said. "You know, for the proceedings, in case we have someone miked up."

"Right." Jake did a thorough walk-through, videotaping everything he looked at. He examined the floor, the ceiling, the walls, the platform, the door from the other side, all while prat-tling off the top of his head about how glorious this would look during the memorial proceedings and how that was the perfect accent for this particular part of the service. As he checked out the door, he noticed a small button on the wall next to it.

"What's that, Rick?" he said.

The three of them were crowded in, so Rick merely had to turn his head to see where Jake was pointing. "That's the emergency exit. Safety feature, in case someone's in here and the door accidentally closes behind them."

"So if we're in here and the door closes, it automatically locks outside, and we're stuck unless we push that button?"

"Pretty much."

"What about air?" Jake said.

"What's that?" Rick replied.

"What do you do for air if you're stuck in here?"

"Well, you wouldn't be hermetically sealed. Air gets in around the door. It's heavy, but it ain't covered in rubber gaskets."

"Gotcha." Jake lowered the camera and looked at Rick. "Can we try it?"

Rick looked panicky. "I'm sorry?"

Jeremy looked doubly panicky. "Dude!"

"Can we try it out? You know, just for fun. I've never been locked in a mausoleum before. Also, I'd hate for one of my people to get stuck in here accidentally and not know what to do."

"Uh, I guess," Rick said. He made short tracks for the exit. "I'll wait outside just in case there's a malfunction. Wouldn't make sense for me to be stuck in there."

"Yeah, since you're the only one who knows how to open it."

"Well, maybe . . . yeah."

He'd hesitated. Someone else knew the combination, Jake was sure. Probably Mrs. Rick or Rick's mother. Jake knew Rick had probably thought of this very scenario. Working at a cemetery probably gave him all sorts of ideas for creepy deaths.

Jeremy rocked back and forth on the balls of Chuck-Taylor-shod feet. "Yeah, I think I'll hang outside, too, dude."

"No, come on, man," Jake said. "I need you to run point on this mission."

Rick was almost out the door, and Jeremy looked ready to bolt. There was no handle on the inside, so just after Rick stepped out, Jake grabbed the edge of the door and swung it hard toward himself. He wanted to get an idea of the door's weight, and he also wanted to make sure he could lock himself in.

Success. The door was heavy, which made it tough to get going, but once it started swinging, it swung home with a clang.

"Seriously, man!" Jeremy's voice was more panicked-sounding than angry. "This is *so* not cool!"

"Oh, relax," Jake said. "What if you wind up having to come in here? You have to get acclimated."

"Not cool, man. Not cool."

Inside, it was black, save for a few slight crevasses of dim light showing through the minute space at the bottom of the door frame. Jake started to feel for the button.

"This is way darker than I thought it'd be. We're going to need a flashlight or something."

"Yeah," Jeremy said. In the darkness, his breathing had the pace and heaviness of a freshly run racehorse.

"'Bout time you said something, anyway. I was thinking you were going to let me do all the talking."

"You talk plenty for both of us. I prefer an air of silent mystique."

"Silent mystique," Jake said. "That has a good ring to it. If you ever start a band, that's what you should call it."

"I'll keep it in mind," Jeremy replied sardonically. "You found that button yet?"

"No." Jake continued to feel along the smooth, cool wall for the magic button. "I heard your little sarcastic eye roll, by the way."

"What?"

"You rolled your eyes just now. When you said, 'I'll keep it in mind.' I heard it."

Jeremy was quiet for a second. "Whatever, man."

"You're so busted," Jake said, retracing the wall, and, instead of feeling a button with his fingers, he began to empathize with Jeremy, as he felt a slight panic rising in his guts. "I wonder if homeboy out there can hear us in here."

"No telling."

"Hey! Rick!" Jake yelled at the top of his lungs. "I can't find your button!"

The echo of Jake's voice died away as he pressed his ear to the door to listen for a reply from Rick. Nothing.

"Hurry up, man!" Jeremy said. "I'm, like, barely clinging to life here."

Jake chuckled. "Older brother lock you in a closet when you were a kid?"

"Yeah. You, too?"

"Of course. Show me a younger brother who *doesn't* have that story, and I'll show you someone who needs some serious psycho-analysis to unlock the memory he's obviously repressed."

"Whatever. Just find the button, bro."

The door popped open as Jake's hand finally brushed the button. A sliver of light penetrated the gloom, ushered in by a wave of cool, fresh air that made them realize how quickly the modern tomb had gotten stale. They rushed the door as it swung open, and they both stepped out.

"Lazarus," said Jake, "come forth."

§

Jake and Jeremy bid Rick farewell and went to seek out Bo. They found him in his well-secluded shop wrestling with a gas-powered weed trimmer.

"Stupid thing keeps losing its spindle," he said. "Almost chipped a headstone the other day. What's up, Jake?" Jake nodded. "Hey, Jeremy. What're you doing here?"

"Chauffeuring Jake around."

"Chauffeuring or chaperoning?"

They all laughed, Jeremy and Bo with sincerity, Jake in mocking tones.

"Very funny, guys, very funny."

"Seriously, Jake," Bo said, "what can I do you for?"

"I need to look at some recent burials. Preferably as far away from the Cruz mausoleum as possible."

Bo drew back in bewilderment. "What for?"

"Just trying to get an idea of how to accommodate the media for tomorrow's funeral service. I want them to be far, far away from the action."

"Oh, they're bloodsuckers, aren't they?"

"They're the worst."

Bo nodded in agreement. "You aren't kidding." His face brightened. "Hey, speaking of—I saw your picture on the news when I went home for lunch!"

Jake's ears stood to attention as the hair on the back of his neck rose on end. "Oh, yeah?"

"Yeah. I live right down the street, so I always go home at lunch and watch the midday update. They had a picture of you and Miss Cruz standing in front of her dad's mausoleum."

"No kidding."

"Yep."

"Did they say anything?" Jake was playing it cool, but inside he was boiling over. Molten lava temperatures.

"Not much. Just mentioned the funeral being in a couple of days, and here's the daughter of the famous deceased spending time at the cemetery with a worker from the funeral home."

"Get out of town."

"Honest. But that was all they said about you. Then they started talking about a talent search in town for some new reality show."

"Yeah, *Hamster Cage.*"

"Crazy idea, isn't it?"

"Aren't they all?" Jake's mouth was on autopilot while his mind spun with this new information.

"Can we take a look at some of those burials?" Jeremy said irritably.

"Oh, sure," Bo replied. "This way."

He led them out of the shop and to a nearby golf cart. "Hop on."

Jake let Jeremy have the passenger seat while he took the backward-facing bench. They started driving, the rushing air drowning out whatever conversation Bo and Jeremy were having. Jake thought about his sudden appearance on that afternoon's news and deduced there would be more unauthorized footage of him and Louisa. He'd considered the possibility that this would happen and had altered his plan accordingly, but he didn't want to use that variation unless he was forced into it. Looks like he was. Louisa wasn't going to like it. Neither was he, for different reasons.

A couple of minutes later, they'd arrived at the site of Brownstone Avenue's most recent burials, a stretch of grass that extended all the way to the cemetery's wrought-iron fence, and Jake forced his mind back to the task at hand. These dear souls had been buried in the last few days, six-foot-long mounds of freshly tilled earth marking their passage into the ground. Their headstones hadn't been cut yet, so the only thing that marked their graves were small metal stakes with plastic sleeves attached at the tops. Inside the sleeves were cards, grave markers written with a blue ink pen.

One, two, three, four, five. Five of them. Perfect. That should work out well. Jake looked across the cemetery, shielding his eyes from the sunlight. He could just barely make out the white cube on the other side of the expanse. He swung around and investigated the nearby surroundings. This would be easy.

Dotting I's and Crossing T's

LOUISA HADN'T GOTTEN much done at the office that day. For starters, there wasn't much to be done. Most people knew she'd just lost her father days before, and so they were keeping their distance. Many of the volunteers were determined not to let any calls go through to her, so as not to burden her during this difficult time.

But besides that, she couldn't bring herself to focus on her work. She was too excited about this scheme, this adventure she was involved in. It was so unlike her, yet it seemed the perfect thing to apply some salve to her wounded soul. True, part of her subconscious was pleading with her to abandon the idea altogether and let God sort it out.

She told her subconscious to shove it.

She was about to leave for home when the phone rang. It had to be Jake, calling to report that afternoon's activity. She picked it up. "Hello?"

"Hello, *mija*."

The shock of hearing her older brother's voice drained her of all excitement. "What do you want, Sand Crab?"

"I just wanted to let you know I saw you and your friend on the news today."

"What?"

"You make a cute couple. Are you interested in him?"

"What are you talking about, Santiago?"

"He'll break your heart, sister. He isn't what he seems."

"Neither are you."

"I'm keeping my eye on you, Louisa. Let him know that. And then get away from him. He will amount to nothing."

The line clicked as Santiago hung up.

If she didn't know any better, she'd think that was a threat.

S

Chiffon took a deep breath before she picked up the phone. All she had to do was dial the number and say what Jake had told her to say. He'd said to think of it as another audition. She punched a few buttons and listened to the rings. When the receptionist answered, "NewsChannel 2," Chiffon did her best to imitate her favorite female anchor, the one who always wore tasteful shades of lipstick and flashy gold brooches.

"Yes, hi, this is Chiffon Brown with White Hall Funeral Home. I need to speak with someone about coordinating the media during the Benjamin Cruz funeral."

"Please hold. I'll connect you."

That went well enough. Chiffon's focus on the task was nearly blurred as she listened to a prerecorded message that told her how NewsChannel 2 was the only news channel in town that really cared about her safety and how their special "Consumer

Crackdown" features were one of many ways they fought for her interests. She was just hearing about how their weather guy gave the city's most accurate forecasts when a voice interrupted the recording.

"This is Staci, can I help you?"

"Hi, Staci, I'm Chiffon Brown with White Hall Funeral Home, and I'm calling about the Benjamin Cruz funeral, trying to coordinate the on-site media. I have some information to give you."

"All right. Go ahead."

Chiffon gave her the information, then got off the phone as quickly as she could, breathing a sigh of relief. That had gone well. She'd sounded professional enough. She could do this again.

Six phone calls later, Chiffon had contacted three other news stations, the two main news radio stations, and the city paper. She'd also heard competing prerecorded messages that all boasted of the most accurate weather, the latest breaking news, the greatest consumer alerts. She wasn't sure who to trust to be her news authority anymore.

She hoped Jake appreciated the job she'd done. She picked up the phone one last time to reach him on Jeremy's cell phone.

S

"That your hearse?" The hardware store clerk was pointing an inquisitive finger toward the parking lot.

"Yeah, man," Jeremy replied, a tinge of pride in his voice.

"Sweet."

"It ain't bad."

The clerk began bagging Jeremy's purchases. A couple of pocket flashlights, some batteries. Ten-pound fishing line. The tiny store was packed to the rafters with all sorts of fun items—well, if it actually had rafters. Instead, it had corrugated aluminum and exposed ductwork. "You want this backpack in its own bag?"

"Um, I don't know. Seems kind of stupid to carry a bag in a bag."

"Yeah." The clerk set the backpack aside and picked up a pair of gardener's gloves to put in the bag. "You ever carry any dead people in there?"

Jeremy gave a wry nod. "All the time, bro."

The clerk stopped bagging for a second, staring at Jeremy with a mixture of amazement and fear.

Jake's approach broke the silence. He set a tall, thin glass jar full of fireplace matches on the counter. "These, too."

Jeremy gave him a sideways glance. "What are those for?"

"Well, you swipe 'em on something really quickly, and they turn into fire. Then you can take that fire and put it on something bigger and turn that into fire."

"Funny."

"And then you use that fire to make yourself warmer or, you know, cook things and stuff."

"You can stop."

"Drop and roll?"

The clerk interrupted Jake's riff. "That'll be $32.73."

Jake paid with some rumpled bills he found in the murky depths of his jacket. Jeremy grabbed the sack with their purchases while Jake picked up the backpack.

"You didn't get a bag for this?"

Jeremy's cell phone rang before he could respond. He fished it out of his back pocket and looked at the display.

"It's Chiffon."

"Answer it then."

Jeremy flipped it open and put it to his ear. "Hey. What's up?"

Chiffon's high voice nearly pierced Jeremy's eardrum. "I'm all done with my phone calls? So tell Jake I said, 'Mission accomplished!'"

"Okay, hold on." Jeremy lowered the phone and said to Jake, "Chiffon says she's done calling."

"Great," Jake said.

"That is not what I said, *Jeremy*," Chiffon said. "What I said? was to tell Jake 'mission accomplished'?"

"What?"

"I would like for you? to tell Jake? 'Mission accomplished'?"

"Come on, Chiffon."

Jeremy was sure he heard a tsk. "Jeremy?" Chiffon said. "Why are you not saying 'mission accomplished'?"

"Because it's stupid," Jeremy said.

Jake leaned his head toward Jeremy's. "What's the matter?"

Jeremy lowered the phone again to talk to Jake. "She's mad because I told you 'she's done calling' instead of 'mission accomplished.'" Back to the phone. "I know that's what you said to tell him, but don't you think it's a bit much?"

"No?"

"Whatever, Chiffon."

Chiffon let out an exasperated sigh. "You? are *so* not fun!"

"Okay."

"Ugh," Chiffon said. Jeremy was glad to hear that her voice had more standard punctuation. "Oh, by the way, Boring Man? Tell Jake that Louisa called, like a few minutes ago? And, like, she sounded kinda freaked? And so she's coming over here."

"All right," Jeremy said. "Can I use my own words, or do I? have to say? exactly what you said?"

"You are *so* rude right now," Chiffon said, though Jeremy could tell she didn't mean it. "Like, at least I? can talk without saying 'dude' all the time? Right, *dude*?"

"Okay, that's enough," Jeremy said. "Bye."

He hung up his cell phone, but not before he heard her say, "Bye, *dude*?"

Jake looked at Jeremy expectantly. "Did you get it all straightened out?"

"Sure did, dude. Chiffon's laid out all the bait."

"Great."

"Oh, she said Louisa called a minute ago, too. Said she was on her way over, and that she sounded pretty freaked out on the phone."

"Well, then," Jake said, "let's get to work. Phone?"

Jeremy handed him the cell, and a couple of rings later, Jake was headed to the hearse, on the phone with Cindy Pennington from Channel 9 News.

❦

"So let me get this straight, Mr. Abrams," Cindy Pennington said.

"You can call me Jake."

"Jake," she said. "Mr. Cruz's will did indeed stipulate that he be buried with his fortune, and White Hall has been put in charge of carrying it out under a strict veil of secrecy."

"Yes."

"Why are you telling me this?"

"Because you've already figured it out. And I don't want you to say anything about it on the air."

Jake listened intently to the phone as she paused.

"Are you just hoping I'll be nice?" she said.

Jake chuckled. "No. Well, yes. But I'm also a realist, so I understand you expect something in return."

She was silent some more. "Such as?"

"An exclusive interview with Louisa Cruz. No holds barred."

"Except about the estate?"

"You got it."

Boy, this woman sure was quiet on the phone.

"And we can still cover the whole funeral?"

"Sure," Jake said. "Except the cemetery. We're not allowing cameras in there." He bit his lip, hoping she'd go for it.

"No dice," she said. "I have to have the cemetery. The story's no good without that footage."

Jake's heart sank. "I can't agree to that."

"Then I'll have to go forward with my rumor."

"I'll deny it to the day I die."

"I don't care."

He was pinned down and he knew it.

"Okay," he said. "Deal."

The Plan Takes
a Detour Downtown

SANTIAGO'S PHONE CALL had rattled Louisa's already frazzled nerves, and, as she drove to White Hall, she began to consider panicking. She felt she was starting to lose it, that instead of heading to the funeral home, she should just drive herself to the nearest insane asylum.

Did they put up road signs for those like they do for hospitals and airports? Then she started wondering what sort of icon a helpful directional road sign for an insane asylum would have (a cuckoo clock, perhaps? a cracked bell?), but then she remembered that if you think you're nuts, you probably aren't. Too bad. She was just going to have to face whatever Santiago wanted to dish out, without being able to plead insanity.

But having Jake made it bearable somehow. She knew she was probably just developing an attachment to him out of the tension of the situation, but at the same time, she was afraid that she was developing deeper feelings, a notion that she promptly ground her heel into. No. There was nothing deeper. She just liked his relaxed attitude and the way he made her laugh. Nothing more.

Right?

Her arrival at White Hall pushed her nagging thoughts away. She walked in and back to Jake's workstation, only to find Jake and a man she'd never seen before sitting down, apparently in a competition to determine who could crane his neck the farthest over and turn his head the most upside down. She couldn't tell who was winning.

"Hey," she said.

Jake refocused his eyes in her direction and immediately snapped his head back up to a normal position. Almost instantly after doing this, he grabbed the back of his neck, grimacing, and seemed to totter momentarily like one of those weighted, inflatable punching dummies. He offered a dazed "Hey" back in Louisa's direction.

The other man stayed put, intensely focused on a television set Louisa hadn't noticed when she entered the room. If he'd won the gold medal in Neck-Craning, he hadn't said anything about it. She wondered how he saw anything through that mess of unwashed hair that strewed down into his upside-down face.

Jake got up and welcomed Louisa back to his work area. "This is Jeremy," he said, introducing her to the other man. "He works here, and he's going to be helping us."

Jeremy unbent his head more carefully than Jake had and gave a cheerful wave. "'Sup?"

"Hi. Nice to meet you."

"Same."

Louisa looked at the image on the TV and couldn't make it

out. Whatever it was, it was upside down. Her head involuntarily began to turn upside down as well to comprehend what was on the screen. She hadn't noticed it when she came in, but Jake also held a remote control in his hand, and he kept pointing it at a VCR sitting on his workstation.

After a few seconds of study, she put together that he and Jeremy were watching an upside-down home video, and that Jake was using the remote to play a portion of it, then rewind it, then play it, then rewind it.

Chiffon entered, her oddball fashion sense making her look like she'd been standing next to a rainbow when it exploded. Jake made the introduction formal. "Hey, Chiffon. You remember Louisa?"

"Yes, of course? Like, I've only met her, like, three times now?" Chiffon rolled her eyes at Louisa. "How are you, Ms. Cruz?"

"I'm doing okay, thanks. Thank you for pitching in here."

"Oh, don't even worry abou—What are you guys doing?"

Jake and Jeremy had gone back upside down. "We're trying to look at this tape I shot upside down," Jake said.

Chiffon walked around to see the TV. She studied it for a second, then strode up, grasped it, turned it upside down, and set it back on the workstation, resting it on its top. "That better?"

The men slowly assumed normal posture, and everyone finally got a good look at the video. They grumbled thanks at her.

Jake reached for a black plastic tray that contained some slices of luncheon meat and processed cheese singles. He grabbed one of each and rolled them together as the crew examined the TV, clearly watching a hand pushing buttons on a keypad. It was slightly off center and soft on focus. "I gotta say," Jake said, taking a bite from his meat/cheese roll, "that is some pretty good aim, what with it being at waist level while not even looking."

"What are you eating?" Louisa said.

"Leftovers," Jake said, mouth full of low-grade ham and American cheese. "From a viewing we had earlier." He picked up the tray and held it toward her. "Want some?"

She wrinkled her nose at him. "Where's the bread?"

"It's all gone."

"I'll pass."

"Not me," Jeremy said, doing his best to keep an eye on the TV while assembling a meat/cheese roll for himself. "Dude, it's a good thing Rick didn't notice that you left the camera rolling when he made us turn around."

"I wish we were in a TV show right now," Jake said. "One of those prime-time dramas where they're always using video surveillance to solve crimes. Then I could just tell some technician to 'Enhance this right here,' and he'd punch a few buttons and then we'd get a perfect image."

"I can make it out," Jeremy offered. "Play it one more time."

Jake played it again, and they all squinted to follow Rick's hand as he punched in the mausoleum's combination.

"Yep. That's what I thought," Jeremy piped up, downright excited. Well, as excited as he got. "2-4-2-7-3-1."

"That's what I was thinking." Louisa had seen the same sequence, as well as she could. It was more like following Rick's fingers and seeing where they landed in respect to the other buttons. But she was sure she'd seen the combination the same as Jeremy.

"Okay, that problem's solved."

"We have another one, though," Louisa said. She relayed the contents of her phone call with Santiago and his strange attitude toward her and Jake.

"That's crazy," Chiffon said. "I mean, sorry Louisa, but even if he is your brother? that's, like, totally weird?"

"Yes, it is," Louisa said. "It's not a very brotherly way to act, is it?"

"No way."

"It's very strange." Even Jeremy was a little rattled.

Jake didn't say anything the whole time Louisa was talking. Instead, he sat still, his hands together, covering his mouth and nose. Finally, he spoke. "I got it."

They all turned to look at him.

"What do you mean?"

"I mean I know how to throw off Santiago and Cindy Pennington at the same time."

Jeremy clicked the TV off. "So what'd you have in mind for this occasion, Jake the All-Seeing Eye of Media?"

Jake closed his eyes, as if entering a trance. His eyebrows furrowed. He inhaled slowly and confidently, then nodded his head slightly. It was apparent that he'd entered some internal realm of Deep Thought.

"We just have to go over her head," he said. "The main news producer for Channel 9 — her boss — is a big fan of karaoke. He hangs out at this lounge downtown all the time."

"How exactly," Louisa interrupted, "do you know that?"

Jake snapped out of Deep Thought Realm and back into The Land of VCR Code-Breaking. "Oh. I go to their Christmas party every year. Great buffet. Anyway, I met him a couple years ago and it came up in the conversation. He's single, too."

They looked at him, baffled. He drew out the suspense for just a moment, then: "Jeremy, Chiffon, what are you doing tonight?"

§

Jake had gone to Sing Sing Lounge once, and he found the place to be aptly named. It looked and sounded and smelled like a karaoke lounge, but Jake saw only a prison. He couldn't understand why people would want to frequent an establishment that didn't just host a bunch of bad singing, but loudly proclaimed it as a feature attraction. It wasn't entertainment—it was punishment, and every second in there felt like doing time.

Off-key warbling? They had it covered. Worse dancing? They had a corner on the market. A performer onstage who's either really uncomfortable or really hammered (or both)? Sing Sing—that's your place.

Top it off with the downtown location flanked by a Denny's and a very old beauty shop that gave off the stench of syrup and perming solution, respectively, and there were about ten thousand other places he'd rather be this unseasonably chilly night. He was ill just standing on the sidewalk outside.

Jeremy wasn't in his element, either. He'd said he preferred music venues that were the size of one-bedroom apartments and that featured scraggly performers making artful noise with guitars, feedback, and whiny voices. But they'd all agreed that Jake's face was now too well-known to assume he wouldn't be recognized by the producer of the very TV station that the story was running on, so it was up to Jeremy to bite the bullet and join in on this part of the plan. He'd even gone so far as to put on a suit jacket over his band T-shirt.

Naturally, it was a perfect place for Chiffon.

After reaching into the nether regions of his brain, Jake had found the words "Sing Sing Lounge," "Chris Walters," and "Channel 9 News producer" all associated with each other. Armed with this knowledge, he, Jeremy, and Chiffon had made the journey downtown in the hopes of finding Mr. Walters in fine form.

"How're you feeling, Chiffon? Ready to knock 'em dead?"

Chiffon's eyes were wide with . . . fear? Excitement? Nervousness? Dread? Jake couldn't really tell. However she felt, she wasn't telling him. She wasn't even paying attention to him. Her eyes were locked on the door to the lounge.

"Chiffon?"

Chiffon looked over at him, irritated. "*What?*"

Jake put up his whoa hands. "I asked you if you were ready to go in."

"Oh, sorry," she said, fingering the hem of her shimmery gold tank top. "I don't know, Jake. I'm kind of nervous."

"You don't have anything to be nervous about. You're going to do great. Just go in and pretend you're in an audition. Hey, you kind of are—this news producer could probably help you get on TV if you play your cards right."

The ethereal quality of the streetlights made it so Jake couldn't tell for sure, but he thought she went pale.

"O-okay."

"Come on, this is what you've always wanted," Jake said. "TV!"

"I'm not so sure."

"Chiffon, for real," Jeremy said, "you're going to do great. Let's go."

Chiffon relented and the three of them walked through the door to find a mishmash of sounds, smells, and decorating ideas from different eras. The pastel floral prints on the furniture were like an official badge for the 1980s, while the carpet and wainscoting boasted proud allegiance to the previous decade. It smelled of stale cigarette smoke and cheap, overpriced beer, but it was surprisingly busy, with people dressed in all manner of regalia from all manner of recent fashion eras.

Once his eyes adjusted to the dim lighting, Jake began looking around for a man who matched his memory of Chris Walters, while Chiffon went to the bar to sign up for a performance. As luck would have it, the man onstage struggling through Kenny Rogers' "Lady" at this very moment looked like their mark. Jake had been in the lounge no more than two minutes before he spotted his target. These things always worked out for him like that.

Jake pointed him out to Jeremy. "There's your guy."

"Man, Kenny Rogers sure looks different without the beard."

"Sounds different, too," Jake said. "All right, you know what to do. I'm going to head outside."

He felt a tug on his arm and turned to see Chiffon looking at him. "Hey," he said. "You sign up?"

She nodded weakly.

"You going to be sick?"

Her eyes got panicky. "I hope not?"

"Chiffon, seriously, you're going to do fine."

Her breathing sped up. "But what if I'm terrible?"

"You won't be terrible," Jake said. "People who have big dreams are never terrible at what they dream about. Maybe they have to work for it, but they're usually pretty good at what they love to do."

Chiffon's breathing slowed to normal, and her shoulders moved into a more relaxed position. Good thing, too, because Chris Walters was just putting the finishing touches on his very amateurish song. The man had given it a shot, but it's hard to sound like your voice is soaked in whiskey when you're holding a club soda with two limes.

Jeremy pointed toward him. "Jake said he's the guy."

"Where?"

"Wrapping it up onstage."

"Really? He's cute?"

"As these things go, I suppose," Jake said. He gave her a final thumbs-up and clapped Jeremy on the back. "You got it." Then he slinked outside to enjoy the night air.

§

Walters finally got to "You're my ladyyyyy-yy," gave a few extemporaneous "oohs" and "mmms," then handed the microphone to the emcee and exited to lukewarm applause. Jeremy and Chiffon made a point to clap loudest.

Walters headed straight for the bar. "Okay, I guess this is me," Jeremy said. "You'll be great." Jeremy squeezed Chiffon's elbow in encouragement as he walked away from her and toward Walters.

"Do good," she offered back.

Jeremy made his way through the maze of tables and patrons and finally reached the bar. He glanced at the bartender. "I'll have a Dr. Pepper with a shot of vanilla, please." The bartender went to work on Jeremy's drink while Walters relaxed against the bar.

Jeremy drew a breath, psyching himself up, then looked straight at Walters. "That, my friend, is one *strong* rendition of 'Lady' you just pulled off there."

"What's that?" Walters replied.

In the back of his mind, Jeremy wondered if Walters was asking because he legitimately hadn't heard the compliment—it was noisy in there, especially with a new singer striking up "Gypsys, Tramps & Thieves"—or if he was so vain he wanted to hear it again. Either way, Jeremy answered his request.

"I said you did a great job with 'Lady.' That song is *not* easy to pull off. All you needed was a white beard and you'd be Kenny."

Walters smiled sheepishly. "Thanks. It's one of my favorite songs, so I try to do it justice."

"I felt like I was listening to the record."

"Wow. Thanks," Walters said, nodding his head like he was diggin' it. "Thanks a lot."

The bartender handed Jeremy his drink, from which he took a sip.

Walters continued. "What are you going to do tonight?"

Time to play the Walters game. "What's that?"

"What song are you going to sing?"

Jeremy smiled and waved off the question. "Oh, you don't want to hear me. I'm not here to sing. I'm here with a client of mine."

"Oh, I see. Business?"

"Yeah, sort of. I'm her agent. She's just about to go on a little tour, and I wanted her to come out here to warm up her performance voice before we hit the road."

Walters lit up like a Christmas tree. "You're a talent agent?"

Jeremy nodded and took another sip of his DP. "Yep."

§

Jake was wishing he'd brought a jacket. The nighttime air clung to his T-shirted frame, fingering its way into his pores, despite his frail attempts at achieving warmth. He crammed his hands into his pockets, doing what he could to still look cool and fight off the slight nip to the air, but it didn't work.

It wasn't cold, necessarily, but it was chilly enough to make Jake contemplate heading into the Denny's and risking saturating his clothes with that greasy smell he knew would be murder to get rid of.

His mind was made up for him by a booming voice, coming from the street, waist-level. "Jake! How are ya, buddy?"

Jake looked around for the unmistakable person of one Del Ciccolella to match the unmistakable voice he'd just heard. He found them both in a Honda Civic in the far lane of traffic. Jake waved to his boss, hoping that would take care of the encounter.

His hopes were dashed when he saw Del whip the car into a parking space and hop out joyfully.

Del picked his way through the traffic, smiling and waving at Jake. "Hey, man. What're you doing out here?"

Jake wondered if the man had already tied on a few. He was pretty jovial. "Oh, I'm just, uh, waiting around."

Del officially arrived on the sidewalk, and Jake could tell from his breath that his joviality was one hundred percent natural. "Waiting around for what?" Del said.

"You know," Jake said. "People."

"Oh, right," Del said, winking. "People." Getting serious, he took hold of Jake's arm and focused his eyes directly on Jake's. "This isn't about drugs, is it? You waiting for a deal?"

Jake matter-of-factly cocked his head to the side. "Please."

Del busted up laughing and smacked Jake on the shoulder. "Aw, I was just playing with ya."

"You sly dog."

"You know me. Sly as they come," Del said. "I was just coming out here to have a Grand Slam." He gestured to the Denny's. "Thought I was going to have to do it all by my lonesome, and then here you are on the corner doing nothing. How 'bout that?"

"Yeah, how 'bout it," Jake said warily.

"So, you up for some breakfast?"

"It's nighttime." Please don't make me go in there.

"Best time for it. Come on. My treat."

"I don't know, Del. I'm kinda busy."

"Standing on the corner? Looking like you're half-froze to death? Nope. You're coming with me. We're gonna round those bases and hit us a couple o' Grand Slams."

Jake started to protest again.

"Jake, I'm not going to take no for an answer," Del said. "Now, I just have to step inside here to say 'hi' to a friend, and we'll be on our way." He started toward the lounge.

"Whoa," Jake said, surreptitiously stepping in front of him. "What do you need to do?"

"Oh, I have a friend who tends the bar there at Sing Sing. I always pop in and chew the fat with him for a few minutes when I come out here."

"You know what?" Jake said. "I am *really* hungry. Think you could talk to him after we eat?"

$\mathscr{S}$

"So what's that like, being a talent agent?" Walters was lapping up every word Jeremy was dishing out.

"Oh, it's great," Jeremy said. "You never know where you're going to find greatness. Take my latest client, for example. I found her working as the receptionist in a funeral home, if you can believe it."

Onstage, Chiffon was stepping up behind the emcee. Behind

his fake managerial exterior, Jeremy was sending comfortable thoughts to Chiffon, but he could tell by the way she was smoothing out her skirt that they weren't getting to her. "Well, there she is now." Jeremy pointed her out.

Walters' gaze followed Jeremy's finger to the stage, while Jeremy's eyes followed Walters'. Jeremy studied those eyes and recognized the look of a romantically interested man. Jeremy lowered his finger and scoped out Chiffon, who took the microphone from the emcee just as the track began the intro to "My Heroes Have Always Been Cowboys." Chiffon clumsily tapped her heel as she listened to the intro, and her hands were shaking so badly that the microphone looked like it was giving the results of a lie detector test. Jeremy's insides were turning somersaults as he hoped against hope that Chiffon would perform at least up to the standards of a karaoke lounge frequenter.

Suddenly, as soon as she opened her mouth to sing, the nervousness fell off her, and she soared into telling the assembled throng how she grew up a-dreamin' of bein' a cowboy. It was magical. It was beautiful.

It was Chiffon. Singing.

It was like the slow-movin' dream she was singing about. Time became a crawl as the audience turned one by one to watch this greenhorn perform like a pro. She could've reached out her hand and grasped the entire crowd. And they would've loved every second. Heck, Jeremy would've loved every second.

And just like that, it was over. Jeremy breathed a deep sigh of relief as the audience applauded wildly for the performance they'd just witnessed. He gave Chiffon a wave, and she headed toward him.

Jeremy could've sworn he saw Walters wipe drool from his

chin. "Want to meet her?"

"Very much!"

Chiffon ambled over, giggly over her drop-dead performance. She reached Jeremy nearly bubbling over with glee. "They clapped! They clapped!"

"Of course they did. You're a natural. You did great."

"Thanks, Jeremy."

"Don't mention it." He gestured toward Walters. "Chiffon, this man would like to make your acquaintance. Chiffon Brown, meet . . . what's your name, buddy?"

"Chris Walters." Walters stuck out his hand like a third grader meeting his favorite ballplayer. "You were awesome."

Chiffon accepted his offered hand gently. "Thank you. Thank you so much. You were great, too?"

"I was just telling him that," Jeremy interjected. "See, Chris? I wasn't full of it. I meant it. I know how to spot talent; that's my job."

"You really think so?"

"Oh, yeah. Talent's everywhere. Take Chiffon here."

Chiffon preened for him. Jeremy wasn't sure how much of it was an act.

"Yeah," Walters said. "You say she works for a funeral home?"

Chiffon and Jeremy both nodded. Jeremy continued the story. "Yep. Right here in town."

"Really? Which one?"

"White Hall Funeral Home?" Chiffon said "You know where that is?"

Walters's face lit up. "Yeah. Hey, I'm actually going to be out there in a couple of days."

"No way. Why's that?"

"Oh, I work for Channel 9 News. I'm one of their producers, and one of our new reporters is covering the Benjamin Cruz funeral."

Chiffon spoke up. "Ooh. Yeah, that's a big deal?" She was hanging on Jeremy's arm, comfortably assuming the look of a diva.

"Yeah, we've been leading the area coverage of it. Cindy Pennington—she's going to be big in this town—she's the one heading up the story. But she's kinda new, so I've been, you know, keeping an eye on her."

Chiffon literally batted her eyes at him. "Sounds like you really know what's going on?"

He tried to downplay the compliment, but he fooled no one. "I guess you could say that."

"So, you're going to be coming up to White Hall for the day?" said Chiffon. "That is so cool!"

"Well, not all day," Walters said. "Just for the service, and then it's off to the cemetery to tape the burial."

Chiffon made the saddest face Jeremy had ever seen on her. "Oh, that's so sad. I mean, like, I think that stuff is so interesting? But I'd hate for you guys to interrupt the actual burial, though? You have to draw the line somewhere."

"R-really?"

"Yeah. I mean, that's, like, such a private moment? I think it should just be between family, you know? I mean, that's what *I'd* want, anyway?"

"Definitely."

"Besides," Chiffon said, "you seem really cool to hang out with?"

Jeremy sensed the seed had been planted. Now it needed time to germinate. "Chiffon, enough of this death stuff! Like you don't hear enough about it all day. Not for long, though, dollface." Dollface? That slipped out accidentally.

Jeremy turned his attention to Walters. "Chris, how 'bout you? You want to sing in karaoke lounges for the rest of your life?" The bartender handed Jeremy another DP, which he held up. "By the way," he said to Walters, giving the glass a little shake, "you got this?"

⅌

Jake sniffed his shirttail as he walked across an undeveloped tract of land next to the cemetery. He hated that greasy syrup smell that always attached itself to him every time he ate at any of the all-night pancake places. Oh well. He hadn't washed his jeans in probably three weeks. They could stand to be run through the laundry.

After leaving Del, sufficiently gorged on breakfast food, Jake had stopped by his apartment to pick up a jacket and a flashlight, both of which he was using now. He shone the light on his watch. Just after midnight.

A few minutes of walking brought him close to the cemetery's fence, which he walked along in the direction of the mausoleum. His thoughts distracted him as he made his way through the flashlight-illuminated darkness, carefully stepping through the tall grass.

Louisa was cool, but Jake had to face the facts: There was nothing there and no hope of anything there. And it had nothing to do with her—well, maybe it had something to do with all the

Jesus stuff. But mainly this was about Jake. He was who he was, and nothing could change that.

How much was Benjamin Cruz worth, anyway? A few million? Whatever it was, it was a lot. A person didn't get an opportunity like this every day. This was no unattended box of fortune cookies at a Chinese restaurant — this was a once-in-a-lifetime shot at eternal happiness.

Jake's flashlight beam fell on a few trees in the near distance just as he heard the high-pitched motor of a golf cart approaching from behind. He quickly clicked off his flashlight and ran toward the trees for cover, hoping he didn't bash into them in the darkness.

He crouched behind one of the tree trunks to watch the golf cart go by. Two security guards sat in it, one of them chattering rapidly, though he was too far away for Jake to hear what he was saying. This was quickly resolved, though, and as the cart drove by, Jake heard the guard say, ". . . Look, I just don't know why the lightsabers are all different colors, you know? It's like me having a purple gun and you having a green one. It just doesn't . . ."

Jake looked at his watch. 12:15. He slid down and sat on the ground, resting his back against the tree, listening to the golf cart's engine fade into the distance. His thoughts turned once more to the greatest freeloading opportunity that had ever presented itself to him.

He couldn't let this chance pass him by. Thinking logically, he basically had to make a choice between the money and Louisa. She was intent on getting the money for her NPO, which was a fine and noble thing to do. But her NPO was doing okay without it, and since it was a good cause, she could probably raise money for it anytime she wanted.

Jake, on the other hand, was not a good cause. This was his chance, and he had to take it. There would be other women, maybe not like Louisa, but there would be others.

But there would never be another chance for this kind of money.

Eighteen

Jake and Louisa Split Up
(Don't Worry: It's for a Good Reason)

THE NEXT DAY Louisa woke up to the ringing of her cell phone. Sleepily, she fumbled for it and managed to punch the "answer" button. "Hello?"

"Hey, Louisa, it's Jake. Did I wake you?"

"No, I had to answer the phone anyway," she said in a lazy voice.

"Please, it's too early in the morning for jokes scrawled next to the cave paintings from the Mesozoic Era."

"Huh?"

"Never mind."

"Mm-kay," Louisa mumbled. "So, what's going on?"

"Just thought I'd give you an update on last night's outing."

"Okay, shoot." Louisa rolled back onto her pillow and hoped she wouldn't go back to sleep in the middle of Jake's recap.

"Well, first things first: Del knows how to put away a late-night breakfast."

"Um, I'm not following you," she said.

"I got stuck pounding down a Grand Slam with him, and he went into extra innings."

"I think that's all I need to know about that."

"Wise decision," Jake said. "Secondly, Jeremy tells me that Chiffon actually sings pretty good. She turned a lot of heads at the lounge."

"Get out of town."

"You'll have to drive me," he said. "Anyway, Walters bit — hook, line, and sinker. After she'd finished her song, he'd have put prairie dogs in the lead story every day."

"She's that good, huh?"

"Guess so. He pretty much agreed to keep the cameras away from the graveside. Hope Cindy Pennington doesn't mind. I wish I could be there when he tells her."

"Great," she said.

"Thirdly, I went to the cemetery last night and found our entry point. I also timed the guard rounds. They drive by the mausoleum every fifteen minutes."

"That's good to know."

"It'll come in handy."

Louisa felt like she should say more, so much more, but didn't know how to get there. "I wish I could see you today."

The other end of the phone was silent.

"Me, too," Jake said finally. "But we have to keep all these cameras off us. We can't get spotted together; you know that."

"Yeah, I know. I still wish, though."

He paused again. "Tomorrow."

"Yeah, tomorrow."

"Call me if you need anything. I'll have Jeremy's cell."

"Okay."

"Okay."

She hovered on her end of the phone, waiting for him to say something else. Maybe he was doing the same thing, and that's why he wasn't talking? Hopefully?

"Uh, bye," Jake said.

"See ya."

$\mathcal{S}$

When Jake arrived at White Hall that morning, he immediately walked to his workstation and saw that his workload for the day was light, thankfully. He'd been sloughing off a little lately—scheming does that to you. Turns you into a slougher. Fortunately, Del was taking it easy on him in return for handling the newspeople.

Jake went into the Prep Room and found Jeremy already there, putting the finishing touches on Benjamin Cruz's fully dressed body, which was laid out on a rolling stainless steel table. At the moment, Jeremy was repeatedly stuffing and unstuffing a gray satin handkerchief into the breast pocket of Mr. Cruz's suit.

"I can't get this thing to look right," he said, pulling it out again. He folded it carefully and started stuffing it into the pocket one more time.

Jake took one look at the man and wished he'd been able to have a better conversation with him at that party. Mr. Cruz had been gruff then, but Jake had no idea that Mean Mr. McSurly was so selfish as to gyp his own children out of their inheritance. Looking at him again, face-to-face, Jake had no problem wanting his fortune. Served the man right.

"You did a good job, Jeremy. Made him look nice."

Jake turned his attention to Benjamin Cruz's casket, which was along the wall of the Prep Room, resting on a collapsible four-wheel dolly. He opened the lid and examined the inside for any new secrets it might contain, but found nothing. Just a plain old casket with a safe in it.

The safe was so small that he began to wonder how much money could fit in there. He didn't know much about treasury bonds, but Kimbrough had said they were high dollar, which he assumed meant each one was worth quite a bit. It wouldn't take too many to amount to a fortune, so the small size of the safe seemed appropriate. Worked fine for Jake: The smaller the treasure, the easier it would be to haul.

"How big do you think a treasury bond runs, Jeremy?"

Jeremy's muffled voice came from the other room. "I don't know. Like, car registration-sized, maybe?"

"Yeah, that's what I was thinking." He hoped he was right.

S

Louisa intentionally skipped work that day—she figured the volunteers would understand—and instead made an arranged visit to Brownstone Avenue Cemetery. She spent a quiet half hour walking the grounds, taking care to stay far away from the mausoleum. She could almost feel the cameras pointed at her, so when she checked her watch for the fiftieth time that day, she was glad to see it was time for her appointment.

She headed toward the cemetery gates, and there they were, right on time—a cameraman whose camera had a large sticker on the side with the Channel 9 News logo on it, a boom microphone operator, some random person holding a stack of papers and a highlighter, and a sharp, pant-suited young lady who had apparently never learned the basics of applying makeup.

"Miss Cruz?" the pant-suited lady addressed her. "Cindy Pennington, Channel 9 News." She seemed nice enough, especially considering that she wasn't going to have the cameras in the cemetery that she thought she would. Louisa surmised that Cindy Pennington hadn't spoken to her boss yet today.

"Oh, hi," Louisa said. Time to play the part of the grief-stricken, bewildered daughter. Shouldn't be too hard.

"First of all, from everyone at the station, we extend our condolences to you and your family."

"Thank you."

"Second, thanks for working this interview into what I'm sure is a very hectic schedule. We really appreciate it."

"Oh, no problem."

Pennington pointed to a bench off to the side, under a shady tree. "Would you like to go sit down while we talk?"

Louisa shrugged. "That'd be great."

The two of them made their way toward the bench, shadowed closely by the rest of the crew.

They situated themselves on the bench, the crew got into position, and Cindy Pennington began the exclusive interview she'd fought so hard for.

"How are you holding up in the face of this tragedy?"

"Well, fine, I guess," Louisa began. She heard a tiny whirring noise that made her look at the cameraman, who was turning a big dial along the lens. She could see the aperture inside the camera narrowing. The close-up shot she knew he was taking right this second made her go tongue-tied. "You know, we're just, uh, just, trying to . . . keep on."

"I understand. How will your father's passing affect the operations of The Cruz Agency?"

"Oh, Thomas Chenoweth and everyone out there is doing a great job. Papa made sure they'd be able to handle anything that came up. That was just the type of man he was." In her own ears, her words sounded like meaningless blather, a steady, flatline tone.

"Miss Cruz, The Agency had been in a negative trend for awhile, but just recently saw some positive growth. How do you think your father's death will affect the overall business?"

Louisa began to loathe Cindy Pennington. She wasn't qualified to answer these questions. How come no one ever asked about Maria House? "I think business will be just fine. Like I said, Tom knows what he's doing."

"How are you feeling about tomorrow? That's going to be tough, being the only family member in attendance."

Oh, you are a crafty one, Cindy Pennington, throwing out the casual crack at her family's dysfunction. Louisa cynically figured this question was an attempt to get her to cry on camera, which Channel 9 would then turn into a promo that would run every fifteen minutes during prime time tonight and then lead the late news. She resolutely made her eyes as dry as Cindy Pennington's withered soul.

"I agree, it is going to be tough," Louisa said. "But I firmly believe my father is sitting with Jesus right now and is having a much better time than the rest of us. That's what I've been focusing on the past few days, and it's what I'll continue to focus on tomorrow when we bury him."

"We just saw you walking around the cemetery. What were you doing, if you don't mind me asking?"

"Taking a look at where I'll be spending some time tomorrow, and the next few days, weeks, and months."

"Thank you for your time, Miss Cruz."

"You're welcome."

The camera went down off the cameraman's shoulder, the boom microphone operator lowered the long, microphone-tipped pole he carried, and Pennington and the assistant immediately started consulting each other over the assistant's stack of paper. They walked to their news van, hopped in, and drove away.

Louisa drove home to watch herself on the news.

She got a call instead. Sometimes Louisa just got tired of her cell phone. The thing just would not leave her alone. She glanced at the screen and saw that the number was from Maria House. Better answer it.

"Hello?" she said.

"Hi, Louisa." Helen. "There's someone here to see you. She says it's important."

"Who is it?"

"A girl. She said she spoke to you a couple of days ago?"

"What's her name?" Louisa asked.

Helen's voice went distant as she apparently took the phone away from her mouth to address the girl. "What's your name, hon?" Louisa could hear the girl's voice, but couldn't make out the reply; Helen remedied the situation seconds later when her normal, present voice came back. "Elizabeth, she says."

The girl spoke again, and Helen paused to listen. "She says you'd know her as Sugar."

"I'll be right there."

A few minutes later, Louisa walked calmly yet purposefully through the doors at Maria House. There was Sugar, on the waiting area couch, her nose flushed and red, a tear escaping from her eye. Helen was seated next to her, one arm around her shoulders.

Sugar — Louisa figured she should think of her as "Elizabeth" now — looked up at her. "Hi, sweetie," Louisa said.

Elizabeth managed a wave. Helen managed more. "Hi, Louisa," she said. "We were just having a little chat. Woman to woman."

Louisa nodded. "Am I interrupting?"

"No, no," Helen said quickly. "We'd just finished." She got up from the couch and helped Elizabeth do the same. "You go on with Louisa," she said to her. "She can really help you. We all can. You can do this."

Elizabeth closed her eyes and nodded. Louisa walked over to the pair, put her arm around Elizabeth's shoulder, and directed her toward the office. "Come on in here, hon. Let's have a chat." She looked back over her shoulder at Helen and mouthed the words "thank you."

Helen gave her a confident nod and a thumbs-up.

In the office, Louisa directed Elizabeth toward the couch. "Why don't you have a seat, Elizabeth? Can I get you anything? Water? Coffee?"

"No, thanks," the girl muttered, sitting down.

Louisa gave her a moment to compose herself, sitting down on the chair opposite. "So, what's going on? Why did you need to see me?"

Elizabeth looked like she was ready to start crying again. "I just — I just . . ." she stammered. "I don't know what to do."

Louisa reached toward her desk, easily within arm's distance, thanks to the office's lack of abundant square footage, and retrieved a box of tissues. She offered it to Elizabeth, who took several and immediately began to use them.

"What don't you know?" Louisa asked. "What needs to be done?"

"Well, I don't have anywhere to go," Elizabeth said. "I want to be finished. I want to give my baby something better."

"That's good. Just giving him life—that's courageous, Elizabeth. I'm proud of you."

Elizabeth smiled through her tears. It was barely a smile, but it was a smile nonetheless. "Thanks."

Louisa took a deep breath. "So you say you want to do those things. Why can't you? What happened?"

"I told Sand Crab that I wanted to be done. And he told me . . . lots of mean things. Mean words. He said I'd never make it without him. No one would want me, an ungrateful little b—" she stopped herself and began to sob anew.

"It's okay, honey," Louisa said, gently rubbing the girl's forearm. "It's okay. He's just as scared as you are. Deep down."

Louisa gave her a moment to calm down, not wanting to say too much and break the girl's trust. After a careful pause, she continued. "So what'd you do?"

"I called my dad. I hadn't seen him in forever, and I thought maybe he could help."

"Did he know," Louisa asked, "what you'd been doing?"

"No," Elizabeth said. "I've been with my mom for years. He hasn't really been too interested in dropping by. But my mom's gotten worse and worse. She's so busy with her boyfriends and . . . other things . . . that I've been on my own for a while."

Louisa considered asking what Elizabeth meant by "other things," but figured that was another story for another time. "Is that how you got involved in the life?"

Elizabeth nodded her head. "I was just hanging out with the wrong people. Older guys. Sand Crab told me I could make some good money, so I started up. And then . . ." she looked down at her belly and ran her hand down the length of it.

"Yeah," Louisa said. "So what did your father say? Did you tell him?"

"No, I just told him that I'd run away, that I couldn't take it at Mom's anymore. That I wanted to come stay with him."

"What'd he say?"

"That'd he pay for a hotel for me and think about it."

Louisa tried to hide her frustration. "Well, that's something, right?"

Elizabeth's chin trembled with emotion. "Yeah, I guess."

"It's scary, isn't it? Being pregnant, with no one to help?"

The girl nodded slowly.

"Sweetie, we can help you. You can start over. But only if you want it."

The girl nodded again.

Louisa smiled. "I think that's a good decision."

Elizabeth smiled back at her, but only for a moment. Suddenly, her face fell. "But what about Sand Crab? He'll be so mad at me if I leave."

"Don't worry, hon. I'll take care of him for you."

The Last Supper

"YEAH, THIS IS it. Right here."

Jeremy pulled the hearse over to the side of the road, got a little too close to the curb, and tweaked the tire on the hard concrete. He swore.

"Don't sweat it," Jake said. "I'm sure it'll buff right out." They opened their doors and climbed out onto the sidewalk. "I hope the neighbors don't mind a hearse parked on their street."

"Just don't take too long."

"We'll be out of here in a jiffy."

They'd stopped in front of the neighborhood park, populated at the moment by only a few birds. The park wasn't much: a small jungle gym enclosed by the requisite railroad ties, surrounded by a half acre or so of grass. It backed into a greenbelt of trees, which Jake slowly began to scan, squinting around the midday sun.

He approached a small break in the trees and saw a faint path leading into the wooded area. He heard Jeremy's cell phone ring as he bent down to examine the surface of the path. It would be rough, but it'd do.

"Jake! Phone!" Jeremy was kneeling by the curb, checking out the hearse's wheel while holding the phone toward Jake.

Jake hustled over to him. He gave Jeremy a "who is it?" face as he received the phone. In return, Jeremy gave him the "I don't know" shoulders.

"Hello?"

"Hello, Jake." The accent was unmistakable.

"Hello, Santiago."

"How are the funeral arrangements coming?"

"Fine. Just fine."

"I didn't see you on the news today," Santiago said.

"I guess my fifteen minutes are up."

"I did see Louisa," Santiago continued. "They were very impressed with her today. Poor girl — she's a terrible interview."

"What's this have to do with me?"

"I'm beginning to wonder if you're worth your price."

Jake feigned shock. "*What?* Why? What's going on?"

"My dear sister was on TV walking around the gravesite. I'm sure I can get pretty close just by watching the news. And that doesn't cost me anything."

"Now w-wait a minute, Santiago. We had a deal."

"So we did. Tell me why I should keep it."

"Because I'm good for it. I'll get you to the precise location, lot number and everything. I'll tell you what: I'll even meet you there tomorrow night so you know you're in the right spot."

The silence was unbearable. Come on, Santiago. You know you want it.

"*Bueno.* Call me tomorrow with a time and location. Use the number on your caller ID from this call."

Jake beamed. "You got it."

Santiago had ended the call before Jake said the word "got." No matter. He handed the phone back to Jeremy.

"Thanks. I'm going to need that phone tomorrow, so be prepared. And don't go erasing your caller ID tonight."

"Sure," Jeremy said as they sauntered back to the hearse. "You should really get your own phone, you know. Everybody has one."

"Nah. It's a shackle, my friend," Jake said. "A mighty expensive shackle. I used to have a cell phone, and I could never get away from it." He gave Jeremy a brotherly pat on the shoulder. "My cell phone diet is the best thing I ever did for myself."

"Yeah, but what do you do when you need to make a call?"

"I just borrow yours."

§

Louisa reached over to smooth down Jake's tousled, helmet-affected hair. He put down his fork and playfully smacked her hand away in protest.

"Hey!"

"Sorry, you just had this one bit out of place. It was really bugging me."

"Messed-up hair: one of the many dangers of scooter-riding." Jake dug back into his fajitas.

"Oh, yeah? What are the others?"

"Rickets, scurvy, dysentery—the usual."

Louisa made a grossed-out face. "Thank you for the pleasant mental image to go with dinner."

They were knee-deep in a feast at Ramon's Mexican Kitchen, provided by the restaurant's namesake himself. The place was busier tonight than Jake had ever seen it, so Ramon skittered by them frequently, rushing from the kitchen to the dining room and back again. Despite his busyness, he heaped many portions of his finest cookery before them, which they delightfully devoured.

They'd invited Jeremy and Chiffon to come join them for their early dinner, but Jeremy had wanted to take a nap before staying awake with the casket all night, and Chiffon had declined for non-Mexican-food-liking reasons. Jake secretly thought she really wanted to head back to Sing Sing Lounge. So Jake and Louisa were left to dine by themselves.

"How're you feeling about tomorrow?" Jake asked between bites.

Louisa paused to swallow some *arroz con pollo* she'd just put in her mouth.

"Sorry," Jake apologized, "I hate it when people ask me questions right after I put a bite in my mouth. And here I am, inflicting the same thing on you. How callous am I?" He picked up the chip basket on their table and, noticing it was empty, leaned over to the recently-deserted-but-not-yet-bussed table next to them and swiped its half-full basket.

The chip swap had given Louisa ample time to swallow. "Don't worry about it," she said, taking another swallow and a sip of soda. "I'm feeling . . . okay, I guess."

"It's going to be a busy day." He sifted through the mostly broken chips in the new basket and found a complete triangle that was to his liking. "You know, with all the funerals and stuff."

Louisa sighed. "That's an understatement." She stopped for a moment. "It's weird, you know? I forget that he's gone. And I'm already kind of starting to get used to it."

"Strange," Jake said, mouth crunching. "I've never . . . lost . . . anyone that important to me before."

"Both of your parents are still around?"

"No," he said. "They weren't important to me." He shifted uneasily in his chair.

"Sorry. I didn't mean to pry."

He waved her off. "It's a long story. I'll tell you the full version sometime, but basically it starts with them taking off when I was in high school and ends with me getting a call from my grandmother six years ago telling me they'd been cremated. Not a whole lot of contact in between."

Louisa reached out her hand and laid it on his as her eyes began to moisten. "I'm . . . so sorry, Jake."

This type of stuff that she did — the sincerity and the reaching out — this stuff was making it hard for Jake. He did his best to remain logical: He needed the money more than he needed her. He needed the money more than he needed her. He needed the money more than he needed her.

If he kept repeating it to himself, it'd eventually sound true. Right?

But oh, how he liked the feeling of her hand on his. The second they touched, he shivered internally. He forced his mind back to the Logic Place: She wasn't his type — no one was his type. Only he was his type. Smiling, he withdrew his hand and used it to pick up his soda. "It's okay." He held the cup in front of his mouth, about to take a sip. "Honest."

Thankfully, Louisa changed the subject. "I had a fairly uneventful day today," she said. "It's hard work being a media target. You have to be so bland."

"And yet you still made the news."

Louisa laughed. "Wasn't I horrible? That lady kept asking the stupidest questions, and I didn't know how to answer them."

"I didn't see it. I just heard about it."

"Oh?"

"Yeah, your brother saw you, though. He called me. Totally fell for it."

She smiled, and Jake saw mischief flash in her eyes.

"Which are you more excited about," he said, "getting him off the street, ruining his personal narcotics and human trafficking empire, or getting even for all the pranks he played on you as a kid?"

Louisa laughed. "Would it be bad if I said all three?"

"No way. I have an older brother. I know the feeling."

Louisa laughed some more.

"You're giddy today," Jake said as he took a bite.

Louisa dropped her arms on the table. "I know! I think I'm nervous."

Jake swallowed and surveyed the restaurant for listening ears. "Well, I'm not. I pull these types of high-dollar capers all the time. Almost every day."

Louisa giggled again. "Sorry! I have to stop that." She closed her eyes and took a deep breath. "So, anyway, you talked to Santiago today?"

"Yeah. He called on Jeremy's cell, though, which was weird. I don't know how he got the number."

"He has ways of doing stuff like that," she said. She stopped chewing, and the mischief left her eyes. "Are you sure we're going to beat him at this game?"

Jake took one last bite of cheese enchilada. "We're sunk if we don't."

They both chewed the remnants of their food for a long while. Jake's elementary school cafeteria lady/nutritionist, who'd always encouraged him to chew each bite thirty times for better digestion, would've been proud.

"Well, I'd better get home," Louisa said. "Like you said, we have a big day tomorrow, and I need to get my beauty rest."

"So that's your secret." The subtle compliment popped out of Jake's mouth before he was quite aware of it. *I need the money more than I need her. I need the money more than I need her.*

Louisa smiled and looked down, bashful, flustered. She got up and knocked over her soda glass. *Table, meet ice. Ice, table.* "Oh!" she exclaimed and immediately began to put the ice cubes back into the glass. Jake got up to help. Astonishingly, their hands never touched.

Ice back in its proper surroundings, the two of them broke for the door. Louisa turned around to find Ramon and give him a parting wave. He did the same and hollered across the restaurant, "*Adios*, Louisa! *Adios*, Jake!" Jake gave him a thumbs-up.

They exited and walked to their respective vehicles, conveniently parked next to each other. Jake bowed low, doing an impression of a medieval serf. "Until the morrow, your highness."

Louisa smiled and followed suit with a very princesslike curtsy. "I thank thee, young squire."

Jake gave her a goofy grin. "Man, our British accents are horrible." He plopped down onto Princess Tangerine. "I'm off to witness the insertion of the envelope. It begins."

"Good luck."

"Same to you."

The scooter had a small electric start button, but it also had the more traditional kick-start lever near the rear wheel. Guess which one Jake used. He dropped the scooter off its kickstand and putted off into the darkening dusk.

I need the money more than I need her.

Twenty

A Video Game All-Nighter
Threatens to Mess Up Everything

JAKE ARRIVED AT White Hall moments before Kimbrough and his security guard. He pulled into the parking lot and immediately noticed Jeremy's car wasn't there. Probably running late, as Jeremy was wont to do on occasion.

He unlocked the front door and went in to wait for Kimbrough, whom he saw pulling up just behind him, followed by a dark sedan that Jake assumed contained the security guard of Kimbrough's choosing.

The two men exited their vehicles. As the guard got out, he seemed to keep rising far after he should've stopped. When he finally stood to his full height, Jake decided that Kimbrough had not hired a guard but a six-and-a-half-foot-tall side of beef dressed in a black suit.

The men walked up to Jake, who held the door open for them. "Greetings, gents."

"Mr. Abrams," Kimbrough said, "this is Darren. He will be maintaining this evening's security."

Jake offered his hand. "Pleased to meet you. Put 'er there."

Darren's hands remained at his sides as he looked disdainfully upon Jake's salutatory mitt. Looked like Jeremy was in for a long night.

"Well," Jake said, "let's go inside and get this over with."

He led the men to the casket containing the body of Benjamin Cruz. A few seconds later, he had the lid open. He'd never noticed it before, but he could see the familial resemblance, especially to Santiago. Like father, like son.

Edgar Kimbrough opened wide the already slightly ajar door to the safe, glancing inside. He then moved to a nearby counter and set his briefcase on top. He worked the combination with some difficulty, but managed to get the case open and produced from it a trim, letter-sized manila envelope.

Amazing what fortunes fit into these days. Those big wooden treasure chests of pirate lore? Gone. The manila envelope now ruled the world of booty.

Kimbrough took the envelope to the safe, placed it inside, shut the door, and spun the combination lock. He gave the clasp a tug to make sure it was secure, then went back to his briefcase and shut it. "That's all I have, Mr. Abrams," he said to Jake. "I trust you can take care of lowering the lid?"

Jake was already in progress. "Yeah, I think I got it," he said as the lid went home.

"And you've arranged for someone to stay the night?"

"Yeah, my coworker Jeremy should be here any minute now."

"Very well." He turned to Darren. "You have my number.

Call me if any situations arise." At the word "situations," he rolled his eyes toward Jake.

Darren nodded and stationed himself next to the casket, legs spread apart, arms down, hands together. Jake figured Darren had been — or might still be — a football player, but when he assumed this pose, he looked like a *fútbol* player readying himself to receive a penalty kick. A kick that had no chance of getting around his enormous, goal-blocking body.

"Good evening, gentlemen." Kimbrough wheeled around and headed for the door. When Jake made to follow him, Kimbrough stopped him. "Mr. Abrams, I don't know what you are doing, but part of our agreement is that you would have someone with the remains at all times. That includes now."

"But I have to find Jeremy."

"I'm sure he can find his way to you, Mr. Abrams. Good evening."

The door swung open, and out went Edgar Kimbrough. Jake went back to the body and settled in to wait for his friend.

§

Jeremy had every intention of taking a nap when he got home that afternoon, but he got wrapped up in a video game he'd been playing the night before. He was obsessed with beating it, so last night he'd unwittingly stayed up into the early morning hours trying, unsuccessfully, to get his dinosaur to fly through all the right jungles and defeat the evil cave people. But he hadn't spent any time on it yet today, so he decided to give it five or ten minutes before he went to sleep.

Three hours later, he collapsed on the couch, exhausted but

triumphant. The guys on the message board weren't going to believe this. He'd actually beaten it. He was spent and tired, but it was totally worth it. And he'd done it in time to go meet Jake at the funeral home. He'd leave in ten minutes. Right after . . . he took a . . . little . . .

S

"What's up?" came Jeremy's prerecorded voice. "You got Jeremy's cell. Hit me with your message."

Jake slammed down the desk phone in frustration. It was twenty past midnight, and Jeremy still hadn't answered his phone. That was approximately the one zillionth time Jake had called, each time getting Jeremy's outgoing voice mail message, which kept growing more and more obnoxious the more times Jake heard it.

"That's really, really annoying," Jake said to Darren, more to vent than to start a conversation.

Darren paid him no mind.

Jake walked over toward the towering behemoth. "You're a very sociable guy, aren't you, Darren?"

Darren continued to stare straight ahead.

"How much is he paying you, huh? Kimbrough? 'Cause I can beat it."

Nothing.

"See, I need to leave for a second to go track down my friend. I'll give you a hundred bucks if you promise not to say anything to your buddy, Edgar."

Still nothing.

"Two hundred."

Stone face.

"Five hundred."

Darren was an oak. But bigger.

"A thousand. Come on, Darren. One thousand dollars. Tell me where you'll find a better deal."

Darren folded his arms.

"Okay, I understand. You're sworn to silence. Probably one of those monks who took a vow or something. That's cool." Jake waved his hand in front of Darren's face. "How 'bout this? I'll leave, come back with your grand, and you don't say anything to Kimbrough. If you're cool with that, blink twice."

Darren's eyes remained open.

"Okay, blink once."

Still open.

"Keep your eyes open."

Blink.

"Shoot."

He had no choice but to stay. Even though it was a mind-numbing, excruciatingly boring task, he had to stay. He worried that if he left, Darren the Meaty-but-Straight-Arrow would find his tongue and call Kimbrough, who would find some loophole in the will that said the fortune now belonged to him, or Santiago, or the country of Costa Rica—all because Jake took off. Kimbrough would be like that, Jake could tell. No, he had to sit tight and hope Jeremy came through for him soon.

And there weren't even any leftovers to snack on.

*

Tick. Tick. Tick. Tick.

The stillness and unique silence that accompanies the middle of the night had settled in for a comfortable rest at White Hall Funeral Home, except for the motion of Darren's wristwatch. Jake was on the verge of going a little bit crazy and was thinking of writing a letter of thanks to whomever had invented digital watches.

Tick. Tick. Tick.

It wouldn't be so bad if Darren would just say something, or at least go to the bathroom. Just give Jake a break from the relentless ticking. He remembered a story he'd read in one of his middle school English classes, where a guy heard a heartbeat in his head that drove him nuts. Caused him to confess about something he'd done.

Tick. Tick.

Jake began to empathize with that guy in the story. At last, he understood.

Tick. Tick. Tick. Tick. Tick.

Okay, time to do something active with the brain. Mental gymnastics. Run the multiplication tables or something.

Think about the plan. That'd be good.

Tick.

It was weird to think that less than twenty-four hours from now, Jake would be considerably wealthier, and his imaginative brain began to fantasize. He had visions of long trips to fast towns, throwing money around casinos and hotels, living the rock star life.

He could definitely see himself in those visions, and he tried to imagine Louisa alongside him, but it never looked right. She didn't fit into that mold, no matter how much he tried to cram her into it.

So what then?

Leave her high and dry. He dug Louisa, that was for sure, and he was happy to have her along for the ride, but he also knew that the ride would have to end soon. She could never be as selfish as he was.

Tick. Tick. Tick.

He remembered the ending of *Potato Thief*, how the guy had double-crossed the girl. He thought of the manila envelope currently inside the safe inside the coffin. He could get one of those envelopes out of his own desk drawer. Fill it with newspaper or something. Pull the old switcheroo. Be on a beach, cigar in his mouth, laughing at how good he'd swindled her.

She'd be fine. She was tough.

Tick. Tick.

Jake had the urge to tear off Darren's wristwatch and stomp on it many, many times, all while yelling, "Shut up and let me think!" He wondered how Darren would react to the crazy person in the room.

Jake Prays

8:13 A.M. THE exact moment Darren's watch stopped ticking backward. At least, that's what the long night had felt like. He was positive each minute had taken at least up to seventy seconds, the elongated warp in time extended all the more by Jake's internal wrestling and Darren's refusal to say even one word.

8:13 was the magical time Jeremy finally showed up, embarrassed and apologetic. He told Jake what happened, and Jake, being no stranger to video game all-nighters, had to admit that it was a valid excuse.

"Did you at least beat the game?"

"Oh, yeah."

"Sweet." He was going to say something else, but his fatigue prevented him from remembering what. "Can you hang out here for a second?"

"Sure."

"This is Darren, by the way. He's a mute."

Jake went to his workstation and sat down, relieved to be looking at different surroundings. His long night of ticking wristwatches and forced awakeness through contemplation had left him physically *and* emotionally drained. Great way to start the day.

He knew there was a reason he'd come back to his workstation, but he couldn't for the life of him remember what it was. He stared blankly at his computer for a moment, his eyes closing to a level of minimum openness. His foggy mind fought for clarity, and for a moment he had a vision of himself hooking coffee up to an IV already started in his forearm. Caffeine. Needed. Badly.

"How's it going, there, Jake?"

Jake decided then and there that he hated Del's uncanny ability to pop up at the worst times. He tried to reply, but honestly couldn't think of anything to say.

"You look terrible," Del said.

"Yeah. I was up late. With Mr. Cruz."

"Oh, I see," Del said, nodding his head. "I tell you what. You've been doing a great job this week. Why don't you knock off after the funeral and get some shut-eye?"

Jake didn't mention it, but he'd already planned a variety of activities that day that didn't involve his job. "Del, that would be very, very helpful."

"Well, it's settled then."

Del stood there for a moment, watching Jake for a reaction, then slowly turned around and walked out. "See ya," he said.

"Thanks," Jake said.

He then spent a good thirty seconds trying to remember what he had been about to do before Del had interrupted him. Ah, yes: six hundred milligrams of caffeine in a single cup of coffee.

To the deli he went, which fortunately was also a bakery that did brisk morning business. The rush of patrons and the smell of baked goods and brewing coffee snapped him back to his senses. He had to be on top of his game today, or the whole plan would go to the sewer. Wait, what was the plan again? Were there combination locks? What were the combinations? He ordered a large coffee in the hopes it would jog his memory.

He essentially sleepwalked through the rest of the morning, and if he would've gone on the witness stand in a courtroom, he wouldn't have been able to recall with any accuracy what he did. A lot of computer-staring and coffee-drinking, but those were the high points. Come to think of it, it was pretty much a normal day.

Jake opened his desk drawer and rummaged through it until he found a package of manila envelopes. Holding them up, he examined them and determined they were the same dimension as the envelope Edgar Kimbrough had placed in the safe. He used the scissors on his desk to cut through the shrink wrap and removed one of the envelopes, placing the rest of them back in the drawer.

He took a few sheets of paper from the trash can he stowed under his desk. Old spreadsheets Del had given him for some budgetary thing. He folded them in two, then placed them in the envelope. He sealed the package shut and set it on his desk.

There. Would Louisa buy that?

He heard a beautiful voice address him very politely.

"You look awful."

Jake swiveled his head to see Louisa standing near his workstation, hands on hips. Despite her hand placement and the arm shifting that made it possible, her tasteful, simple black dress wasn't even bunched around the waist. He resisted the urge to panic, but her sudden presence startled him enough to wake him up.

"Aw, you're just saying that to be nice," he said.

"What happened? Didn't you sleep last night?"

Jake took another sip of coffee. "No. Jeremy never . . . it's a long story." He rubbed the back of his head. "What are you doing here?"

"The funeral starts in half an hour."

Of course it does. Get your act together, Abrams, or you're going to get found out. "Oh, yeah. I lost track of time. How're you doing?"

"Okay, I guess," she said softly. "I figure it'll hit me once the funeral part's over and my life starts to get back to normal."

"Nice thought, normality." Jake had seen enough funerals to know that there was no going back to normal after the death of a loved one. If he was honest with himself, he'd even see it with his own parents, how much he'd changed as a result. But then, he was rarely honest with himself.

"My old normal doesn't exist anymore, does it?" she said. It didn't sound so much like a question as a realization.

"No, it doesn't," Jake said. "You have to redefine it."

"I don't know if I like the sound of that."

Jake shrugged. "You do what you have to."

She nodded. A tear began to form in her eye, and Jake instinctively wanted to comfort her. He knew he should be pulling away, preparing her emotionally for her envelope surprise, but she was just too beautiful to resist. His arms enveloped her shoulders, and she sank into his embrace, shuddering as she let the tears flow.

Your arms. I made these arms the perfect size to fit around her shoulders. Your chin is the right height to rest upon her head. I gave her your favorite scent. I gave you her favorite personality. I made you two for each other.

Fatigue. That's what it was. His brain was playing a trick on him by going off on some tangent. Because if Jake hadn't known better, he'd have sworn he'd just heard God.

♪

White Hall's fairly sizeable chapel was packed to the gills with scores of well-wishers from the community, as well as a few of the higher-ups from The Cruz Agency. And, of course, all the news stations in town, though they had to stand along the back wall, behind the rows of mustard-yellow pews, made all the more mustard from the afternoon sunlight streaming through the orange and yellow stained-glass windows.

The funeral itself went as well as a funeral can go. Louisa's pastor delivered the eulogy with the appropriate air of practiced solemnity that Jake was very, very familiar with. The hired keyboardist wrought "Great Is Thy Faithfulness" and "Amazing Grace" from the chapel's keyboard (using the "pipe organ" setting) with the expected stoicism (and zero syncopation).

Jake, wearing the dark suit he kept on a hanger at his workstation, stood at the back of the chapel. He watched Louisa on the front row, sitting by herself. He scanned the crowd. He knew Santiago wouldn't be there, but he'd half-expected Ramon. Nothing doing.

Soon it was over, and people began to file by the casket to give their good-byes. Jake stood at the back of the chapel watching the procession when he felt a not-so-gentle tap on his shoulder. He'd seen Cindy Pennington approaching out of the corner of his eye, but hadn't acknowledged it, hoping she would just keep on walking. Instead, he was forced to turn to her and smile broadly. "Hello, Ms. Pennington."

"Mr. Abrams."

"It was a nice ceremony, wasn't it?"

She glowered at him. "I don't know how you did it, but I know it was you."

Jake put on a bewildered air. "Did what, Ms. Pennington?"

"Don't play pretend with me, Jake," she said. "You went over my head to get my camera yanked from the cemetery."

"Why, Ms. Pennington," Jake said, "I had no idea your boss had done that to you. I'm so sorry. In fact, if I wasn't just about to head out to the cemetery, I'd call him for you and let him know I'm fine with it."

She huffed. "Please, Mr. Abrams. Jake. I know it was you."

Jake continued smiling. "Honestly, Ms. Pennington. Cindy. I don't know a thing."

Pennington sighed in defeat. "Look, I'm not mad," she said. "Well, not that much. I just wanted to congratulate you on turning the city's most rule-bending news producer into a stickler for family privacy. Kudos."

Jake desperately wanted to take credit, but instead just said, "Really wish I knew what you were talking about, Cindy."

It was her turn to smile. "I'm sure you do." She turned to leave. "You beat me at the game this time, but next time I'll be on you like nobody's business. See you around, Jake."

"Whatever you say," he said, waving.

The chapel had now emptied except for Jake, Jeremy, and the deceased. Those visitors who'd planned ahead were already driving to the cemetery for the interment service. Jake thought of the envelope, still lying on his desk, and how easy it would be right now to switch it out with the one in the casket. So easy.

Too easy. Where was the fun in that?

Jake and Jeremy emptied the chapel of its last occupant, using a gurneylike device to roll the casket out of the building and into the waiting hearse.

Jeremy closed the door, and Benjamin Cruz began the short journey to his final resting place.

§

Jake and Jeremy got to the cemetery after most of the crowd had arrived. They drove the hearse to the appropriate spot near the mausoleum and parked. Jake got out to scan the crowd for media while Jeremy went to round up the pallbearers.

Jake was pleased. No newspeople in sight, thanks to the karaoke stylings of Chris Walters and Chiffon Brown. Come to think of it, Jake hadn't seen Chiffon all morning. Had she overslept, too?

His thought train jumped the tracks when he saw Louisa talking to a man he recognized, but couldn't place. He was a definite clod, though.

Jake approached the pair to see how Louisa was doing and caught part of their conversation. The Clod was speaking.

". . . wish more people from The Agency had come, but you know how it is."

"Sure, sure. Of course," Louisa said to him. "I'm just glad you could be here."

"So am I. Your father meant a lot to me. I wouldn't have missed it."

"Well, thank you. Oh, hi, Jake!" Louisa had finally spotted

him and greeted him with a warm smile. She gestured to The Clod. "Jake, this is Thomas Chenoweth, executive vice president of The Cruz Agency."

The Clod stuck out his hand for a shake, and Jake reached out to complete the transaction. It was at this second, forward motion already in progress, that Jake's fuzzy mind cleared up and found this man's file in its memory banks.

Too late. Jake was now shaking hands with Stall Man.

"Jake Abrams."

"Nice to meet you," Stall Man, a.k.a. Tom Chenoweth, said. "How did you know Ben?"

"Oh. I, uh—"

"Jake works for the funeral home, Tom," Louisa said. "He's been taking very good care of Papa the past few days."

"Excellent. I've heard nothing but good things about your business."

Jake downplayed the praise. "Oh, thanks." He turned to Louisa. "Anyway, I just wanted to see how you were doing, Ms. Cruz. Anything we can get for you?"

"Uh . . . no," Louisa said, taken aback. "No, thanks."

"Very well. Pardon my interruption."

Jake bid them farewell and walked back toward the hearse, replaying the conversation he'd overheard in the bathroom the night of the party. So Tom Chenoweth was Stall Man, The Clod who was out to hook up with Louisa at the Downtown Hilton.

He filed this information away for later as he stationed himself next to the hearse, eager to get Benjamin Cruz in his rightful place so he could get going with the rest of the day. He was too far away to hear anything, but he saw the minister say a few words, saw the pallbearers carry the casket into the mausoleum, saw them walk out, saw them push the door closed.

Everything was in place. No turning back.

Jake saw the minister say a few more words, and then the assembled crowd bowed their heads to pray in unison.

For the first time since he was a kid, Jake said a prayer with them. Two prayers, really, both with equal earnestness. The first was that he would wake up enough to pull off the plan without a hitch tonight. The other was that God would somehow, some way, make Louisa forgive him for double-crossing her.

The Setup

THE PEOPLE WENT their separate ways, mostly at the same time, with a few stragglers hanging around to admire the mausoleum's handiwork. It wasn't long until they, too, were gone.

When it was all over, Louisa strode over to Jake. "'Ms. Cruz'? What was *that* all about?"

"Sorry. I don't know—I just don't trust that guy. I thought it'd be better to not clue him in on how well we know each other. That's all."

"Well, from now on, if I introduce you to someone, you better act like you know me."

"Yes, ma'am."

She gave him one of her fiery looks (patent pending). "I'm serious, Jake. If we're going to—" she stopped before she finished the sentence.

"—pull off this plan, we need to stick together?" Jake said. "I agree."

"Good."

"Great."

"Great."

"Good."

They were both smiling now. "I used to say a prayer like that when I was a kid," Louisa said. "Right before I ate."

"I usually just ate."

"That doesn't surprise me."

They began to walk back to the limousine White Hall had provided to Louisa as a ride to the cemetery. "So," Jake said, "you all set for this evening's festivities?"

"Yeah. It's going to be very . . ."

"Exciting?"

"Weird."

"I almost said 'weird,' too," Jake said. "In fact, I thought 'weird' and 'exciting' at the same time and almost said 'wexciting,' but caught myself at the last second."

Louisa laughed that musical laugh of hers. "You're something." She climbed into the limo and rolled the window down as she shut the door. "See you tonight." It was all she said before the limo pulled away.

Jake met Jeremy back at the hearse. "You 'bout ready, bro?"

"Yeah. I'm good to go."

"All right. Let's get started."

S

"Haven't you guys already delivered a body today?"

Jake and Jeremy were in the hearse, back at the cemetery, fielding a friendly question from a security guard they each kind of knew, though they'd failed to come up with his name when they discussed it on the drive over. And while he had a generic blue security-type uniform, it was devoid of any nametag to clue them in.

"Yeah," Jake said, his memory wheels turning as they tried to produce the guy's name. "It's crazy. A big mix-up."

"What's goin' on?"

"You wouldn't believe it," Jake said, making too much of the production. He leaned forward confidentially and spoke in a voice just above a whisper. "We accidentally put the wrong wedding band on the guy." Bruce? Bill? It was one syllable.

"Yikes."

"Tell me about it," Jeremy said.

"Yeah," Jake said. Lee? The guard's feathery, sandy blond hair didn't look like it belonged to a Lee. "Anyway, we need to switch 'em out, pronto, before it's too late."

"Okay, fine by me," the guard said. "Just let me radio over to Bo and let him know you're coming." The guard raised his walkie-talkie to his mouth, about to speak.

"Actually," Jake said, "we already talked to him. He's expecting us."

The guard lowered the walkie-talkie. "Oh, okay. Head on in, then."

Jake smiled. "Awesome." He leaned his head a little closer to the guard. "By the way, could you do us a favor and keep this between us?" "S"-something. It started with "S."

The guard chuckled. "I seen it all now," he said. "Sure, it'll be our little secret. Take it easy, fellas."

Ding!

"You too, Stan," Jake said with a smile and a wave.

Jeremy eased the hearse through the gate and toward the mausoleum. Jake looked into the back. "I think we're good. This is going to work out great."

"I better not have any drips on the floor of my hearse, man," Jeremy said. "That's all I got to say."

"Nah, she won't drip. No worries."

Once they arrived, Jeremy brought the hearse around, facing the gate. He'd parked near enough to the structure itself that the vehicle and the building's walls obstructed their path from view.

"Last stop, Cruz mausoleum," Jeremy said.

They got out and hurried to the back to release their passenger. Jeremy opened the door to reveal the only orange, fiberglass, two-wheeled, 150cc guest his hearse had ever carried.

"I think the Princess enjoyed her trip, don't you?" Jake said.

"Seriously, dude, there better not be any drips."

"Let's find out."

The two of them grappled the hefty scooter, lifting it out of the hearse, righting it, and successfully setting its two dinky wheels on the ground. Jake wheeled it stealthily behind the mausoleum while Jeremy went over the hearse's interior with studious precision.

The back of the mausoleum was conveniently landscaped with some tall shrubs that accented the marble. Jake stashed the scooter behind one of these as well as he could, then looked around, scoping out the surroundings.

The back of the building faced the cemetery's iron fence, and beyond that was just a patch of trees, so Jake was fairly confident that no one could see the scooter from outside the cemetery and that the evening security patrols would miss it once the sky got darker. As it was now, the late afternoon sun bathed the whole grounds in orangish light; Princess Tangerine looked like a mere anomaly of light playing between the shrubs and the wall of the mausoleum.

When he got back to the hearse, Jeremy was scowling into the back.

"How is it?"

Jeremy frowned and pointed at two small dark oil spots on the floor.

"Huh. Who would've thought?" Jake said. "Sorry, man. It'll buff right out."

8

Jeremy piloted the hearse back toward White Hall as Jake snapped up the cell phone from its resting position on the dashboard.

"Mind if I use this again, bro?"

"I guess."

"Thanks."

Jake flipped it open and found the "received calls" list so he could make his planned phone call to Santiago.

But he only saw the same number. Over and over again.

An all-too-familiar phone number.

The call list noted the last twenty calls made to the phone, and all of them were from the funeral home. Jake closed his eyes and sank his head back against the headrest as the realization washed over him. Every time he'd called Jeremy out of frustration last night, he'd forced Santiago's number closer to caller ID oblivion. He didn't know when it'd happened, but he knew he'd accidentally erased the number himself by calling too many times.

He cursed himself for not having written Santiago's number down. Why didn't he just write it down? His whole plan was coming apart thanks to this stupid cell phone and his lack of a pen and a scrap of paper.

"What's wrong, man?" Jeremy asked.

"Nothin'."

"Come on," Jeremy said. "You're all sighing hard and stuff."

Jake suppressed the hard sigh he was about to let out, unaware he'd been doing it. "Okay, when you were asleep last night, I kept trying to call you. Why didn't you wake up?"

"Phone was on vibrate," Jeremy said. "I was out of it, man."

"Well, I wound up calling you so many times I erased Santiago's number from the caller ID."

"So?"

"So? So, I'm supposed to call him and give him the—" Jake made finger quotes around the word—"'location' of the grave."

It was Jeremy's turn to sigh hard. "Oh."

"Yeah."

"So what're you going to do?"

"Wait for him to call, I guess."

They drove on in silence. Jake leaned his head back, eyes closed again, and felt the sticky fingers of sleep threatening to pull him into their world. He wished he could just take a little nap, something to clear his head before his big night. Those fingers were persuasive, they were. Yes, he would obey them, at least until the hearse pulled into the parking lot at the funeral home. But the fingers suddenly lost their grip as a voice, vaguely sounding like Jeremy's, began to draw Jake back to the real world of the hearse.

". . . isa has it?"

"What?"

"You think maybe Louisa has it?"

Of course! Louisa! Surely she had it. She seemed pretty

on top of things. Jake flipped open the phone and dialed her number.

"Hello?"

Success! Never before had her voice sounded so beautiful. "Louisa! It's Jake. I need your brother's cell phone number."

"Which brother?"

Why did she have to be so literal all the time? "Santiago."

"Oh, yeah. I thought you had it."

"It got erased."

"How?"

"I called Jeremy's phone too many times. Look, it's a long story. Just give me the number, please."

"Okay, okay. Don't freak out, Jake."

S

Seconds later, Jake was dialing Santiago.

"You're late."

"Sorry. I was making sure they'd officially buried him."

"And?"

"And they have. He's in the Wildwood section at the northeast end of the cemetery. Plot number P-29. Third one from the left, about twenty yards from the fence."

"That's where Louisa was walking yesterday."

"Yeah. I'll meet you there tonight at midnight."

"Very well." Jake would've sworn he could hear Santiago smiling through the phone. "You've earned your money."

"Good. You'll have it for me tonight?"

Was that the sound of a suppressed chuckle Jake heard? "Sure thing, Jake."

A click let Jake know Santiago had hung up on him. Mission accomplished. Hopefully, Santiago wasn't a man of his word. Jake was counting on him showing up early.

S

Louisa sat in her office, not really doing anything as she waited for zero hour. When her office phone rang, she was both surprised at the lateness of the call and thankful for the interruption in her patient anxiety.

"Hello?" Louisa said, picking up the receiver. "Louisa Cruz, Maria House."

"Hi, Louisa, it's Elizabeth." The girl sounded as if she were smiling.

"Hi, Elizabeth. How's it going, hon?"

"Good," she said. "I already went to the doctor you sent me to, and he said everything looks fine so far."

"Great."

"And I talked to my dad again. He said I can stay with him!"

Louisa smiled broadly. "That's great, Elizabeth!"

"Yeah. I'm really excited."

"Did you tell him about your baby?"

The line was quiet for a moment.

"Elizabeth? You need to tell him, sweetheart. He'll figure it out soon enough."

"I will, Louisa. I just need to wait for the right time."

"Sooner is better than later," Louisa said.

"I know. I know."

"Well, anyway," Louisa said, "I'm glad to hear you're being taken care of. You keep me posted, okay?"

"Okay. Thank you."

"You're welcome."

Louisa heard the phone click, then hung up her end of the receiver. She realized that Elizabeth had not once asked her about the funeral or her own father. She wondered if Elizabeth even knew about that whole situation. She was grateful for the chance to talk about something else.

She began to think about the evening's festivities, approaching as rapidly as they were. She thought about all the girls like Elizabeth, girls she was helping make something of themselves. She thought of the way her father had begrudgingly helped Helen all those years ago and how he was now going to help other women like her, and again do it begrudgingly, in a sense. She'd had to work to get the initial help from him, and now she was going to do it again.

So help her, God.

S

Jake passed the next couple of hours in a daze. The cemetery closed at six, but it wouldn't get dark enough to start until nine or so. Figuring in travel time, that left Jake roughly two and a half hours with nothing to do, so he decided to forego dinner and take a nap. He lay on the floor of the Interview Room with a rolled-up jacket for a pillow, running through the basics of the plan as he closed his eyes.

Seconds later, he was swimming in a sea of money. Hundred dollar bills. He kicked off his shoes and dove down into the currency, which took on a fluidlike appearance. The money was real and present, but translucent enough to see through.

Down, down he went into the unending ocean of bills. Golden fish swam by, apparently evading a predator of some sort. Jake's eyes were wide at the sight of the ocean, thousands upon thousands of faces of Benjamin Franklin pulsing in a liquid state. Sensing a need to breathe, Jake began to swim upward.

His head broke the surface, and he took deep breaths of the money-scented air. He treaded water and looked around at the vast body of money in which he swam, made all the greener with the hot illumination of the setting sun. He wondered how much of it he could get.

A slight engine noise caught his ear, and he turned his head to see a small boat with a piddly outboard motor, navigating the currency a few hundred yards away and moving toward the sunset. A speck on the horizon, growing tinier. He instinctively knew that Louisa was driving the boat, though there was no way he could actually make her out. He waved his arms and called out to her. "Louisa!"

Her tiny head turned around. Her tiny arm waved back. A few seconds later, he heard the reply. "Hi, Jake!"

"Come over here!" he called out.

But he never saw whether she did or not. He was too distracted by the sudden, intense pain in his leg. He was forcefully dragged down into the depths, becoming more aware of a searing, piercing sensation in his ankle. He looked toward the pain and saw a dazzling, bejeweled shark gnawing on his limb, swimming down into the depths and taking Jake with him. Jake gave the shark a kick in its diamond snout, only to find that the rumors were true: Diamonds were indeed very hard.

Nevertheless, the shark let go, and Jake made immediate haste for the surface. He came up, sucked a lungful of air, and began hailing Louisa. "Louisa! Help!" He waved his arms frantically, hoping she'd catch sight of him if she didn't hear.

"Bye, Jake!" The strains of her voice reached across the ocean just as the pain in his leg returned. Jake barely saw Louisa waving good-bye as he was dragged underneath the surface of the not-water again. He looked down through the bills and saw the bejeweled shark again gnawing on his ankle. He reached down to pry its teeth off when another shark, this one made of rubies, bit down on his wrist.

He instinctively tried to cry out in pain, but got a mouthful of money instead. As the sharks dragged him down, down, he tried to spit the money out, but it only led to more getting in. And more. It was forcing itself down his throat, into his stomach and lungs. And Santiago was laughing in his head. He couldn't breathe. The pain. The depths.

He was being rolled over now. Something was attacking his shoulder, shaking it. He tried to turn his head to see it, but got more money in his mouth. His gag reflex tried to kick in, but failed.

For a second, just a brief second, Jake thought of Louisa and her childhood Bible. And the thought was nice, and he felt okay. For a second.

The creature wouldn't let go of his shoulder. Relentless. Santiago's laughing grew louder. Another shake. And another.

Jake was going to die.

Breath. He needed a breath. He needed to get to the top. But the sharks were too heavy. His lungs were too full. He was choking. Choking. Santiago. Cackle.

He awoke with a start, quickly focusing his eyes on Jeremy, who was shaking his shoulder.

"Wake up, dude. Louisa's here. Time to get going."

Jake had never been more glad to be alive. He checked out his wrist and ankle, glad to see there was no sign of shark teeth marks.

It was time, finally time. He took a moment to gather his thoughts, then hopped up and transformed his makeshift pillow back into the jacket it was designed to be.

"Let's go."

Twenty-Three

Stage One

"LOOK AT THAT sky."

"Those stars are beautiful. God sure knew what he was doing."

"Uh, yeah. I guess. What I meant is that it's perfect light for a robbery, wouldn't you say?"

"Jake, this isn't a robbery. It's a . . . It's . . . Well, it isn't a robbery."

The moon was full, which, combined with the adrenaline pumping through both of them, made the night sky feel brighter and more alive. Dressed in comfortable, dark clothing, Jake and Louisa were slowly making their way toward the cemetery perimeter across the undeveloped field that would soon be a new housing division. It only made sense to pass the time with a little conversation about the nature of their visit to the cemetery that evening.

"Is it a plan? A scheme? A mission?"

"It's a . . ." Louisa fumbled her lips around for a moment. "It's a noble quest."

"Fair enough."

They reached a patch of trees that stood near the fence and crouched behind a couple of thick trunks. Jake looked at his watch. They were ahead of schedule.

He had to admit that he got a little thrill being out here with Louisa. He was really starting to enjoy her company, which made it all the worse that they were so incompatible.

"Louisa?" he said.

"Yeah?"

"Do you think people can, like, change who they are?" He didn't think so, but that dream he'd had made him wish he could. "Like, their fundamental natures?"

Louisa thought for a moment, her face difficult to read in the moonlight. "No."

Aha! He was destined to rip her off, and he knew it, and she knew it, and she was already preparing herself for it.

She shifted her weight and leaned fully against the tree. "I don't think people can change themselves, but I believe God can change them."

Or maybe Jake was all wrong about her.

And himself. "Really?"

"Yeah. Look at my dad—lived his whole life for himself, and then God changed him at the last minute."

Jake still wasn't sure. "Hmmm. I guess."

Their conversation was interrupted by the dull whine of a souped-up golf cart driving down the path on the other side of the fence. The full moon compensated for the lack of lighting in this area of the cemetery, and the cart soon came into view. Jake noted that the two security guards in it were once again paying more attention to their heated conversation than to their surroundings.

Over the sound of the engine, which Jake now noticed sounded very much like Princess Tangerine's, he overheard one of them saying, "So you've got two Jedi masters who fade away when they die, and two *other* Jedi masters who leave bodies behind. How do you explain *that*?" Sadly, Jake missed out on the reply.

The sound of the cart faded into the distance, leaving only the faint smell of tires and traces of fossil fuels. "Okay," Jake said, "we should have about fifteen minutes before the guards come by again. *Vamanos*."

Jake and Louisa stood up, left their hiding places, and approached the fence, a vertical iron-bar number with pointed spires at the top of each bar.

"Well," Louisa said, taking a deep breath, "this is it."

Jake nodded and held his hands down low, palms up and fingers entwined. "You first, champ."

Louisa began to put her foot into Jake's bare hands for a boost when he suddenly pulled them away, causing her to lose her balance and stumble forward into him.

She quickly righted herself.

"Sorry. So sorry. Really, really sorry," Jake said, flustered, holding up his hands. "Forgot my gloves."

"It's okay. No problem. Fine, just fine," Louisa replied. "I don't think you did it on purpose, or anything." She chuckled too loudly.

Jake took off the backpack he was wearing, unzipped it, and fished through until he found two pairs of gardener's gloves. He handed the smaller pair to Louisa and pulled on the larger pair. He set the backpack by the brick base of the fence, then remade the "boost" offer with his hands.

"You ready now, your highness?" she said.

"Hey, watch it."

Louisa put her foot in Jake's hands and, with his help, vaulted herself to the spire portion of the fencing. The rubberized surface of the gloves helped her grip the squared-off iron, while her rubber-soled sneakers found decent footing on the fence itself. She walked her legs up the fence until she was bent nearly double. "Okay."

Jake had picked up the backpack while she was making her way up the fence and now cocked his hand back to toss it. "Here you go."

He let it gently fly while Louisa reached out a hand and snatched it from the air. Perfect grab. She laid the backpack across the tops of the spires. Then, using it as a buffer between her and the pointed spire tops, she leaned over the top of the fence and swung around until she was on the other side. Her feet quickly found footing against the bars. She took a moment to steady herself, then jumped backward onto the soft ground, the backpack following her. She didn't stick the landing like a gymnast, but she was over, and that was all that mattered. "Your turn."

"I'd say that was a bronze medal performance," Jake said.

"Oh, like you could do better."

"I'd like to think I'd be a little more graceful, yeah."

"Well, let's see what you got, Mary Lou Retton."

"Oh, you're *on*," Jake said. "Hey, did the backpack fall on your side or mine?"

Louisa scoured the ground until she saw it. "Mine."

"Okay. Here I go." Not having the luxury of a boost, but with a height advantage, Jake shimmied up the side of the fence until he'd assumed the same bent position Louisa had. "Toss it." She heaved the backpack a little too eagerly, nearly throwing it over Jake's head. But a well-timed thrust of Jake's arm brought the backpack back into safe hands. He repeated the procedure Louisa had, but when he got over, he lost his balance and had to jump off without steadying himself. He'd meant to yank the backpack down with him, but instead, it rolled over toward Jake and Louisa, then stopped, seemingly in midair, its top loop caught on one of the spires.

Jake hit the ground hard and felt like smacking his forehead the whole way down. Stupid backpack. In fact, he'd almost cut that loop off before they came out here, just in case something like this happened.

"At least I'm on the medal stand," said Louisa. "You all right?"

"Sure," Jake said.

"You know, you really should try to get some sort of workout routine going," she said. "I think it would help you." She looked up at the backpack. "What now?"

"I'll get it down." Jake gripped the fence again and started climbing. In a few moves he was underneath the backpack and able to reach it. He gave it a tug.

No go.

A harder tug, this time with a little jolt upward.

Still nothing.

He set his teeth, climbed a little higher, grabbed the backpack, and gave it a hard pull, snapping his wrist up in one fluid motion.

The backpack came free.

So did Jake's grip.

The momentum of the pull carried Jake farther away from the fence than he could compensate for, and his body weight began to drag him down. Instinctively, he tightened the hand holding the fence as he tried to contort his body against the laws of physics and back toward stability. Instead, his gripping hand became a pivot as his feet slipped off the fence and between the bars.

Louisa stifled a scream. The backpack landed at her feet.

Pain shot through Jake's wrist as it bent in a most unnatural direction. He wasn't sure, but it felt like it might be swelling up at that very moment. For a few grotesque seconds, his injured hand was all that kept him from falling the six-foot distance to the fence's brick base. Finally, Jake had the presence of mind to bring his other hand around to ease the load. He forced his legs back through the bars onto his side of the fence until his feet found the solid iron. Now that he was vertical once again, he jumped lightly backward onto the ground.

He came up clutching his wrist, wanting to put immediate pressure on it. He squeezed it tightly, feeling the thorns of a sprain and the comfort of compression simultaneously. "That hurt."

"Are you okay?" she said. "What's wrong with your wrist? Is it broken?"

"I don't think so." He gingerly tried to move his hand up and down. Agony struck him as his wrist screamed its disapproval of Jake's attempt. "No, it's probably just a sprain. Hurts, though."

"So what do we do?"

"We keep going. It shouldn't get in the way." Jake removed his gloves with his teeth. His injured wrist was his right, so he tenderly used it to remove the watch from his left wrist and hold it out to Louisa. "Here, can you put this on me?"

"Sure." She wrapped one of his gloves around his wrist to act as crude compression, then cinched it tightly but comfortably with his watch. "That feel okay?"

He tested it out with a rotation of his hand. "Not bad," he lied. "A little better." He glanced at his watch: 9:25. "We better get going. We have to get into the mausoleum before the guards come back." He winced a bit. "I mean, I would like to hear how they explain the Jedi master death thing, but I guess it will have to remain a mystery to me."

Jake snatched up the backpack in his good hand and led Louisa along the fence line a few yards until they came to the mausoleum. They looked around for signs of security or unwelcome visitors. The coast was clear.

They stepped away from the fence and toward the shrine to Benjamin Cruz. Jake approached the keypad and prepared to enter the combination. But suddenly he came to the crushing realization that he was dealing with a tricky combination of his own: the combination of a night without sleep and the sudden pain of his wrist. For the life of him, he couldn't remember what he was supposed to punch in.

"What's wrong, Jake?" Louisa asked. "Type it in."

He looked at her quizzically. "I — I can't remember."

"What?"

"The combination. I don't remember it."

"Well, surely you wrote it down."

He smiled ironically. He hadn't. The second time today he'd gotten burned by not writing down a number he needed. And this time there was no one he could call.

"Jake. You have to write these things down."

"Yeah, I know that, Professor! Lesson learned."

"Easy."

"Sorry."

They both stared at the keypad. Jake was at a loss.

"Would Jeremy know it?" Louisa said.

Jake's eyes brightened. Yes, Jeremy would know it. "Call him."

Louisa nodded and reached into her jacket pocket for her cell phone. She flipped it open and dialed the number. As it rang, decided he was definitely going to get himself a cell phone tomorrow.

"Jeremy? It's Louisa. . . . Hey, this is kind of silly, but Jake doesn't remember the combination to the mausoleum. . . . No, he didn't write it down."

Whatever Jeremy was saying, it was loud enough that strains of it reached Jake's ears. Jake immediately took offense. "Hey, tell him if he has a problem with that, he should've been there last night. It's only 'cause I'm so sleepy that—" Louisa shushed him with a stern finger.

"Okay. Okay, we'll try it." She looked at Jake. "He doesn't have it offhand; he thought you wrote it down. But he thinks he remembers it. Try 27-42-31."

Jake punched in the code.

Nothing.

"No good. Try again."

Louisa listened to the phone again, then spoke to Jake. "That's all he's got."

"Great. Just great." Jake almost kicked the building, but decided he didn't need a broken toe in addition to the wrist.

"Wait a minute, wait a minute." A figurative light bulb had come on above Louisa's head. "When did Papa order this?"

"I think it was, like, two years ago."

She smiled. "I was there when you guys cracked the combination. I thought the numbers sounded familiar."

"Huh?"

"Try 24-27-31."

Jake punched it in. A slight click let them know to look door-ward just in time to see the heavy brass panel open slightly.

They were in.

"Wow," Jake said. "That's some memory."

"It's simple. That's how old my brothers and I were two years ago."

"That's . . . creepily ironic," Jake said.

"Yeah, it —" Louisa was cut off by the sound of a souped-up golf cart in the distance.

"We'd better . . ."

"Yeah."

They wasted no time walking to the door. They both gave one last look around, then pulled the door open wide enough to squeeze into the mausoleum. Jake, with his one good hand, and Louisa, with both of hers, grabbed the door and gave it a heave toward themselves, stepping backward at the same time.

It swung shut and locked, bringing complete darkness with it.

S

"I guess your dad cared more about you guys than you thought," Jake said as he felt through the backpack for a flashlight. "Strange he'd use your ages as a combination."

"Yeah, to a room we were never meant to go into."

"Maybe it was a test." His hand found a flashlight, and he brought it out of the backpack to turn it on. "Maybe he wanted you guys to come after the money." Despite the pain, Jake used the thumb from his injured hand to press on the flashlight's power button. It was tougher to turn on than he remembered, probably because he didn't have a whole lot of strength in that hand. "Maybe he wanted to see which one of you . . ." Finally the button gave and light illuminated the small room. ". . . was brightest."

"Very dramatic of you," she said. "Did you draw that speech out because you couldn't find the flashlight?"

"Couldn't get it turned on."

"Ahh." She took the flashlight from him, an easy enough task since they were alarmingly close to one another. The beam from the flashlight reflected off the mausoleum's gleaming marble interior surprisingly well, brightening the room considerably, but without the harsh directness that usually comes with a flashlight.

Louisa shined the beam into the backpack so Jake could find the other one they'd put in there. Her head was right next to his, so close he could smell her shampoo. Lavender. It's supposed to help you go to sleep, but Jake found himself more awake than he'd been all night.

"You could be right, you know," Louisa said. "He could've been testing us."

"Could be." He produced the other flashlight and traded Louisa for the one that was already on. "You ready to do this?"

Louisa nodded. "It's weird," she said. "I thought this would be different. That doesn't really seem like my father in that casket over there, or that there's really anyone in it at all. This doesn't seem like a mausoleum—just a stuffy, tight little room with shiny walls and a really tall couch in the middle of it."

"Is that good?" Jake asked.

"Let's find out." Louisa reached toward the casket handle, grasped it, and, after taking a deep breath, opened the final home of her father's body.

Jake purposefully shined his flashlight away from Louisa's face and onto Benjamin Cruz's. He wanted to give her some time to herself, time to get the closure that she needed. The flashlight's beam took on a different appearance in the light-absorbing coffin. Benjamin Cruz's face had never looked more grotesque. He took a good hard look at the dead man, and, in the quiet interlude, began to daydream.

He thought of his money ocean, where he'd been adrift in his dream. He saw Benjamin Cruz, in his coffin, sitting at the bottom, doing nothing. Immersed in a sea of wealth that went on without him. He saw Louisa on top in her boat, far from her father.

And he saw himself treading water again, knowing the shark attack was coming. He was back where he'd started his dream — only this time, he knew what to do.

He swam toward the boat.

Powerful stroke after powerful stroke, each one taking him closer and closer. He covered the distance in record time, as if the boat itself was drawing him in, and he was only going through the motions. He now knew that the boat — or rather, its occupant — had been tugging on him the whole time, and that he'd just been resisting. Now that he was going toward it, the trip was easy.

He reached the boat and hauled himself in.

Louisa was not there.

It was a dude who looked exactly like Jesus.

Hmmm. This was unexpected.

"Where's Louisa? How'd you get here?" Jake asked.

"I walked," He replied.

"Naturally."

The Jesus-looking dude laid his hand on Jake's shoulder and looked into his eyes. "Jake, it's time to give it up, son."

Jake looked back into those deep, deep eyes, simultaneously longing to dive into them and resisting that urge with everything in him.

"You know what needs to happen," the Jesus-looking dude said. "What are you going to do?"

A mighty sob stirred Jake awake from his reverie, and he noticed that Louisa was crying voluminously. Startled at his strange vision, he put his arm, damaged wrist and all, around Louisa and gave her the strongest hug his injury would allow. She leaned her head against his torso and put her hands to her face. And she wept.

"Jake, is this wrong?" Louisa's muffled voice sounded broken.

"What?"

"I'm just thinking that we shouldn't be doing this, Jake."

Jake was shaken from his daydream, but not so shaken that he didn't know how to handle this. He put the Jesus-looking dude out of mind and got to the business at hand.

He released Louisa and turned himself to look into her face. He shined the flashlight against the wall to create some decent indirect lighting. She had to be able to see his face.

"Louisa," he said, "I know this is tough, this situation, but think about all that we know."

"I know, Jake, I'm just—"

"No, hold on," he said, giving her shoulder a minor squeeze, which was more than he should've. His wrist fought back. "Louisa, this is what your father wanted. Maybe he didn't want it to happen *exactly* like this, but come on: the will that has the loophole, the new will that said this money was supposed to go to you, the combination that has everything to do with you and your brothers." He opened his eyes wide in earnest. "I mean, it sounds like your dad wanted you to get this money from the get-go and then decided, after you guys, you know, patched things up, to just give you the money anyway."

Louisa's shoulders and head sank.

"Don't you see, Louisa? This is your father's gift to you." He let go of her shoulder, reached down, and gently guided her head up so her eyes met his. "Take it."

She leaned her head against him once again, and his arm instinctively went back around her shoulders in a half embrace. They stood there for a few minutes, Jake propping up Louisa, Louisa looking down at her Papa.

More lavender hair, made all the more powerful by the warmth of Louisa's body against his. Maybe she really was worth more than the money. Maybe they should just split, leave the old man to rest in peace. Maybe Jake was just tricking himself into believing something that wasn't true.

And then Jake felt Louisa steel herself. She glanced at his watch. "We'd better hurry up and crack this safe. We still have a lot to do.

Maybe not. "You okay?" Jake said.

She gave a simple nod. "I feel a lot better." She looked at his arm, still around her shoulder. "Now."

Jake gave her a slight squeeze, then dropped his arm and set his attention on the safe. He had to lean over the casket to read the numbers, so he handed the backpack to Louisa and bent over the body. She shone her flashlight onto the dial.

"I remember this one," she said. "Fortunately, I wrote it down and memorized it when Tom read it to me."

"I'll take it into consideration, this strange practice of 'writing things down,'" he replied. "Fortunately, I remember it, too." Jake worked the combination easily and had the door open within seconds.

There it was.

The envelope that would change Jake's future.

The one on his desk matched it surprisingly well.

Jake found himself at a loss for breath. He forced himself to inhale through his nose and exhale through his mouth. He reached in and carefully took the envelope in his hand, passed it to Louisa, and closed the safe. He stood upright, took hold of the casket handle, and lowered the lid back into place.

"That was easy," she said.

"Yeah, I thought it would be harder. I keep expecting arrows to shoot out of the walls or a big boulder to come rolling after us."

Louisa shined her flashlight around the enclosure. The effect reminded Jake of a disco ball at a roller skating rink, only a lot faster. "Nope. Nothing."

"Okay, then. That's that. Stage One complete." Jake rummaged through the backpack.

"Did you really just say, 'Stage One complete'?"

"Yeah. Kind of makes it feel more official. More caperish, you know?"

She chuckled and shook her head.

"Stop laughing so much," Jake said, "or you'll use up all our air."

"It is getting stale in here, isn't it? Let's get going."

"Hold on," Jake said. "Aha." He looked up from the backpack, removing the long, thin glass jar he'd bought at the hardware store, emptied of its matches. He'd taken those out at the funeral home.

He quickly opened the lid and held the jar out to Louisa, who rolled up the envelope and inserted it. Perfect fit. Because of Jake's injured hand, Louisa replaced the lid and handed it back to him.

"Cinch it tight," he said.

"I cinched it as tightly as I could."

"Tighter."

"Okay." She gave the lid a death grip and torqued it shut with all the strength she had in her.

"Much better." He held out a length of fishing line, about two feet long, ending in a hangman's noose Jeremy had tied into it. "Now. Put this on it."

8

They made it out of the mausoleum without a hitch, Jake finding the button much more quickly this time. The door opened slightly. Jake put his ear to the crack, and upon hearing nothing, hurried out. Louisa was close behind, eyes roving around to make sure no one was watching. One hefty push later, the door was closed and locked, looking very undisturbed.

As Louisa hustled around to the back of the structure, Jake took a few tentative steps away from the mausoleum to avoid the moon shadows it was casting in his direction. He peered at his watch, cocking it at an angle to catch the moonlight on the face: 9:57. They'd spent longer in there than he'd planned. Better get moving. He raced to the scooter, where Louisa was just flipping her cell phone shut.

"Is he ready?" Jake asked.

"Ready."

"Good. Time to execute Stage Two."

"Should I synchronize my watch, Commander?"

Stage Two Gets Dodgy

PRINCESS TANGERINE'S HIGH-PITCHED engine motored Jake and Louisa across the cemetery landscape. They'd gone in a wide arc away from the mausoleum and now were approaching the gravesite coordinates Jake had given Santiago over the phone. They were there easily two hours before they were supposed to be.

So was Santiago.

As Jake and Louisa approached, they saw two men feverishly digging in the precise location Jake had named. A battery-powered work light sat on the ground, casting a wide beam that backlit the men in silhouette. Peering through the moon-illuminated night, Jake made out the rungs of an extension ladder leaning against the outer side of the enclosure and deduced they'd scaled the cemetery fence as well.

The men heard the scooter approaching and stopped their work. Funny, Jake had expected them to scatter when they heard what sounded like a golf cart containing security guards coming their way. Something wasn't right here. Jake eased up on the accelerator, forcing a motion his wrist didn't want to make. In order to ease suspicion from Santiago and make nothing seem out of order, Jake had removed his rudimentary wrist compression and replaced his watch on the correct arm. Driving the scooter, he wished he could have the compression back—it would've made the twists of the accelerator handle easier. The pain felt like a dozen ball-peen hammers. She was a demanding mistress, Princess Tangerine.

Jake slowed the bike to a stop and killed the motor.

Santiago was already stepping toward them, covering the few yards between the grave and the scooter with a handful of strides. "Well, well. The little mortuary man brought along my dear sister. I should've known I couldn't trust you, Jake."

Jake stood stock still as he tried to put on some bravery. "We're just here to help. Get you out of here faster."

Santiago chuckled. "You expect me to believe that? You're here," he looked at his watch, "two hours early."

"So are you," Louisa said coldly. "Planning on digging up the grave, taking the money, and disappearing—leaving us to hold the shovel?"

"I guess you just can't trust me to show up on time next Thanksgiving."

"Look," said Jake, "we want the same thing as you. Just let us help dig. We'll get our fifteen grand and go."

"I don't think so."

"Are you trying to mess with me?" Jake was acting tougher now than he'd probably ever acted in his life. Come on, Santiago, step up.

S

Jeremy sat in the hearse, trying very hard to avoid looking conspicuous. A dim blue light shone from the vehicle's interior while he wrapped up his current cell phone conversation.

"Just some suspicious activity," he said in what he hoped sounded like an older man's voice. "I think someone's messing around out there at the cemetery. There was a ladder and a light. Looked like they were digging something up."

He looked in the rearview mirror at some teenagers walking by for a late night stroll. Shouldn't they be eating pizza and watching a horror movie? The squawking in his ear stopped. It was his turn to talk.

"So you're going to check it out? Thank you, officer. I'm tired of these kids ruining the neighborhood."

δ

Santiago was raging angry, inches from Jake's face. "You think you can come out here and try to cheat me out of my money?"

"You're trying to cheat me out of *my* money!" Jake was hot, and he was beginning to feel himself cross a line from acting to *acting*. He refused to back away from Santiago, even though the work light was shining directly in his eyes. Still, he made sure to keep himself between Louisa and her crazy brother.

Santiago's steely face pulsed, veins bulging from his neck. He took a deep breath, then reached into his jacket and removed a very shiny, very handsome, very deadly Ruger handgun.

And touched it to Jake's forehead.

So *that's* why they hadn't run when Jake and Louisa had approached.

"Don't move."

Jake's eyes widened as he froze. Louisa, slightly behind him, clutched the backpack in terror. This was definitely not part of the noble quest.

Without taking his eyes off Jake, Santiago called out. "Marcos!"

The other man was still standing by the fresh hole he'd helped dig, but had raised his shovel off the ground and was holding it like a weapon. He looked ready to pounce on Jake and Louisa if something went wrong. "*Sí?*"

"I think these two are up to no good," Santiago said coolly. "In fact, I fear for my very safety. Please search them and their belongings for weapons."

"*Bueno.*" Marcos set down the shovel and started with Jake, patting down his jacket, looking in his belt for obvious fire-arms. He moved to Louisa and patted her down, too, gently and not lasciviously. He removed the backpack from her hands and searched it, using a flashlight he'd taken from his own jacket. He peered inside, looking annoyed, and then upended the backpack and dumped its meager contents onto the ground. He shone the light on the pile and looked at Santiago.

"Flashlights? Gardening gloves?" Santiago's suspicions were confirmed. "You came here to dig! You came here to cheat me!"

"We just came to help! We don't even have any shovels."

"Oh, come on. The landscape shed is just over there! You know the groundskeeper. He's probably in on it with you!"

Jake shut his mouth, wanting Santiago to believe it, but not wanting to get shot.

Santiago turned his attention back to Marcos. "Search the moped."

"It's a scooter," Jake said. He was so used to hearing people mislabel Princess Tangerine as a moped that he automatically fought for her honor as a knee-jerk reaction to the offense.

Santiago didn't appreciate it. He pushed the gun barrel's cold metal harder into Jake's perspiring forehead. To Marcos: "Search it."

Marcos went over to the scooter and felt along the edges of the body, underneath the footstep, the wheel wells. He pushed a few buttons and tested the latches. He opened the glove box, a narrow compartment located just under the handlebars. He peered into it with his flashlight for a moment, then closed it.

"*Esta limpio,*" he said. "Sunglasses. Paint. *Es todo.*"

Santiago removed the gun from Jake's forehead and lowered it until it was pointing at Jake's chest.

That's it, Santiago. Consider the evidence.

‑

The hearse's interior lit up again as Jeremy dialed one last number. He listened for a single ring, then ended the call and flipped the phone back down.

The hearse was dark once more.

‑

Louisa's cell phone buzzed in her jacket pocket one time, but did not ring. She looked at Jake and gave the tiniest of nods.

‑

"You're lucky," Santiago said. "Instead of getting fifteen thousand dollars, you get to live." He gestured toward the scooter with the gun. "Go."

"Jake," said Louisa, grabbing his arm, "let's go."

Jake looked at her, reading her eyes. "No," he said. "I don't like that arrangement, Santiago. I came to get my money, and I'm going to get it."

Santiago cocked the gun and swung it back to Jake. "If I see you again," he said, "I will not repeat this offer."

Louisa let out a tiny scream. "Jake! Come *on!*"

Jake wordlessly followed Louisa to the scooter and climbed aboard. He stared at Santiago with all the machismo he could muster, then pressed the electric start button, and Princess Tangerine's engine sputtered to life. Jake put the scooter in gear, eased out on the clutch, and gave it some gas.

A few gears later they were speeding down a cemetery path, the ghostly white flashes of headstones whirring by. Then, open space, and the end of their time on the path.

"Time to go off-roadin'," Jake said, guiding the scooter onto the freshly mown grass that stretched all the way to an unused corner of the cemetery.

"Good job back there, Jake," Louisa hollered over the minor wind noise.

"Same to you."

"Were you nervous?"

"Nah. I've had a gun stuck into my forehead dozens of times. Hundreds."

"You're such a liar."

Jake smiled. "By the way," he said, "Stage Two complete."

"Couldn't resist, could you?"

S

Santiago and Marcos watched the scooter disappear into the blackness. Santiago was still agitated at the nerve of that little man to try to outsmart him. He hadn't gotten where he was by being stupid. He was glad to have a reason to show off his new gun, though. He'd just recently gotten it and was eager to pull it on someone. It was with imminent satisfaction that that someone had been Jake.

He ordered Marcos back to work. "*A trabajar!*" Marcos dutifully obeyed, stepping into the roughly two-foot hole they'd already dug. Santiago joined him, and they were back to work.

They heard a high-pitched engine approaching.

Unbelievable. The little funeral man was coming *back*?

Suddenly, heavy spotlights shone on them from three directions.

A siren let out a chirp.

A voice, through a loudspeaker, said, "Stay where you are. Put your hands up."

Santiago had no choice but to comply.

A Capture and an Escape

PRINCESS TANGERINE EDGED her way through a narrow gap in the cemetery fence and onto a rough path that cut through the nicely wooded greenbelt behind Brownstone Avenue Cemetery. From here, they were only about a hundred yards away from freedom, provided that the scooter's single headlight could find the way out.

Louisa finally dared to look back and saw a bright light turn on just as they disappeared into the trees. "Security's there!" she yelled into Jake's ear.

"Great!"

It had all worked as planned, and Jake was ecstatic. Despite the hang-ups, metaphorical and literal, he'd managed to pull off this noble quest and come out with only a sprained wrist. Too fun.

The gun had been an unexpected wrinkle, and Jake would've been lying if he'd said it hadn't scared him to death. He'd almost lost it all right there. Frankly, he'd nearly wet himself. But he'd maintained his cool (and the sanctity of his bladder), and now he, Jake Abrams, was driving away with a ton of money *and* the girl.

He was starting to come down from the initial adrenaline rush of having a loaded firearm touching his person. His body was unwinding and his mind was unraveling as he congratulated himself on his success.

Jake tried not to be too hasty, though. They weren't out of the woods yet (somewhere in his subconscious, he noted the irony that phrase implied), and they needed to be careful if they were going to see the path that led out of the wooded greenbelt.

And then he saw it. The straight line, leading through the remainder of the trees. The straight line that would take them home much, much richer. Nothing left to do now but gun the throttle and get the heck out of there.

It was at this precise moment that his fatigue chose to return with a vengeance. Jake meant to shift up to the next highest gear.

Instead, he shifted down.

This, naturally, was a mistake.

The second he reengaged the clutch, Princess Tangerine shuddered in midscoot, jerking wildly backward. This had happened to Jake a couple times before, but he'd always been by himself, and healthy. Now here, with a sprained wrist and an extra passenger, he wasn't prepared. He tried to maintain control, but the force of the scooter's sudden backward motion was too much for him. He had to lean to the right to compensate for his wrist's inability to make sudden moves, and in so doing he lost control of the clutch.

Jake Abrams and Louisa Cruz tumbled over the handlebars and skidded to a stop next to a tall maple tree.

§

Santiago had nowhere to go—four uniformed security officers were closing in on him from two directions.

The loudspeaker rang out again. "Put your hands behind your head and lie facedown on the ground."

He obeyed.

They were on him in seconds. He felt the handcuffs tighten first around his left wrist, then his arms pulled behind his back, then the other cuff on the right wrist. How had cemetery security known to be there? He answered his own question immediately. His dear sister and her boyfriend must have had something to do with this.

"There were more of us," Santiago said. "Two more. They just rode a moped away from here, in that direction." He gestured with his nose.

"Sure, pal," said the officer. "I didn't hear nothing—"

"I mean it! They drove off on an orange moped, a man and a woman!"

"Right."

"Those are their things. That backpack, the gloves, the flashlights. Right, Marcos?"

"*Sí.*"

"Check it out if you don't believe me."

The officer looked toward the goods, then spoke into his shoulder-mounted radio. "Hey, Stan, we have detained an individual captured during a grave theft attempt."

"Roger that."

The officer stood Santiago to his feet, then sized him up through narrow eyes. "All right, pal. Which way did these so-called people go?"

Santiago nodded his head toward the greenbelt. "Into those trees."

§

"Are you okay?" Louisa asked.

Jake had had the good fortune of having Louisa land directly atop him, so he knew she was probably fine. Oh, he was a wreck, but who cared? That lavender fragrance was darn near surgically implanted now. She leaned against the tree and climbed off of him. Jake gave a groan and rolled over, trying to focus his eyes on Louisa in the dark woods. Nope. Too difficult. The sticky fingers of sleep suddenly weighed slightly less than a spoonful of neutron star, and they were Super Glued to his brain. He closed his eyes again.

"Good night."

"Jake. Jake." She smacked his cheek with her hand. "Wake up!"

Startled, he opened his eyes and regained awareness of what had just happened. "Princess! Jeremy! We need to go."

"Yeah. Let me help you up." Louisa aided Jake into a standing position, brushing off his shoulders and back with her hands. "Does it hurt anywhere?"

"Not too bad," Jake lied. It did hurt. He must've absorbed the fall with his left knee, which smarted beyond belief. He tested some weight on his leg and felt a shooting pain not just in his knee, but also in his ankle. Gingerly, he knelt down to investigate and noticed that his ankle seemed much bigger than it should be. He tested it with his fingers and felt swelling. "Well, looks like I got a sprained left ankle to go with my sprained right wrist."

"At least you're balanced."

Jake gave a disgusted chuckle. "How's the Princess?"

"Don't know. I was worried about you."

Jake hobbled over to the scooter and saw immediately that she wouldn't be heading out of the greenbelt on her own steam.

The cable that operated the clutch had been torn away from its connection on the bike, severing it roughly. It must have caught on something—a rock or branch—when the scooter hit the ground.

"Well, Princess isn't going anywhere without a clutch. Looks like we're walking out."

"Okay," Louisa said. "Can you handle it?"

"I don't have much choice."

Using his good hand, Jake tipped the scooter from the ground back onto its wheels. Fortunately, nothing was bent or broken in the rolling or steering departments. Princess Tangerine looked less than beautiful, but she could still move.

Jake grasped one side of the scooter's handlebars, Louisa the other, and together they began to make their way down the path through the trees.

§

Marcos was flat-out sulking. It was bad enough that he and Santi had gotten caught, but they'd gotten caught by *security guards*. Not even real police. He'd done time—hard time—for grand theft. Twice. And now he was getting busted by rent-a-cops? *No bueno.*

And this kid messing with him. Trying to do the cuffs all professional. Kid's probably on summer vacation from the eighth grade, trying to make enough to buy a new video game or something.

Freakin' kids.

Santi was mad. When the guards found the gun on him, Marcos knew it was over. He chuckled to himself. He was only an accomplice, and he hadn't done anything really criminal since last time he got out. Santi, though . . . he wouldn't be back for a while.

The guy checking out Santi called out to the kid. "Hendricks, come here." Kid walked like the uniform didn't fit him. Marcos suppressed a shudder at the chill that had descended on the cemetery as the night had progressed. He didn't realize how much heat the work light had generated until the security guards had moved him away from it and cuffed him to their golf cart.

He was handcuffed to a golf cart. He hoped he could keep this fact to himself when he went back to the big house for the third time.

Hendricks approached the head guard. "Yes, sir?"

"What are you doing right now?"

"I've detained the other suspect and secured him to the golf cart," Hendricks said.

"Okay," said the officer. "See that line of trees down there?"

"Yes, sir."

"Check it out once you're finished. Looking for an orange moped with a man and a woman on it."

"Yes, sir!"

Hendricks looked back at Marcos, smiled, pulled a flashlight from his belt, and set off on foot for the greenbelt a hundred yards away.

Kids.

S

It was slow going for Jake and Louisa, since scooters don't roll nearly as fast as they drive. But they plodded steadily, Jake bravely not wincing with every other step. He'd even managed to suppress the limp most of the way.

"Do you think the money's okay?" Louisa asked.

"I hope so. That was a nasty tumble."

"It's snug, though, right? In there? Think it cracked? It couldn't crack. Should we check?"

"We might as well just head back," Jake said. "We'll know soon enough."

They wheeled the scooter through the last of the trees and stood on the edge of the park. Jeremy's hearse was waiting at the curb.

❦

Hendricks eyed the break in the fence at the edge of the greenbelt. He stooped down and examined the ground with his flashlight, hoping for a clue, but the earth was too firmly packed to yield any information. He reached for his radio.

"Stan? This is Hendricks. I see a break in the fence down here, and a path leading into the trees, but no moped and no suspects. Shall I proceed?"

"Negative, Hendricks," the guard replied. "We hooked up with the police database and ran these guys' IDs. The leader has quite the history. No way was he telling the truth. He was just trying to do something—anything—to keep from getting busted."

The rookie sighed, not really wanting to go back to his world of paperwork. Maybe he could stay out here just a little longer? Just to see what he could find? "Actually," he said, "I think I hear something in the trees back there. I'm going to go check it out."

His radio crackled. "All right, go ahead."

"Roger. Proceeding." Hendricks drew his revolver, held it up, and stepped onto the path.

$\mathscr{S}$

Jake was almost ready to collapse on the suddenly comfortable-looking grass when Jeremy came rushing up to him and Louisa. He nudged Jake out of the way and took control of the scooter-pushing duties. Jake began a more brisk walk toward the hearse.

"What happened?" Jeremy asked.

"We fell off," Jake replied. "I missed a gear, and . . . I'll tell you in the car, I promise."

"Well, let's go, then. There've been some kids wandering around the neighborhood, and I think they're a little too interested in the hearse."

$\mathscr{S}$

Hendricks thought he might've heard voices, but he couldn't be sure. He was being overly cautious, he knew, but he had no idea what would be out there, and truth be told, he was scared. He took step after tentative step along the path, partially hoping he'd find something, partially hoping he wouldn't.

But those sure sounded like voices. And they were fading.

$\mathscr{S}$

Between the three of them, they managed to wrestle Princess Tangerine back into the hearse. Jeremy had thoughtfully brought along a thick blanket to cover the hearse floor.

"No drips."

§

"Hendricks, you found anything yet?" His radio cackled loudly into the quiet of the surrounding trees.

"No, sir." He didn't want to add that he was almost to the other edge of the greenbelt. He figured he should've been there long ago.

"Okay, come back, then."

Disappointed but relieved, Hendricks took one last look at the trees' edge before heading back down the path.

§

Jake, Louisa, and Jeremy climbed into the hearse, quietly shutting their doors so as not to wake the neighbors. Jeremy started the engine, put the hearse in gear, and stepped on the accelerator.

§

Hendricks heard it. Clear as day. An engine starting. They had a getaway car! He hurried back toward the trees, hoping to catch a glimpse, some type of clue.

He burst through the line of trees and looked furiously in both directions. He heard a distant car engine, but whatever the vehicle was, it was already gone, and he couldn't tell where.

Shoulders slumped, he began the long walk back into the cemetery.

The Envelope, Please

THE RIDE BACK to the funeral home was a quiet one for Jake. He elected to let Louisa tell the story of their adventure while he sat in the back and focused his attention on not hurting. At this point he was glad they were through and on their way back. He looked forward to a long night's rest, a long morning of sleeping in, and a visit to the drugstore to get a big bottle of aspirin and some real bandages for his injuries.

The rhythm of driving put him to sleep—an exhausted, dreamless sleep that seemed to last only an instant before he woke to a violent shove on the shoulder. Jeremy. "Ease up, man," Jake said.

"Sorry, dude. You were out. I've been shaking you for like five minutes."

Jake rubbed his eyes with his left hand, willing the sleep out of them. They'd arrived at the funeral home. "Okay," he said. "Let's get her out."

The three of them made their way to the back of the hearse

and again wrestled the scooter to the ground, mostly pulling it out by the blanket. The crispness of the night air brought renewed vigor to Jake's body, and now the excitement of counting the haul began to come over him.

He wheeled Princess Tangerine to the sidewalk, where he normally parked, then removed the key from the ignition. Jeremy and Louisa crowded around as he inserted the key into the back of the seat.

"Time to work some gas cap mojo," Jake said, for no real reason.

Despite his persistent fatigue, Jake performed the snake-charming ritual to get the seat open and all the way forward. He delicately unscrewed the gas cap, finding a thin strand of fishing line coming from inside the gas tank. He gripped the line in his bad hand as he finished removing the cap, then pulled it directly up from the tank.

On the end of the line hung a narrow glass jar with an envelope in it.

Jake breathed a sigh of relief. "Catch of the day. Should I throw it back?"

Louisa, too, looked relieved. "I'm just glad it didn't crack." She took the jar from Jake's hand and inspected it. "Nope. Nothing."

They admired it for a few seconds before Louisa said, "Let's take it inside."

In they went. "Hey, where's Chiffon been today?" Jake asked. Jeremy gave a shrug. Louisa didn't know either. "Crazy kid."

When Jake first started working at White Hall, he'd had to come up after hours once to make a lengthy long distance phone call. He'd expected the place to look all foreboding and creepy, what with it being a funeral home at night and all. It surprised him when it just looked like a dark building.

And so it was now, the moonlight streaming through the front windows and illuminating a path to the Interview Room. The trio hurried in and Jeremy flipped the light switch, banishing the darkness. Jake went to a storage area in the back and, after a little rummaging, returned with some plain letter envelopes and some duct tape. He delicately tore off some strips of the tape and then, after rolling an envelope around his wrist like a bracelet, wrapped the tape around the envelope as tightly as he dared.

Chiffon had a first aid kit in her drawer, and Jake cursed himself for the time he used the compression bandages out of it as wrist-bands to complete his tennis player costume at last year's company Halloween party. He knew he should've put those back.

On his way back to the Interview Room, Jake stopped by his workstation. He clicked on the lights and eyeballed the manila envelope, still resting on his desk. Though it had no features, no face, it looked extraordinarily guilty.

Jake knew what to do. He'd known it all along.

He hobbled to his desk, picked up the envelope . . .

And threw it in the trash.

§

When Jake got back to the Interview Room, Louisa had set the jar on the edge of the table, and now she and Jeremy were sitting on either side, looking at it with awe and trepidation. Jake rolled over a chair and joined them.

"I'm nervous," she said.

"Go ahead, open it," Jake said. "How much did you make?"

She furrowed her brow, took a deep breath, then picked up

the jar and worked to undo the cinch she'd given it back in the mausoleum, which seemed like days ago.

It wouldn't budge.

Jake laughed. "That thing's stuck like a new jar of pickles."

"Maybe we should tap on the edges with the back of a knife," Jeremy said.

"You two manly men are welcome to try," Louisa said, thrusting it toward Jake and Jeremy.

Jake held up his recently taped wrist. "Can't."

"I still think we should tap on the edges," Jeremy said. "I can go find a butter knife or something."

"Typical," Louisa muttered, going back to work on the jar. She gripped it tightly and threw all her weight into the task.

Pop!

The lid came undone suddenly, momentarily throwing Louisa off balance. She quickly recovered and set the jar on the countertop. Steadying herself, she reached two fingers into the jar and gripped the rolled-up envelope between them, pulling gently until she'd freed it from its round glass prison.

"Open it up and see what Papa got you for Christmas," Jake said.

Louisa nodded and took a deep breath. She reached her finger underneath the seal and slid it along the length of the envelope. She opened it, saw a small stack of papers inside, and removed them. She flipped through the stack, her face registering first bewilderment, then shock, then anger.

"What is it?" Jake asked.

Without a word, Louisa showed them the papers, rifling through them like a professional blackjack dealer.

They were all blank.

Louisa Goes Nuts

LOUISA WAS PUSHING the Volvo to its limits as she and Jake sped toward Edgar Kimbrough's house.

"Look, Louisa," Jake said, "there's no use going off half-cocked. You don't know for sure what happened."

Seeing blanks in the envelope had messed with Jake's head in unimaginable ways. To think that he'd almost wound up on the wrong side of a double cross—no money and no Louisa. That wouldn't have been *Potato Thief* at all. It put him in a particularly forgiving mood.

"It had to be Edgar, Jake. No one else knew what was going on."

"Maybe your dad set it up like that," Jake said. "Like it's a test, to see who would be smart enough to get the fortune."

Louisa momentarily took her eyes off the road to send Jake a disgusted glare. All he heard was the sound of air rushing past his slightly cracked window (to keep him awake) and the gunning of an engine being pushed beyond normal driving capacity by a half-crazed Hispanic woman who wasn't thinking clearly.

"All I'm saying," Jake said, enjoying the irony, "is that it isn't always a good idea to assume the worst about people. Maybe you need to give Edgar the benefit of the doubt."

"I'm not assuming."

"Also, you're driving angry, and I am afraid for my already bruised self."

Louisa began muttering under her breath in Spanish, but she slowed down enough to make Jake a little more comfortable. He strained his memory to full capacity trying to recall his ninth-through eleventh-grade foreign language classes. From what he could tell, Louisa was praying. Something about God preventing her from committing the sin of murder? He couldn't really tell.

"Louisa, I don't know much about God, but I'm pretty sure He'd want you to calm down."

She sped up. "Jake, I refuse to calm down. He stole from us! He stole from my family! That money was not his!"

"Well," Jake countered, "technically it wasn't yours, either."

"Stop being so practical. This is the spirit of the law here!"

He nodded. "You have a point."

"Thank you!"

"I just don't like to see you like this," Jake said. "All out of control. You're always so peaceful. It's just strange."

"Well, I don't think this is a time for peace."

Jake turned in his seat to face her. "So you're just going to barge into Kimbrough's house and say, 'Hey, you stole my money!'?"

"Yes."

"And what are you going to say when he asks you how exactly you know that?"

Jake had expected this point to give her pause, but if it rattled her, he couldn't tell. "I'll think of something," she said.

"Okay."

They drove in silence the rest of the way.

⚜

Jake's first thought as the Volvo pulled into a long, circular driveway was that Edgar Kimbrough lived in a nice house on a nice street in a nice part of town. He gawked at the magnificence of the home. It wasn't a mansion, but it was close.

"Look at all this," Louisa remarked. "Like he needs more money. Like he has to take it from me."

"I think it's kinda cool." The look she gave him—he never wanted to be on the receiving end of it again. "I mean, replace the word 'kinda' with 'very' and the word 'cool' with . . . 'evil.'"

"Come on." She stopped the car behind a late-model Mercedes-Benz, the signature three-pronged logo flashily reflecting the Volvo's headlights. Louisa threw open her door.

Jake took a little more caution extricating himself from the car. He gestured toward the Benz. "Nice ride. I guess he can afford it though, huh?"

Louisa was already striding toward the front door. She stopped and looked back. "That isn't Edgar's." She took a few small steps toward the vehicle. "But I recognize it. From somewhere."

"Car of your dreams, maybe?"

"Oh, come on."

They walked up a winding path toward the front of the Tudor-style home, its sharply angled, perpendicular features virtually ablaze with security lighting beaming up at it from the perimeter.

"Bruce Wayne live here?" Jake said.

Together they approached the heavy wooden front door, and Louisa pounded the doorbell three times.

No answer.

Louisa pounded the doorbell again, five times.

The porch light suddenly shone from above them, and they heard the deadbolt turning in the lock. The door squeaked open, and there stood Edgar Kimbrough, standing by himself in too much house, answering the door in the dead of night. By the look of his attire, he hadn't been sleeping. He was still fully dressed from the day, without the tie.

"What? What are you doing here, Louisa? Mr. Abrams?"

"Just paying you a visit, Edgar," replied Louisa. "Mind if we come in?" She pushed past him and into the spacious living room, furnished to match the style of the home. Lots of ball-and-claw legs, red and purple velvet upholstery, all blending well with the fabric wallpaper and heavy velvet curtains. Edgar stepped aside to allow Jake in, who hobbled over the threshold with his usable ankle.

"What's going on here, Louisa?" A voice that wasn't Edgar Kimbrough's came from the top of a wide set of thickly carpeted stairs, branching off from the left of the living room, heading upward to a vast second-floor landing that overlooked the high-ceilinged first floor.

Louisa looked up to address the speaker. It was Tom Chenoweth—The Clod, Stall Man—also in full business attire. She did a physical double take. "Uh, hello, Tom," she said. She regained her composure quickly, though. "I wasn't expecting to find you here. Why're you hanging out at Edgar's so late?"

"A personal business deal. He agreed to see me after hours."

"Yes, Louisa," Edgar said. "As you can tell, I don't always need an appointment to talk." He closed the front door and walked into the living room, seating himself on a plush sofa in front of a massive picture window. There was another sofa opposite him, a dark cherry coffee table between the two. He motioned Louisa and Jake toward the other sofa. "So what's on your mind?"

Louisa followed him into the living room, but refrained from taking a seat. "I want to know what happened to my father's money."

Sigh. There went Jake's hopes for diplomacy and tact.

Edgar went motionless, then slowly drew his hand into a tightly clenched fist. "What do you mean, Louisa?" he said.

"What did you do with Papa's money?" Louisa articulated each word, punching them for emphasis.

"Louisa," Tom said, descending the stairs, "what exactly are you getting at?"

"I — I put the envelope in the safe," Edgar said. He pointed at Jake. "As this man can attest."

Jake shrugged. "I saw you put in an envelope, but I didn't see any money."

"So what'd you put in there, Edgar?" Louisa said.

Edgar regained control of his exterior and acted put out. "Louisa. Mr. Abrams. I don't appreciate your tone, nor your accusatory and defamatory statements."

Louisa had kept her eyes on him the whole time, unwavering. She marched closer to him. "You're dodging the question."

"I am doing no such thing. I've told you plainly what I did. Mr. Abrams and another gentleman witnessed it, and I believe that should settle the matter."

"It's missing." Louisa had the words out before Edgar was finished prattling his defense.

"I'm sorry?" he said.

"The money," Louisa said, leaning dangerously close to Kimbrough and thumping him on the chest with her forefinger. "It's missing. And I think you have it."

Without breaking eye contact, Edgar stood, coolly reaching out his hand and removing Louisa's forefinger from his chest. They were now eye to eye. "How, pray tell, do you know the money is missing?"

"Louisa, are you suggesting," Tom said, sidling next to the lawyer, "that Edgar deliberately misled everyone?"

"It's no suggestion, Tom. That's what happened." She reached into her jacket and pulled out the envelope full of blanks. Without looking, she threw it down on the coffee table, where it landed with an accusatory *smack*!

Edgar eyed the envelope, then looked back at Louisa. "Where did you get that?"

"You know."

Edgar looked at the envelope.

Louisa looked at Edgar.

Jake looked back and forth between Louisa and Edgar.

Tom looked bewildered.

Edgar's eyes took on a steely gaze. "You've been up to some criminal activities this evening, Louisa?"

"I guess it takes one to know one, doesn't it, Edgar?" Louisa said. "Isn't that how the saying goes?"

"When did you get this? Your father's will specifically stipulated that this be interred with him."

"But it didn't say anything about staying there," Louisa said. "Guess you missed that loophole, huh?"

Tom backed away slowly.

Edgar didn't flinch. "Nevertheless, your father's will stipulated that his fortune be buried with him, and, loophole or not, you have specifically gone against your father's wishes. He would be ashamed of you, Louisa."

Smack! The slap came quickly, but it came with power. Edgar reeled backward, his hand shooting up to his face, his eyes wide at Louisa's sudden reaction. Louisa reared back her arm to slap him again, but Jake caught her wrist and held firm.

"Don't you even *pretend* to tell me what my father wanted!" Louisa said, her eyes on the verge of reaching flood stage. "I know about the new will. I know what he really wanted to do. You're a criminal, Edgar! You're a criminal and a liar, and I will make you pay!"

Jake turned his head and fixed his eyes on Edgar. "You said it yourself, hoss. The will said the money was supposed to be interred with Mr. Cruz." He nodded his head toward the envelope. "Looks like you're the one who went against someone's wishes."

Edgar sank to the couch. "I have nothing more to say."

Louisa shook her head, about to boil over with anger. "I think you do."

Edgar slowly shook his head in return.

Jake noticed Tom's slow retreat toward the front door and turned toward him. "Where are you going, Mr. Chenoweth?"

Louisa looked at him, too. "Tom? Why aren't you saying anything?"

He looked stung as he stopped. His eyes darted back and forth between Louisa, Jake, and Edgar.

Edgar leaned forward in his seat slightly and narrowed his eyes at Tom. "I don't have anything to say either, Louisa," Tom finally said.

Louisa recoiled as some realization sank in. She closed her eyes and tipped her head as far back as it would go.

Jake didn't know what Louisa had figured out, but he knew it was big. He ambled over to Tom and guided him back into the living room, to the couch. "Why don't you have a seat here, Tom, and we'll figure this whole thing out, huh?"

Tom complied and sat next to Edgar. He began to fidget, his right leg bobbing up and down rapidly.

All three men waited in silence, their eyes on Louisa.

Jake's ankle wished he would sit down. He began to think he would live the rest of his life like this. Standing here, in this moment, waiting for something to happen. This is how it would be. Forever.

Louisa quickly tipped her head back into place, simultaneously opening her eyes and fixing them on her father's former business partners. "How dare you," she said, beginning to pace along the length of the couch opposite the men. "How *dare* you! Men my father trusted, going behind his back for the fortune he built."

Edgar and Tom held their gaze on her, apparently waiting to see what she would do next.

She thrust her finger at Edgar. "You. You want to talk to me about *shame*? He gave you a new will, and you didn't file it. Was that so you could keep the money for yourself? You knew what he really wanted to do with it! Both of you did. Unconscionable. How *dare you*!"

Jake edged in behind Louisa as a show of solidarity. Tom began to object at being included, but Louisa shushed him with a wave of her hand, still pacing.

"I'm not done," she said. "I can't believe this. I cannot believe what I am seeing. I absolutely cannot believe what you two have done." The men withered under the force of her verbal blows. "And now I'm having a hard time believing where my mind is leading me. Did you two have him *killed* so you could get his money? Is that what happened? Couldn't hold off any longer on filing the will, so you just decided to get rid of him?"

Edgar's face came alive with a strange combination of fear and anger. "No! No way. You're father's death was completely natural."

"I'd like to believe that," Louisa said, "but you can understand why I'm having a problem here."

"Louisa," Edgar began, "I can assure you that we—"

"Edgar," Tom said softly.

"Don't 'Edgar' me!" the lawyer said. "You're the one who called her in the first place. If you hadn't called her, this wouldn't have happened!"

"Watch it, Edgar! That envelope proves nothing."

"You had to call her and tell her about the other will! You put ideas in her head!"

"Stop talking!"

Jake and Louisa backed away as the two men faced each other.

"Edgar," Tom said, "think about what you're doing right now. Think about it. You're a lawyer. You know you should stop talking."

"I've had enough, Tom."

"Don't."

"Louisa," Edgar said, turning to her, "there's something you need to know."

"Edgar!"

"Tom, back off!" he snarled. Turning back to Louisa, he settled down and continued. "All that stuff about your father's will and putting his fortune into the casket and all that—it was all true. One hundred percent truth. And what Tom told you about your father wanting to draw up a nullifying will that would instead give all that money to you, that was truth, too."

"Edgar, I'm warning you," Tom said.

"She won't love you, Tom," Edgar said, his voice breaking. "Not after she hears the truth. You have nothing to hide now."

"Stop it," Tom said. "Stop."

"Accept it, Tom. She won't. You can't make her."

Tom said nothing. He buried his head in his hands.

"Louisa," Edgar continued, "the truth is, your father *did* make out that will. And he gave it to me, and . . . and . . . I never filed it."

Jake reached for Louisa and grabbed her around the shoulders. He didn't know what she would do, but he feared it wouldn't be pretty, especially with all the vitriol he'd heard from her on the way there.

"But I swear to you," Edgar said, "we had nothing to do with his passing. Not a single thing."

Jake had thought before that he knew what the word "tension" meant, but he realized now that all his previous definitions had been incomplete. Louisa's eyes shot daggers at Edgar and Tom, and Jake hoped that her brain was working overtime to call off the assault. Otherwise, things were going to get rough.

He hardly dared to breathe. Louisa's mouth was a thin straight line, as if it'd been sewn shut. Her lips were white, and he thought he could hear her teeth grinding.

"Dad?" A female voice Jake didn't recognize came from the landing on the second floor. "Is everything okay?"

Everyone turned to look. Louisa stopped pacing instantly.

"Everything's fine, sweetheart," Edgar said.

"Oh, my gosh!" the girl said. "Louisa! What are *you* doing here?"

Louisa's face underwent an instant transformation from rage to horror to surprise. "Sugar? Elizabeth?"

Elizabeth came bounding down the stairs, her Tinkerbell-themed pajama bottoms nearly tripping her up as she transitioned from stairs to floor. She rushed across the living room to give Louisa a hug. "Oh, my gosh!" she said again. "What are you doing here?"

Louisa looked from Elizabeth to Edgar and back. "Edgar's your father?"

Edgar stood and approached the pair. "Elizabeth? You know Louisa?"

Elizabeth drew in a sharp breath, and a look of nervousness crossed her face. "Yeah," she said quietly.

"How?"

Elizabeth dropped her hands to her sides. "I just do."

Edgar moved toward her, raising his hand to point. "Young lady, I—"

Louisa took a step in between them. "I just met her a few days ago, Edgar. She's had a rough time lately, and she came to me for help."

Edgar had been leaning aggressively toward Louisa and his daughter, but at this news, he took a step back and put his hands up halfway, as if surrendering.

Louisa sank into the sofa she'd paced in front of. As she sat down, Jake seated himself on the arm next to her, unsure of what to do for her.

And then she started to cry. More accurately, she bawled. Boiling tears rolled down her perfect cheeks, turning her nose red, bringing pink splotches to the corners of her eyes.

Jake still thought she looked beautiful.

"What are we doing? What are we doing?" she said, pangs of regret audible in her voice. "Why are we ruining our lives and wasting time on just a little money?"

Edgar and Tom followed her lead and sat back down on their couch. Elizabeth remained standing.

"This?" Louisa said. "This is not what my father would've wanted. Maybe a few years ago, even a few months ago, but not when he died. H-he used to care about money; he did that for a long time. And he saw it got him nowhere. It wasn't until he stopped caring about it that he was happy again. And here I am, caring about it too much, trying to take it for myself. I'm sorry, Papa." She buried her face in her hands and let the tears flow.

Jake reached over to offer some comfort, by way of touch and words. "But Louisa, we didn't do this just for you. We did it to keep the money out of Santiago's hands. We did it for Maria House. Right?"

She looked up at him. "Jake, I don't expect you to understand, but there's a voice — God's voice — speaking inside me. It's tough to explain, but I've heard that voice telling me from the beginning not to go through with this. And I haven't listened to it. I needed to trust God in this, to trust that God would bring Santiago to justice. It wasn't my job."

"But we did it," Jake said. "They busted him. We saw it."

"They busted Sand Crab?" Elizabeth said, clearly overjoyed.

Louisa nodded at her, then turned back toward Jake.

"And that was good," she said, reaching out and taking his

hand, "but was it the best outcome? Is it what God wanted to happen?"

He had no response. Instead, he thought of a dude who looked like Jesus, sitting in a boat, on top of liquid money, telling him what he needed to do.

Louisa tearfully looked at the other two men. "I'm sad. Sad that you two thought you had to do what you did. I'm sure in time I'll forgive you, but I can't say it won't be hard."

They looked sheepishly at the floor.

She looked at Elizabeth. "I'm sad for you, too. Sad for the life you've lived. Sad for the example you're seeing right now. But I'm happy, too. You're on the right track. And that gives me hope. I look at you, and I see the future. I see renewed promises. I see God taking care of you no matter what."

She stood up slowly, pulling Jake up by the hand. "Let's go, Jake. You need some sleep."

"Hold on, Louisa," Edgar said. "What about the money?"

"The money will take care of itself," she replied, looking at Elizabeth. "God takes care of me, too." She put her hand on Elizabeth's shoulder. "You have to tell your father." She looked at Edgar, then back to Elizabeth. "When you're ready."

Louisa walked toward the door, and Jake had never admired her more than he did at that moment.

"Wait," Tom said.

Edgar shifted his eyes over and looked at him. "Yes."

Louisa and Jake stopped walking.

"What were we thinking, Edgar?" Tom said. "Louisa's right. This money belongs to her."

"You're right," Edgar said, with some difficulty. "We got blindsided by the money. We . . . weren't thinking straight."

"Absolutely not," Tom said. "I think this decision makes itself, don't you?"

"Agreed. I'll go get it from the safe." Edgar stood up and walked up the stairs, presumably to some hidden corner of the house where his safe resided.

Tom motioned toward the couches. "Let's all sit down, hmm?"

Jake and Louisa walked back into the living room and sat down on the picture window sofa as Tom and Elizabeth seated themselves on the opposing couch.

Tom closed his eyes and breathed deeply, then reopened them and began. "Louisa, I have to set the record straight here. Edgar and I are both businessmen. We are men of action, and part of the reason we've been successful is because we use all the resources available to us. So when your father came up with this idea to be buried with his fortune, we got to thinking.

"Neither of us liked the idea of that money sitting around completely useless, so we decided that when the unfortunate time came for your father to pass, we would make sure the money didn't go to waste. Edgar put that loophole you spoke of into the will to allow for an easy removal of the money, and we just left it at that.

"And then your father came up with a new will three months ago. One that included you. We tried several times to discuss it, but were never able to connect in the secrecy and privacy that we needed. Meanwhile, Edgar held off filing the will until we could decide what to do about our prior plan." He leaned back, throwing his arms out in exasperation.

"So, what happened? The unexpected. Your father passed away. We didn't know what to do, because now the only will on file is the old one, so it's the one we had to follow, else the fortune would be contested in court, and then there'd be a big media circus that would bring every criminal in the area out of the woodwork and into the cemetery. We certainly couldn't allow that.

"We didn't know what to do, but we knew that as soon as Ben—your dad—was interred, the money would be lost for good. So on the spur of the moment, we decided to go through with it and figure out what to do with the money later. We'd considered giving it to you, at least a portion, but we didn't really know how or when or what, so we simply held off on it.

"But when you showed up tonight, I for one didn't know *what* to do. I had no idea how much we should tell you or withhold from you. And then you showed us our phony papers—which, how'd you get those by the way?"

Louisa smiled. "I have my ways."

Tom smiled back. "I'm sure you do," he said. "Once I saw the papers, I knew the jig was up, but I just had dollar signs in my eyes." He leaned forward, moving to the edge of the sofa seat. "I'm sorry, Louisa."

It seemed pretty heartfelt. Jake turned his head slightly toward Louisa to see what she would do. She seemed to be having difficulty finding words at the moment, starting to speak and then stopping quickly, like her thoughts were being stolen out of her mouth. Finally she settled down and locked her eyes onto Tom's, holding his gaze for approximately one million years. Finally, her voice came, softly:

"I . . . forgive you," she said.

He breathed a sigh of relief as he leaned back. "Thank you."

Edgar was coming down the stairs, into the living room. "Louisa, I'm glad you came over here, because you made this decision all the more easy. I'm embarrassed and ashamed at my behavior, and I'm proud to give you exactly what you deserve."

He reached into his pocket and produced a pistol.

Elizabeth screamed.

Tom leapt to his feet.

Louisa folded her arms resolutely.

Jake shook his head. "Not again," he said.

Tom strode quickly toward the lawyer-turned-gunman. "What are you *doing*, Edgar?!"

"What should've been done the moment she walked in here," Edgar said. "I can't believe I haven't done it already."

"I can't believe you, either," Louisa said, rising slowly from the couch. Jake followed suit, as best as he could manage. "Is this really how you think this should be settled?"

"You found the loophole in the will. You came into my house and disrespected me. You even struck me. You've done something to my daughter, and now she's fallen in with that rabble you think you help."

"Dad!" Elizabeth said. "She didn't—"

Louisa stood up and reached a calming hand in Elizabeth's direction.

"It's okay, Elizabeth," Edgar said. "You're back with me now, and we'll make sure you get cured of whatever is wrong with you."

"You're not getting it, Edgar," Louisa said. "She doesn't need to be cured. She needs to be loved."

"Elizabeth," Edgar said, "go upstairs, please."

Elizabeth stepped in front of Louisa. "No, Daddy."

Edgar raised the gun so it was pointing where Louisa's chest would be, if Elizabeth were to move out of the way. "Go," Edgar said. "Upstairs. Now."

Elizabeth stood her ground.

Edgar began to step toward her. "I said, 'Go!'"

As soon as he moved, Jake and Tom both sprang toward him.

Jake's ankle was not up to the task, and it rebelled at his commands to support and launch his full weight. It crumpled underneath him, and he began to fall, face-first, arms flailing. "No!"

Edgar reached Elizabeth in the same instant and moved with his free hand to throw her out of the way.

Tom was almost to Edgar.

Jake's arms found Louisa's waist and instinctively grabbed on to support the rest of his body.

Louisa fell forward into Elizabeth.

Elizabeth got caught between the falling Louisa and her gun-bearing father.

Tom reached Edgar.

All five of them collapsed onto the hard parquet floor.

BANG!

Twenty-Eight

What Happened After

FOR THE SECOND time in less than a week, Louisa Cruz was in a hospital waiting room, hoping and praying that God would grant continued life to someone she cared about. She thought of what Elizabeth symbolized for her, how this young girl had brought focus into her life. She thought of her actions over the past few days, and felt regret over her lack of trust in the God she served.

Mostly, she just hoped Elizabeth would be all right.

Also, this time was different. This time she had Jake with her.

A nurse walked into the room and found Louisa. "Miss Cruz?"

"Yes?" Louisa said.

"They have her stabilized. You can see her now."

§

It was your standard hospital room with all the bleeping and blooping machines surrounding one of those beds with all the handles and pedals and levers and hinges. Pastel watercolors on the light brown walls, trimmed in gold metallic frames. A TV/VCR combo mounted onto the wall in one corner.

Elizabeth looked like a princess, albeit one wearing a hospital gown with roughly one zillion tubes and wires protruding from underneath it. Her right shoulder was heavily bandaged.

"Hey, Louisa," Elizabeth said weakly. "How are you doing?"

"How am *I* doing? How are *you* doing?"

"I'm okay. You know, considering."

"Good. Good."

Louisa laid her hand on Elizabeth's, careful not to touch the IV coming from it. "I'm proud of you, Elizabeth."

Elizabeth smiled sleepily. "Thank you."

The door opened, and a shadow fell across the bed. Elizabeth stiffened.

Louisa and Jake turned to see who had entered.

Kimbrough.

He looked surprised to see Jake and Louisa there. "Oh!" he said. "I'm sorry, I didn't know I was interrupting." He began to withdraw from the room. "I'll just come back."

"Dad," Elizabeth said, "you can stay."

"How are you here, Edgar?" Louisa said. "I figured you'd be with the police."

Kimbrough came back into the room, carefully, like a squirrel. "I was. They let me go."

"Really?" Jake said.

"Yeah. They took my gun, obviously, but after listening to our story of what happened, mine and Tom's, and with knowing who we are in the community, they let me come to the hospital to see Elizabeth." He gestured out the open door, and Jake and Louisa noticed the police officer standing just outside it.

"Oh," Louisa said.

Kimbrough walked over to Elizabeth's bedside and looked her in the eyes. "I'm . . . so sorry, honey. For everything."

Elizabeth smiled at her father. "Thank you."

"I should've been there. I should've done more. I just . . . I can't believe what I've become."

"You don't have to stay that way, Dad," Elizabeth said, smiling at Louisa. She reached out her hand and took her father's. "You can start over. But only if you want it."

Louisa gave her a wink.

The door opened again, and this time a real, live, scrubs-wearing doctor walked into the room. He looked competent enough: midforties, balding, glasses, fit. "Hello, Elizabeth," he said, "I'm Dr. Lorenz, and you are one lucky girl."

"Hello, doctor," Elizabeth said. "I know."

The doctor glanced at his chart. "Not only did the bullet make clean entry and exit wounds, but it didn't hit any bones. Pretty clean, as far as a gunshot wound goes." He flipped the chart shut and relaxed his arms. "Also, the really good news is that the accident didn't affect your baby. He's still in perfect health."

Edgar's eyes got wide. So did Jake's.

Elizabeth's got worried. She looked at her father. "Dad, there are a few things you need to know."

He looked down at her and, after taking a moment to overcome the shock, finally shook his head and gave her the best hug he could give, careful to avoid her injured shoulder and wide array of wires and tubes. He stroked her hair. "It's okay, honey. It's okay. We'll figure this out." He looked at Louisa. "I'll make sure of that."

Wrapping Up Loose Ends
(and Sprained Joints)

JAKE AWOKE ACHING like he'd never ached before. Struggling with his good hand, he sat up in bed to take stock of his body's current state. He could see minor swelling in his wrist and ankle, pushing against the envelope/duct tape wrap he'd put on the night before and not bothered with removing when he got home. His foot was a light purple color, looking like it was in need of some circulation.

He slowly eased himself out of bed, looking over to check the time. He'd slept until 12:47 and felt like he could use another eight hours. Maybe he just needed to work some of the kinks out of his joints. Maybe that would help him feel better.

Maybe he just needed a visit from Louisa. Maybe, in the grand scheme of things, this wasn't really about money, but about a relationship. About caring for someone else. Yeah, maybe. But right now it was about standing up and getting dressed.

Jake hobbled into his apartment's sparse kitchenette to find a pair of scissors. A few awkward snips later, his makeshift wraps were in the trash can and he was on his way to the shower.

The shower helped magnificently, its soothing warmth a balm to his creaky joints. His sprains flexed and bowed and took comfort in their newfound freedom. He would need to corral them soon. Nevertheless, he enjoyed the warmth and massaging effect of the shower all the way to a depleted hot water tank. His poor hot water tank was always running low.

A towel applied, a shirt buttoned, a pair of jeans zipped. Jake was ready to visit the drugstore for some much-needed medical supplies. He wasn't quite sure how to get there, since Princess Tangerine was still down for the count, but it was only a couple blocks away, and he figured he could hobble over there with only mild discomfort. He wished he could send his ceramic monkey instead. Maybe the gnome would be up to it.

He was still considering his options when there was a knock at the door. He limped to it as quickly as he could, surprised at his speed, and opened it.

"Good morning, Jake. Even though it isn't morning." It was Louisa, looking more beautiful than Jake had ever seen her. And it wasn't just the simple-yet-fashionable skirt and blouse she'd put together, or her hair (worn loose today) or makeup (applied so sparingly) or anything like that. Instead, her eyes twinkled. It was almost as if this joy had been restrained before, but now it was loose and running wild within her. "I brought you some bandages and breakfast."

Jake couldn't have asked for a better way to spend the first thirty minutes of a day. "The two most important Bs of the day." He smiled goofily at her. "Come on in."

"I hope you don't mind me dropping by unannounced," she said, walking past him and into the living room. "I just had to deliver the news in person."

"What news? And how did you know where I lived?"

"Jeremy told me." She handed him two plastic bags: one from the corner drugstore containing some two-inch rewrappable cloth bandages, the other from the deli by the funeral home containing a turkey sandwich with bacon. "Here. Wrap and eat."

"Don't I have to *un*wrap the sandwich to eat it?" Jake said. "Oh, wait. Wrap the sprains. Got it. Thanks." He took the bags to the couch and plopped down. "So, what's this news you're talking about?"

Louisa chose to sit on Jake's bed, which honestly wasn't that far from the couch. "Well, I got a call last night from Tom, after I dropped you off here."

"Yeah, what'd he want?"

Louisa held up a finger. "I'm sorry — is that a monkey?" She pointed at the ceramic novelty, then waved it off. "You know what? Never mind." She turned her attention back to Jake. "Where was I?"

"Call from Tom."

She nodded her head. "Right. He'd contacted an associate of Edgar's to see what needed to happen now, and it's looking quite good."

Jake raised his eyebrows. "Do tell."

"Well, apparently, since the original wishes of the will weren't carried out, they can now file the new will. Which means . . ." Louisa's voice trailed off in anticipation.

"Holy mackerel."

"Yeah." She stood up and looked like she was about to do a

little dance. "And Tom said he's been in contact with Edgar this morning, and Edgar confirmed it. In fact, Edgar's going to champion it. Soon as he can."

Jake looked up from his bandaging and shook his head with a chuckle. "What a crazy legal system." He turned his attention back to his bandages. "It's almost like someone's just making it up as they go along."

"Tell me about it," Louisa said, sitting down on the couch next to Jake only to bounce back up again eagerly.

"Watch it," Jake said. "The couch is a little springy. Makes it tough to wrap."

"Sorry."

"So, how much did you clear?"

"Well, I've decided to give part of it to Ramon," Louisa replied, "so I called him this morning and told him that Papa had actually given the estate to me in a newly filed will and that I wanted to share it with him to really give his restaurant the kick it needed. I offered him thirteen million, but he only wanted two."

Jake forgot about the bandages. "Did you just say *thirteen* million? A one and a three, put together?"

Louisa nodded vigorously. "Ramon wouldn't take a penny more than two, though. So stubborn. So that leaves twenty-four million for Maria House."

Jake couldn't believe his ears. A broad smile extended his lips farther than they'd ever gone.

"That *is* big news!" And then the realization hit him: He wasn't sad. He was legitimately, honestly happy for Louisa. Maria House was her life, and now she would be able to help more people than she'd ever dreamed. Jake hadn't received a dime of the money, and he was still happy about it. He was happy because she was happy and because the money was going to go to do more than serve him. "That's great!"

"Oh, Jake, I'm just . . . just . . . overjoyed! You have no idea!" She reined in her exuberance, plopped herself down on the couch, and looked deeply into his eyes. "Thank you."

Sprains? What sprains? Aches? What are those? Jake was awash in smittenness once more, and as the waves of infatuation rolled over him, they soothed every part of his hurting body.

But looking at Louisa, sitting there on his couch, he probed inward and found something deeper than infatuation. Something his soul had been hinting at, if only he'd been awake enough to pay attention. And now Louisa was thanking him and he had no idea why, but it was glorious and he didn't want it to end.

"Thank you? For what?"

"I never would have confronted Edgar and Tom if you hadn't helped me in the first place. So . . . thanks." She clapped her hands together joyously and bounced back up again. "And I know you're all set up in your job at the funeral home, but if you'd like to, I want you to come work for Maria House."

Was she serious? What on earth would he possibly do for them? He knew nothing about relating to prostitutes. In the entire realm of his experience, that would be at the distant edge, a place he'd never traveled to. "Really? Why?"

"Because even though we're going to get this major cash infusion, I still need to spend it the best way possible. I've seen you—you know how to get free things. For a nonprofit organization, that's invaluable. Besides, it's time you start putting that talent to work for others instead of yourself."

She was a jewel, and Jake knew it. Sure, he knew it before, but now he *knew it*. And now he began to worry because he was clearly not good enough for her. She deserved better than he could offer.

Sometimes people make life-altering decisions on the spot. Jake did all the time. He wanted the job, and not just because it meant he would be working with Louisa on a daily basis. He wanted to help. He was tired of being the center of his world. He was ready to do something different.

What would the Jesus-looking dude do? Jake already knew. "You got a deal."

"Great!"

"And," he continued, "I wanted to talk to you about something. I've been thinking a lot lately about, you know, Jesus."

She smiled. "I bet you have."

ℰ

Two weeks later, Jake walked limp-free into White Hall Funeral Home for the last time. He heard the familiar ding of the bell on the door and smelled that familiar carpet/particle board/embalming fluid smell. He would miss a lot of things about the funeral home, but the smell wasn't one of them.

"Thank you for calling White Hall Funeral Home, how may I direct your call?"

Who in the world was that? Jake looked at the reception-ist desk and was surprised to see a strange woman who must be nearing retirement age manning the phone. He wandered over to Del's office and poked his head in.

Del looked up from some paperwork and smiled. "Jake, Jake, Jake. How are you?"

"Good, good," Jake said, shaking Del's hand. "Ready to move on."

"Well, we're going to be sorry to see you go. I have to admit, your call came out of the blue."

"You know, Del, I just think it's time to start a new phase in my life."

"I understand. You were good to have around, but I never expected you to be here as long as you were."

"Yeah, me either," Jake said.

"Guess I'll have to put Jeremy on all the odd jobs, too."

"Poor guy," Jake said. "Say, where's Chiffon?"

Del chuckled. "Wouldn't you know it, you aren't the only person quitting on me."

"She quit?"

He nodded. "Yep. The darnedest thing. She told me she went out to that Sing Sing Lounge downtown, where my friend works. She sang her song and some TV producer or something saw her. Offered her a chance to be on some TV show right there on the spot."

"You're kidding!"

"Nope."

"What show was it?" Jake asked.

"Don't know. Something about mice or gerbils."

"*Hamster Cage?*"

Del snapped his fingers and pointed at Jake. "That's the one!" He used his pointing finger to comb his mustache. "I thought it sounded kind of shifty, but Chiffon, she's wanted it for so long she knew just what to do. Turns out her dad's a lawyer, so he worked it all out for her. She's drivin' to Hollywood—" he checked his watch—"well, right now."

Jake was astonished. Way to go, Chiffon. "That's crazy."

"Yeah," Del replied.

Jake pulled two envelopes out of his jacket pocket. These had paper in them, but not blank paper. "Well, you have Chiffon's new address? I need to get something to her."

"Yeah, she gave it to me. Want me to send it on?"

"Please." Jake handed one envelope to Del, then offered the second one. "This one's for Jeremy. Can you make sure he gets it?"

"Of course," Del said, bewildered.

"It's nothing much," Jake said, smiling. "Just some money I owe them."

"Pretty thick envelopes, Jake," Del said, hefting them in his hand. "How much were you into them for?"

Jake played it off. "Oh, I just threw some extra stuff in there for fun." He turned toward the door. "And now, I have to get moving." He gave a wave. "See you, Del."

"Hey, Jake, hold on." Jake complied, turning to see what his former boss wanted. Del lowered his head and looked him in the eye. "Thanks for taking care of that whole thing with Benjamin Cruz. Did you have any trouble?"

Jake grinned. "Not at all."

S

Walking back to the Volvo, Jake felt like a new man. Yes, he was starting a new job, and he was eager to see what would develop with Louisa, but deeper down inside, he felt . . . well, he couldn't put words to it. "Different" didn't really do the trick. Same with "changed." The best he could think was that he felt the most *normal* he'd ever felt in his life. It was as if he'd spent his life being restless, and now he was beginning to get hints of what peace—real peace—felt like. He liked it.

Louisa was leaning against the back of the car, taking in the warm sunshine. Jake never understood how Louisa made jeans and a T-shirt look so great. "How'd it go?" she asked.

"Fine." He held up an envelope containing his last paycheck for White Hall. "Dinner's on me."

"Great. *Vamanos.*"

"Hey, Louisa." He stopped as she turned toward him. He looked in her eyes and wanted more than anything to kiss her right then and there.

So he did.

And she kissed him back.

And it was magical.

And then it was over, and they were looking into each other's eyes.

"Was that an okay first kiss?" Jake asked. "I can do better, I'm sure. In fact, forget that one and let's start over."

She smiled, and kissed him again. And then broke into a laugh, the musical, lovely laugh that Jake so adored. They climbed into the car and sped off into the proverbial sunset, and Jake imagined himself once more among miles and miles and miles of calm, placid waters, his smittenness with Louisa knowing no bounds. Except now he imagined himself not on a boat or ship or any seaworthy craft. He had found an island, a foundational paradise from which he could enjoy the waters all the more. He'd found a friend to keep him company there. He loved her, and she loved him. He needed her more than he'd needed the money.

And they were both in the mood for fajitas.

bonus content includes:

Reader's Guide

1. Which character in *Mooch* do you most identify with? Why?

2. Which character would you most want to have over to your house for dinner? Why?

3. Was Jake and Louisa's plan to acquire Benjamin Cruz's money morally right? Why or why not?

4. Louisa makes a major life change because the Bible reminded her of simpler childhood times. How often do your memories of childhood influence your life today? In what way?

5. Jake says the following about God: "He's like the president or something. Kind of in charge, but I'm not going to run into him anytime soon. He's off in heaven or Washington or wherever, and I'm over here just minding my own." How closely does this reflect your own view of God? Why?

6. Okay, everyone's mooched something before. Maybe not at Jake's level, but we've all gotten something for free that maybe we shouldn't have. What's *your* best mooch story?

7. Jake experiences an internal battle, wondering if there was really a way his fundamental moochlike nature could change and he could care about Louisa more than money. Have you experienced a similar internal battle? How did it end? Has it even ended yet?

8. In our story, Jake's plans keep getting derailed as he learns more and more about Benjamin Cruz's funeral arrangements. How true to life is this for you? Have you ever had plans derail? Explain.

9. What's your favorite Mexican food dish? Why?

Welcome to Sing Sing Lounge! We're glad you've decided to join in the fun this evening. Please know that, while we want your experience with us to be enjoyable, we aren't always able to provide every song you request. After browsing through our catalogs, please fill in your name and your requested songs below, and we'll let you know which song(s) is/are available this evening:

NAME: Chiffon Brown

SONGS:

Cat#	Song Name	Made Popular By
P102	"Never Gonna Give You Up"	Rick Astley
P027	"(I Just) Died in Your Arms Tonight"	Cutting Crew
C017	"My Heroes Have Always Been Cowboys"	Willie Nelson
P224	"Time After Time"	Cyndi Lauper
D512	"I Will Survive"	Gloria Gaynor
C357	"The Thunder Rolls"	Garth Brooks
S657	"Reflection"	Lea Salonga (from *Mulan*)
C001	"Walkin' After Midnight"	Patsy Cline
R831	"Livin' on a Prayer"	Bon Jovi

So You Want to Buy a Scooter

Handy Tips on Scooter Ownership

1. You have a name, right? So should your scooter. This should be the *first* thing you do, before you even learn how to ride it: Name that scooter.

2. Don't go too scooter-crazy at first. If you're unused to high-speed, two-wheel transport, it can be a bit overwhelming. Take some time up front to get used to the sensation and awesomeness of scootering by driving it through low-traffic, low-speed areas such as neighborhoods or empty parking lots.

3. You know what's cool? Helmets.

4. You know what isn't cool? Gray matter on the pavement. Wear a helmet, for crying out loud. Bashing your head on the asphalt will mess up your hair even more.

5. Visualize yourself on the road. You know how there are, like, two sort of "tracks" made by the tires of all those cars that travel the road? Keep your scooter in the left track. Two reasons why: (1) This makes you more visible to those "cars" you keep hearing about, so they don't run over you. (2) Those pesky cars again: They drip oil and other slick fluids on the middle of the roadway (aka, between the tracks). If you ride in the middle of the lane/road, you're riding on the slipperiest part of the road.

6. Never ride your scooter when the temperature is below freezing. Black ice will unseat you quicker than you can correct for it.

7. Never ride your scooter in the rain. Yes, you can do that on a motorcycle, but motorcycles weigh much more than scooters and also have larger tires (and therefore more contact with the road). You, on the other hand, do not. If you insist on riding in the rain, be sure to buy stock in gauze, medical tape, and antibiotic ointment. You'll be using a lot of it.

8. Don't take unnecessary risks while riding. Remember: You're doing sixty miles per hour while essentially sitting on a backless chair. Things can go wrong very quickly.

9. Sunglasses impress chicks. Just make sure they're shatter-proof.

10. Scooter engines are pretty easy to maintain. Just be sure to check the oil frequently and keep up with the service/maintenance schedule. Just like you'd do with a car, in other words.

11. Have you given your scooter a name yet? If so, congratulations! If not, quit reading and get to it!

How to Get Stuff and Influence People

By Jake Abrams

OLD HABITS DIE hard, people. You know, I've pretty much spent my whole life as a getter of free stuff, but I'm trying to do things a little differently these days. Still, it's hard to let stuff just sit around, you know? So while I don't out-and-out steal things these days (except for cable, and I'm addressing that with a phone call on Monday), I still use some of my old skills to make life easier. And now, I share a few of them with you. Just keep 'em to yourself.

Let's start with food, since it's a necessity for everyone. First off, you should never buy condiments again. Ketchup, mustard, mayo, honey mustard . . . these things are available for free in restaurants. Crackers. Pickles, depending on where you go. Jam, if you aren't picky about what kind you get. Really, the only condiment necessity you might have to buy is barbecue sauce, and even then you can get that free, if you find a generous enough barbecue restaurant.

What else? Do you qualify for food stamps? Get on 'em. You're looking at tons of free dairy, at the least, and sometimes you can get pretty much whatever you want at the grocery store. It should go without saying to buy all the generics instead of the name-brand stuff: Stretch those stamp dollars as far as you can.

I don't mess with coupons. Sorry. Call it my tragic flaw. You're more than welcome to cut 'em out if you want.

Moving on to entertainment: Do you have a library card? Because the library is the single most satisfying (and free) entertainment resource you have. Yes, I know you automatically think "books" when I mention the library, but the truth is that most libraries have a full-on media onslaught of stuff just sitting around waiting for you to check out. Movies, CDs, books on CD, magazines . . . all sorts of stuff. A lot of libraries even have free Internet, so you can check your e-mail. Pretty cool. Let's just say I've taken so much advantage of the library that I have my library card number memorized.

Gasoline: Can't help you there, other than to say that walking is free. And if you must use motorized transportation, scooting costs a heckuva lot less than a Hummer, I'll tell you that much.

Furniture: Retail is for suckers. If you must get something relatively new, many furniture stores have an "as is" section (or sometimes they call it a "scratch and dent" section) that is a treasure trove of savings. But I find even this to be way too expensive to be acceptable. If I must buy furniture, I get it from garage sales or thrift stores. It's cheap and it's unique. But my best acquisition was the time I found a couch next to a dumpster in an apartment complex. That was sweet.

If you do find furniture that way, be sure to inspect it before you take it in your house. You don't want your home to be exposed to, like, a rabid chinchilla hiding in the springs or anything like that.

Garage sales are good for clothes, too, though it's tough to really stick to one style. I get most of my clothes at thrift stores, or the clearance rack at mall stores. Again: Retail is for suckers.

Really, the cardinal rule here is this: Always keep your eyes open for opportunity. Again, I can't condone literal stealing, but there's nothing wrong with checking coin returns for quarters or with convincing a fast-food employee that he should just give you that order he prepared wrong instead of throwing it in the trash. Keep a level head—and an open eye. And all that money you save? Give it to something worthwhile. Do it for Louisa.

About the Author

ADAM PALMER is a freelance writer and eater of fajitas who has, in his lifetime, owned a motor scooter, married a half–Costa Rican woman, sung karaoke, and stolen a fountain drink refill or two. He has also written a few books, the most notable being *Taming a Liger: Unexpected Spiritual Lessons from Napoleon Dynamite*. He has never (to his knowledge) stolen millions of dollars from a dead man. He currently resides in fabulous Tulsa, Oklahoma, with his wife and children, who always split the cheese enchilada dinner.

NEW FICTION FROM THINK BOOKS.

Bad Idea

Todd and Jedd Hafer   1-57683-969-9

Griffin Smith is on the road trip of a lifetime as he makes his way to his first year of college in California with his family and best friend in tow. But unexpected detours cause Griffin to revaluate life and what's important as he confronts an absentee mother, a terrible betrayal, and one justifiably angry coyote.

Bright Purple

Melody Carlson   1-57683-950-8

In the newest installation in the TRUECOLORS series, Melody Carlson asks, What's the Christian response to a gay friend? And that's just what Ramie Grant would like to know after her best friend comes out of the closet. Turns out, there's much more to Jessica's story than Ramie knows—but will she stick by her friend long enough to find out?